PRIV.

Private Lessons

Cheryl Mildenhall

First published in 1995
by HEADLINE BOOK PUBLISHING

A HEADLINE LIAISON paperback

10 9 8 7 6 5 4 3 2

ISBN 0 7472 5125 8

Phototypeset by Intype, London
Printed and bound in Great Britain by
Mackays of Chatham plc, Chatham, Kent

HEADLINE BOOK PUBLISHING
A division of Hodder Headline PLC
338 Euston Road
London NW1 3BH

Private Lessons

Chapter One

When Monsieur Guy Ricard first asked her to seduce his seventeen-year-old son, Tara took it as a joke, her laughter a light tinkle filling the air between them like a shower of confetti.

The other customers in the Kent coffee shop glanced up to look at the curvaceous blonde in her late twenties and the dark, handsome man in a sharply tailored suit. Some smiled at the sight of such an attractive couple but all quickly lost interest.

He must be mad, Tara thought, her laughter gradually subsiding. Gorgeous but totally insane. She took a sip of her coffee and smiled at the implacable face opposite. 'I understand your concern for your son's linguistic abilities,' she murmured, 'of course I shall be happy to continue to teach him English but . . .'

She broke off abruptly as he leaned across the white table top, his expression darkening. 'I do believe you are deliberately trying to antagonise me,'

1

he said in a low Gallic growl. 'I told you what I want you to do and it has nothing to do with his English lessons.'

Tara stared at him, her turquoise eyes widening as she realised the gravity of the situation. 'You're serious, aren't you?' she said, stirring her sugarless coffee in confusion. Her spoon clattered against the edge of the thick white cup, giving away the extent of her nervousness.

He put out a hand and stopped her movement, his touch electric. 'I am. Perfectly serious.'

Glancing down at the long, well-manicured fingers, the pale pink nails with their perfect half-moons so white against the darker canvas of his skin, she decided to humour him. 'What makes you think I am the best person for the . . . ahem . . . job?'

The Frenchman stared at her, his gaze softening. 'Because he likes you – a lot.'

'I don't know if that's a good enough reason,' she interrupted, frowning. 'He likes Mrs Morris from the post office a lot and she's sixty-five. I don't suppose you planned to ask her to seduce him?'

She laughed again, amused by her own little joke but he glared at her. 'Please do not be obtuse. This is not a joking matter,' he said, the words carried from his mouth on a heavy sigh. For a moment he hesitated, recrossing his legs and brushing an imaginary piece of lint from his perfectly tailored gabardine trousers. 'Very well,' he added, 'the truth is I found a diary in his room. When I looked at the most recent entries I found he had written some . . . well . . . complimentary things about you.'

'What sort of things?' she asked, intrigued despite his disconcerting behaviour. Leaning forward, she urged him to elaborate.

For a moment or two he hesitated. His eyes strayed to the deep recess of her cleavage where the top button of her simple white blouse looked to be under some strain, as if it might pop undone at any second and expose the golden swell beneath.

'To begin with, he mentions that he finds you attractive,' he said at last. 'Then he describes certain aspects, shall we say, of your physique.'

'Such as?' she prompted.

'He describes the way he watches you when you're not looking,' he said. 'He talks about the shape of your breasts,' his eyes flicked momentarily back to her cleavage. 'He imagines how they must look without the benefit of clothing, how soft and round and generous they must be.' He stopped and cleared his throat.

'Go on.'

Tara was spellbound, amazed that the young man should have been thinking such things about her when all the time she thought he had just been keen to improve his English.

'I . . . I . . . please bring us two more coffees!' He ordered suddenly, catching the waiter's eye before glancing back at Tara. 'This is very difficult,' he added, his expression now almost pleading.

In view of his arrogance she didn't feel inclined to give him any leeway. 'I need to know all the facts if I am to make an informed decision,' she persisted.

The Frenchman paused until the waiter brought their coffees before he continued. 'His diary describes other parts of you also. Your buttocks, your thighs, your . . . sexual parts,' he said, stopping to clear his throat, 'or rather, the way he imagines they look. He tells his diary that he desperately wants to touch all those parts of you and then he talks about himself.'

'In what way?' she murmured, thoroughly entranced.

She leant back, crossing her legs once more, aware that his eyes had now moved to the hem of her tight navy skirt. She wondered if she had inadvertently exposed the top of her stocking but resisted the urge to tug at her skirt.

'He talks about his penis.'

He pronounced it 'pen-iss', she noticed with an inward smile. 'Go on,' she added, taking perverse delight in his discomfort.

'He mentions how much it has grown in the past year or so. How easily he can make it stiff . . .' he sipped his coffee, relaxing a little for the first time since the beginning of their meeting '. . . he confesses that he is still a virgin and that he wants more than anything to have sex with you.'

'I see,' she said, not really seeing at all. In desperation she tried to appear calm, her face a study of

4

composure while inside, her brain whirled and her stomach churned with excitement – and another sensation that she recognised as fear. Fear that she might actually agree to Monsieur Ricard's strange request.

'I do not ask this of you lightly, madame, believe me,' he said, putting down his cup and lowering his voice. 'André and I would be most grateful.'

She stared at him, surprised to find that feelings she thought were deeply buried had suddenly welled up inside her, manifesting themselves in physical sensations that had also been lost to her for over a year. All at once her body was burning.

'Alright, I'll do it,' she said, surprising herself. It was the one response that she hadn't intended to give. How could she possibly agree to accompany this man, whom she hardly knew, and his son, whom she knew only a little better, all the way to France in order to relieve the boy of his virginity? 'Why France?' she asked suddenly.

A slight smile touched the corners of his mouth. 'We always go to our country home every year for the month of August,' he said. 'After André's mother died I started the tradition to maintain contact with his grandparents, now it is just something we do.' He gave a typically Gallic shrug and added, 'Besides, it would be a beautiful location for a seduction, *n'est ce pas*? So warm, so relaxed, so aesthetically pleasing.'

As he spoke she could imagine being seduced by him. The atmosphere between them was heavy with something indefinable that set her heart pounding and caused her nipples to swell and chafe against the fragile lace of her bra. Despite her best intentions, she couldn't help suspecting that the boy's father was the real reason she had agreed to this madness.

When she returned to the sanctuary of her small thatched cottage she wondered if the previous couple of hours had all been a dream. At any moment, she thought, André would knock at the door, and she would greet him with a smile and a glass of cola as she usually did. Then they would sit at her dining table and she would listen while he recited the verbs and vocabulary she had asked him to learn from the time before, correcting his pronunciation, scolding him if he had not bothered to study properly.

Twice a week for the past six months that had been the pattern of their lives. Now it was to be altered irrevocably.

With a small sigh, she made some tea in her favourite brown earthenware pot, glancing at the photograph of her late husband, Lance, as she moved around the small farmhouse-style kitchen. The aluminium frame looked too modern sitting on the pine dresser, she realised and resolved to change it at the first opportunity. Her thoughts turned to Lance. They had started married life so confident of their future, she remembered with a fond smile, certain that they would spend their old age together. And then he had been killed. An army officer, he had returned safely from a peace-keeping mission only to be run down the same day by one of the army's own vehicles. It would have been funny if it hadn't been so tragic.

She was startled out of her reverie by the sound of the grandfather clock marking the hour. Perhaps the chimes were symbolic, she thought, denoting a new era in her life in which sex and laughter would return to chase away unhappy memories.

Sipping her tea, she walked up the narrow, creaking staircase to her bedroom. It was her favourite room, welcoming and sunny at every time of day. Pausing only to glance out of the small leaded window at the deserted lane and her abundant front garden, she sat down at the dressing table and stared at herself in the mirror. When she did this she sometimes expected an old spinster to stare back at her, because that was often how she felt. Today, though, she felt alive for the first time in over a year and, what was more to the point, she felt desirable.

So now when she gazed at her reflection she saw the real Tara Cochrane: a woman who looked younger than her twenty-nine years, with blonde hair framing a strong but pretty face in soft, unmanageable curls. Her huge turquoise eyes sparkled brilliantly in a lightly tanned face now flushed with memories of past carnal pleasure. It wasn't a bad combination, if she did say so herself.

On impulse, she stood up and began to undress, smiling at herself in the mirror as she revealed her body to her own eyes. She wanted to see herself as young Master Ricard saw her – full-breasted and curvaceous, her body soft and inviting, her legs shapely, tapering to small, high-arched feet. Desire curled in the pit of her belly, growing stronger by the second as she cupped her breasts and felt the pleasing weight of them in her hands. They felt good to her, so how would they feel to someone else for the first time? Would they please André? Would they please his father?

Stop it! She couldn't allow herself to think like that. Every time she pictured Guy Ricard's dark, secret smile she felt as though she was losing control of herself. The half-forgotten piquancy of desire gripped her hard and made her sex swell and moisten. She could feel her body responding to the image of him and she gave in to the temptation, imagining his hands on her body. With a groan, she rolled the hard buds of her nipples between her fingers, her actions slow and tremulous as she pinched and pulled them. After only a minute or two of this pleasure she allowed her hands to slide lower, drifting over her belly in an eager quest to reach their destination.

Having been alone for over a year she had spent time getting to know her own body. She knew what she liked and how to make herself respond and, strangely, she hadn't missed having a man in her

8

bed. She didn't go out in the evening very often, nor did she work outside her small country cottage. There was no need. An army pension and various insurance policies kept her well provided for and she supplemented her income by occasionally offering English lessons to foreign students. That was how Guy Ricard and his son, André, had come into her life.

Stroking herself lightly, she tried to think dispassionately about them. First André: about five feet eight inches tall, a medium height for an adult, possibly tall for a seventeen-year-old, his lean body just beginning to develop a sculpted musculature thanks to his efforts at the local gym. Dark wavy hair. Devilish sloe eyes. A full-lipped mouth. Hm, all things considered, he was a very handsome boy for his age.

And his father? Taller, of course, and darker than André – his skin tone quite swarthy. Eyes a surprisingly deep blue, like sapphires. Body? Here she hesitated. On the two occasions she had met him, first when he had enrolled André with her and the second time today, he had worn quite loose-fitting clothes. Nevertheless, she assumed he had a good physique, he certainly wore his clothes well.

Oh hell. Just thinking about him – both of them – was starting to make her feel uncomfortably aroused. She would have to do something about it.

Taking a few paces backwards, she sank down onto the large double bed, her bare skin reacting pleasurably to the cream satin quilt beneath her. Bending her legs slightly she allowed them to drop open and for a moment she remained still, simply revelling in the blissful sensation of fresh warm air caressing her naked flesh. She was in no hurry, there was nothing for her to do but relax and enjoy herself.

Dreamily she stroked delicate fingertips across her small pink nipples, bringing them to life, the uniquely textured skin blushing deeply with arousal. Around and around she traced her fingers, teasing and coaxing with maddening skill. Quelling the urge to hurry herself, she held her breasts in her hands, squeezing the plump flesh that felt as ripe as a summer peach until her sex began to throb insistently. Small frissons of pleasure travelled from her breasts to her womb, forcing her to acknowledge her growing desire for release. She breathed in deeply, trying to quell the demand from her body to give in now. She could if she wanted to. All she had to do was touch herself in a certain way and within seconds she would be satisfied. But she didn't want to rush it. She wanted to prolong the ecstasy and enjoy each delicious moment of torment.

Delaying the inevitable, she slid her hands down her sides, enjoying the curve of her waist and hips, for once feeling like a woman and not an automaton. She was getting closer to her objective now and she brought her palms across her ribcage, over her stomach and further down, sliding over the slight swell of her belly until her fingertips tangled in the silky curls of her pubic hair.

Exhaling slowly and deeply, she felt the fire rise — tingling, sparking, glowing, fermenting inside her — turning her sex to molten lava. She wished André was here now, she wished she could see his young, firm body, wanting him to want her as much as his father claimed he did.

For an endless moment she combed her tangled pubis, drawing her fingers through the blonde curls only to feel them spring back instantly. Sometimes her actions moved the flesh of her outer lips, pulling them back ever so slightly. Her secret flesh was hot now, hot and swollen with lust. She opened and closed the puffy lips, feeling the effect of her manipulations on the delicate area around her clitoris, like ripples moving out from the centre of a pond.

Her breathing was shallower now and coming a little faster. She parted her legs further, sliding a tentative finger between her labia, down the full length of them, feeling the endless folds of flesh beneath, wrapped like petals around the tingling bud of her clitoris. Longing to open herself up, she moved her hands back to her breasts, re-establishing the tautness of her nipples before retracing the fiery trail her fingers had already created.

This time she allowed herself to delve a little, to spread her sex lips open, easing them further and further apart until she could feel the slight breeze of late afternoon against her innermost flesh, drying the moisture there. And even then she resisted the temptation to hurry, pausing instead to circle a fingertip around the outer edge of her desperate vagina, gathering a little nectar as it went. The fingertip slid up hesitantly, like a skater on thin ice, slicking the creamy juices over the hard little pleasure bud that throbbed so incessantly.

She stroked herself again and again, wondering for how long she could keep up the deliberately leisurely pace. Despite her apparent self-control she wanted to let go, to rub herself hard and drive her fingers into herself frantically, knowing that to do so would bring instant relief from the torment. But something held her back, a determination to learn about herself and to learn patience. Before she could teach something she too had to master it.

She was unable to stifle a gasp as the pleasure rose on a high wave, building higher and higher and higher still, suffusing her body with a powerful heat. It was a turning point. Suddenly all her darkest fantasies were there with her in her room, in her head and in her bed – all of them crowding around her and jostling to play in her own private pleasure ground.

She couldn't hold back the urge for gratification now. It was all happening too fast, naked lust overtaking her like an express train and dragging her body into the deep, dark tunnel of desire. There was no turning back, not that she wanted to even if she could. Her legs thrashed, her body writhed and her fingers touched and stroked and probed with a desperation bordering on madness. And, from every part of her body, pleasure heaped upon pleasure in an unfaltering ascent until her climax burst from her in a harsh, continuous scream of ecstasy.

Now, as she felt the waves of desire ebbing away, she felt something more powerful than regret. She needed to have a man in her bed again. In her bed and inside *her*, she realised, wondering all of a sudden how she could ever have denied herself sex for so long. Perhaps that was why she had agreed to Monsieur Ricard's request, she thought. Perhaps she was simply desperate for a man – any man at all.

Smiling to herself, she shook her head. That wasn't the reason, not the real one. Her reason, the only one she needed, was her overwhelming desire for the Frenchman himself.

Guy Ricard had given her some time to think it over, time without the distraction of teaching André and now she found she missed him. She wondered what he had said to the boy, what excuse he'd used. Without André's visits to look forward to, the days seemed interminably long, like a self-imposed exile. She found herself reaching for the phone time and time again to call the Frenchman and tell him she had changed her mind, that she wanted things to go back to the way they had been before. But, of course, they couldn't. Things would never be the same now she knew about André's secret thoughts and desires.

Then one day, just over a week later, she awoke

feeling very positive and decided to go on a shopping spree. After all, she could hardly seduce someone wearing the sort of grey, fraying underwear that currently graced her body and filled her lingerie drawer. She laughed wryly to herself at her glib use of the word 'lingerie' and decided that, rather than shop locally, she would rediscover the delights of Chelsea, Knightsbridge and the West End.

She had not shopped for her own pleasure in ages and she found it an exhilarating experience. For the first time in a long time she was dressing to please a man – men, rather, she realised with a frisson of excitement. Looking at the clothes on display through new eyes, she envisaged how she would look in them from a man's point of view rather than that of another woman. She wanted to look elegant but not too formal, and seductive without looking tarty. Finding the perfect balance between school-teacher and seductress was not easy but finally she felt she had accomplished her mission and returned to the station weighed down with carrier bags.

During the day the journey did not take long but at this time of the evening, the train full of commuters anxious to escape into the suburbs, the delays at each station were horrendous. She glanced at her watch, noting with surprise that it was already six thirty.

'Excuse me, could I trouble you for the time?'

Jolted out of her thoughts, she glanced up in the direction of the polite clipped tones and saw a smartly dressed man. He was probably in his late twenties like herself, she guessed – GQ executive personified.

'Of course,' she said at once, 'it's ... er ...' she glanced at the dial on her wrist again '. . . six thirty-four.'

Her friendly smile was rewarded by his immediate presence in the seat next to hers.

'Do you mind if I sit here?' he said and, without waiting for an answer, he placed a grey leather briefcase and stone-coloured raincoat on the opposite seat and sat next to her.

'No, not at all,' she said, as though it wasn't already a *fait accompli*. For a while they sat in uncomfortable silence, Tara finding to her dismay that she had forgotten how to make polite small talk with a man. Nevertheless, she couldn't ignore his presence. These days it seemed her awareness was automatically drawn to the men she met: ticket collectors, shop assistants, men on trains . . .

'I . . . it's been a lovely day again, hasn't it?' she said at last.

The stranger smiled at her, stretching out his long legs as far as the cramped confines of the train carriage would allow. 'I suppose so. I don't really get to see much of the daylight during the week. I'm stuck in a stuffy office all day, you see?' he explained.

'What a shame,' she muttered, feeling guilty that she should have nothing to do all day except please herself.

Unable to think of anything else to say she stared out of the window and, as she watched the scenery flash by in a blur of fields and industrial estates, she considered the presence of the man next to her. It hadn't escaped her notice that there was no shortage of seats in their first-class carriage, therefore she assumed he wanted more from her than simply the time of day.

'Where are you going?'

His voice came out of the silence with the surprising suddenness of a ship emerging from a thick fog.

'Roebarton,' she said and glanced sideways at him, taking in the warmth of his hazel eyes. 'What about you?'

'Lambton.'

She knew the village, it was about the same distance as hers from the station but in the opposite direction.

'I expect your husband will have a heart attack when he sees how much you've bought,' he said as he glanced at her packages on the rack above their heads.

'I doubt it,' she replied, 'he's already dead.'

She knew her tone was deliberately laconic but sometimes she just liked to shock people. To her surprise, he didn't offer his condolences but simply said:

'Good. In that case you're free to have a drink with me.'

For a second she stared at him open-mouthed,

then her face softened into a smile.

'Okay, I will. Thanks.'

The pace of her heartbeat picked up and the small tingle of excitement that had lain dormant inside her all week was reawakened. Life could certainly be incredible. To think that she could spend such a long time alone, without even the threat of romance, and then all of a sudden to find herself being pro-positioned from all angles – what irony!

There was a pub just outside the station and by unspoken agreement they made their way there, he carrying half her purchases. After he returned with their drinks and sat down he peered inside one or two of the smaller bags.

'Well, well, what have we here?' he said in a slightly mocking voice. He thrust a hand inside one of them and drew out a pair of black silk and lace knickers. 'Very nice,' he said, nodding his approval as the wispy scrap lay in the palm of his hand. Arranging the knickers carefully on his thigh he reached inside the bag again and extracted a matching bra.

Tara blushed, wishing he wasn't airing her brand new underwear in public. 'Do you mind?' she said with a frown, putting out a hand to snatch the gar-ments away from him.

'No, I don't mind at all,' he replied and looked hard at her, his stare challenging. 'In fact I'd like to see you wearing these.'

She hesitated. Inside her tightly coiled body her

heart thumped and her stomach contracted sharply. Every instinct she possessed urged her to finish her drink, take her clothes and walk away from him.

'Alright,' she whispered quietly, her voice barely audible in the general hubbub that surrounded them in the busy pub, 'we'll go to my house.'

He didn't waste any time. Draining his glass, he stood up and began stuffing the fragile items back in the carrier bag. 'Come on, let's hope we can get a taxi,' he said.

With a silent nod she rose quickly to her feet. Fortunately, there was a mini cab waiting for customers outside the station. She gave her address to the driver and they both climbed in. In no time at all it was pulling up outside her front gate.

'This is very picturesque,' he commented, inclining his head in the direction of her small thatched cottage with its white-painted, ivy-laden walls and brightly coloured flower borders.

Too nervous to speak, she merely nodded and began to lead the way up the narrow garden path to the front door. Once inside, she felt more in control. They stood uncertainly together in the tiny hallway. 'Would you like another drink?' she offered hesitantly. 'Wine, scotch?'

Her stomach clenched as he shook his head decisively and took a step towards her, bridging the gap between them. 'No thanks, I just want you.'

It was as though a green light came on suddenly inside her head and she fell into his open arms, returning his kiss with a passion that surprised her. She could hardly get enough of him. Her tongue drove into him hard, her fingers pulling frantically at his shirt, almost ripping it from the waistband of his trousers. Oh, the relief to feel a male body in her arms, so hot and hard and muscular. She allowed her hands the luxury of roaming his back and shoulders for a few moments before coming around to the front of him. Squashed between the heat of both their bodies, her fingers worked to undo his buttons, each tiny one a barrier that had to be overcome.

He pulled his mouth away from hers. 'Stop,' he gasped hoarsely and pushed her gently backwards.

Her legs collided with the staircase and she sat down with a bump. For a moment she sat in a daze, watching him as he pulled off his clothes at speed. Her heart pounded harder as his body came into view. Hard, virile, nicely formed. Then his cock, long and thin, the foreskin already retracted slightly to reveal the tantalising glimpse of his glans. Her eyes widened and she licked her lips in an unconscious action. She wanted to touch him there, to enclose that rigid shaft with her fingers, but he was already hovering over her, kneeling down, pushing his hands up under her skirt.

She groaned as she felt his fingers grip the waistband of her knickers and begin to pull them down. Lifting her bottom, she watched as if this were happening to someone else as the white satin slid down the length of her legs. He pulled them away from her with a flourish and suddenly her sex spasmed and she opened her legs involuntarily.

'Oh, baby,' the stranger moaned hoarsely and pushed himself between her legs, forcing her thighs even wider apart.

Just for a moment she felt his fingers inside her and then the unmistakable hardness of his cock pushing against the entrance to her vagina a couple of times before sliding right inside.

'Oh God!' she cried aloud, wrapping her legs around his waist and grinding her pelvis against him. 'Oh God, it feels so good.'

She was so hot. He made her feel hot, like a furnace. And so full. Although his cock was slender she felt nicely stretched by him, her wet, swollen flesh enfolding him gratefully and tightening around him. She lifted her bottom up from the step and tried to pull him in deeper. Now she had a man inside her again after all this time she wanted as much of him as she could get.

'Don't stop,' she urged. 'Do it harder . . . harder.'

He gazed down at her and tried to smile. His vision was blurred by a haze of lust but he thought she looked beautiful. She was certainly passionate – a joy to fuck. To think when he boarded the train he thought his evening would consist of nothing more exciting than a steak supper, a glass of scotch and the late film. His wife, bless her, was a good mother but she had no real interest in sex. All she did was perform her duty in much the same way as she hoovered and dusted and wiped the kids' noses. He loved her but sometimes he craved a bit more than stoic acceptance, he craved what he was getting now – wild abandon.

Tara wanted to keep her eyes open, to watch him as he came but she couldn't. Passion was making her eyelids heavy and she had to close them for a moment just to savour the feel and the scent of him. Her nostrils quivered, he had the aroma of aftershave overlaid with the musky scent of perspiration and arousal. Oh God. It was all becoming too much!

She arched her back and he changed position subtly, the soft wire of his pubic hair grazing the desperate swelling of her clitoris. All of a sudden white lights exploded behind the dark canopies of her eyelids and she dug her nails into his shoulders hard, her pelvis grinding and thrusting underneath him. Lust rushed in to claim her and she let out a scream.

He began to whimper with the effort of trying to delay his climax. His gluteus muscles clenched and quivered, his scrotum tightening unbearably. How could he be expected to hold back when she was bucking and squirming under him like that? Her scream startled him and then he felt her inner muscles spasming, gripping him hard, threatening to milk him dry. Thank God she was coming, now he could really let himself go.

Chapter Two

She crawled up the stairs on her hands and knees as she didn't have the strength in her legs to stand upright, let alone walk. As she moved she could feel the fluid running out of her, down the insides of her thighs. It made her feel very sluttish to be behaving in that way, crawling on all fours, her bottom swaying in front of his face as he followed her, their combined juices running down her legs. And yet, if she was honest, she couldn't really care less. Why should she – who did she have to answer to?

Just as she reached the last couple of stairs she felt him touch her, his hands pushing her skirt up to her waist, exposing her naked sex and bottom.

'God, you're a sight for sore eyes,' he said and added, 'don't move, stay like that,' when she made to stand up as she reached the landing.

She did as he asked, continuing to crawl with her lower body exposed to his appreciative gaze until they reached the overtly feminine sanctuary of her bedroom. Then she rose awkwardly to her feet and tugged down her skirt. She crossed to the window to draw the floral chintz curtains against the lengthening shadows. 'It must be late,' she said, 'are you in a rush to get off?'

All at once she realised that she knew absolutely nothing about him at all, not even his name.

'No, not at all,' he said, to her relief. She didn't want him to go yet. Her immediate desire had been assuaged but she still felt the need for more. After all, she had a whole year to make up for. She noticed he had brought his clothes and her carrier bags up with him.

'Would you still like to see me in that underwear?' she asked, nodding towards the pile of bags with a coquettish smirk.

'I'll say,' he said and began to rummage through the bags until he found the right one. 'Here it is.'

With a slightly embarrassed smile she took it from him and he sat down on the bed. 'I'll put it on in the bathroom,' she said, much to his surprise, 'I won't be a minute.'

When she came back he was still sitting where she'd left him, naked and a little limp. But when she walked through the doorway he rose quickly to his feet.

'My God!' he said, the breath escaping from his lips in a long wondering sigh as his eyes feasted on her scantily clad body, 'I didn't expect you to look like that.'

For a moment she wondered if he was disappointed, she knew her figure was not perfect.

'Turn around,' he ordered.

Her skin burned under his penetrating stare as she did as he commanded. The next instant he had stepped forward and she felt his hands upon her waist, turning her, pulling her to him.

'Do I look okay?' she said. She had to ask him, had to know if she had been fooling herself every time she looked in the mirror.

'No, not okay,' he replied with a slight smile as he stroked one finger down the deep valley between the soft globes of her full breasts. 'Fantastic!'

His words shattered her doubts and she relaxed visibly, her shoulders dropping back, the sudden movement almost thrusting her breasts into his hands. Silently she allowed him to run his palms over the thin layer of lace that concealed the straining flesh and beneath the scant material he felt her nipples harden in response to the long forgotten sensation of a man's hands upon that part of her body.

A soft moan escaped her lips.

'You like that, don't you?' he said, continuing to stroke her breasts, at the same time easing her legs apart with the insistent pressure of his thigh.

'Oh, yes,' she murmured and allowed herself to dwell on the sensation of his fingers plucking at her nipples for a moment before asking his name.

'Glen,' he replied. 'What's yours?'

She told him, her fingers gently stroking his arms

and shoulders as he caressed her.

'Tara, that's a lovely name.'

He breathed softly in her ear as he reached around her to cup her buttocks. She did look fantastic in the black underwear, so curvaceous and sensuous that he felt himself hardening all over again. He loved the feel of her too, the taut mounds of her buttocks underneath the fragile covering. The silk whispered over her skin – silk on silk – and he slid a hand around to the front of her to gently cup her mound. Her legs parted obediently and he slipped his fingers between them. The crotch of her knickers was soaking wet.

He pressed her gently back against the bed until she sat upon it and then lay down. Then he stretched out beside her and simply looked at her for a moment. 'You're beautiful,' he murmured, his tone seductive.

'No . . .' she started to protest but he silenced her.

'Just believe me when I tell you things, okay?'

'Okay.'

He moved her arms above her head and held them there by the wrists with one hand. The other hand he ran slowly across her stomach and the soft swell of her belly, smiling when she shivered at his touch. Then he moved his hand lower, taking it casually across her lace-covered mound, stroking her thighs until they parted again.

'That's better, just relax.'

His voice was almost hypnotic as he continued to

stroke her, the unfamiliarity of his caress reminding her of the other pleasures that awaited them.

Sliding his hand underneath her, he unfastened her bra, pulling it away from her body slowly until her naked breasts were revealed to his appreciative gaze.

'I usually go for legs but I think you've just converted me to a breast man,' he chuckled, tracing the contours of her smooth round globes with his fingertips.

Tara sighed with pleasure, she had to admit that if there was one part of her body which particularly pleased her it was her breasts. As André had described them, they were indeed large and round and firm, seeming to defy gravity. She glanced down at his hand as he fingered her nipples and suddenly she noticed, with a flicker of disappointment, that he was wearing a wedding ring.

'Won't your wife wonder where you are?' she blurted out just as he was about to cover one of the tingling buds with his lips.

Apparently unperturbed by her lack of tact, he raised his head. 'I often work late, or go to the pub with some colleagues,' he said simply. 'She knows better than to ask.'

She relaxed again under his caress. 'That does feel good,' she said, feeling the swollen buds of her nipples grow even harder as he alternately sucked them and lathed them with his tongue.

As he mouthed her aching teats he took each

breast in his hand and squeezed it gently, moulding his fingers around it until she started to emit tiny gasps of pleasure. 'Tell me what you like,' he murmured, his lips moving against her flesh. Raising his head, he gazed into her eyes, his expression a question waiting to be answered.

'I . . . I . . .' she stammered, struggling with the reply. She didn't know what to say to him, how to convey her myriad wants and desires. In the end she simply shrugged.

Fortunately for her he didn't give up that easily. 'Do you like it when I do this?' he persisted, pinching a nipple lightly.

She nodded.

'This?'

He bit her nipple, then sucked it hard.

'Mmm,' she whimpered, beginning to squirm.

'What about this?'

He cupped her pubic mound and squeezed it, the heel of his hand pressing into the tropical opening between her legs. Her body felt hot and moist. The flesh gave a little, sucking in the fragile fabric of her knickers.

Tara wriggled under his hand, small sparks of desire flickering deep inside the pit of her belly. 'Yes, I like that,' she gasped, 'I like it a lot.'

The desire grew rapidly as she felt both his hands moving over her and the fingers tugging at her knickers, pulling them down her legs and away from her body. Lifting her legs, he bent her thighs back towards her chest so that the whole of her sex was exposed to him: from the triangle of golden hair to the tiny puckered opening between her buttocks. Straight away she felt her body flood with shame. She wanted to hide herself from but he held her motionless with his gaze, his uncompromising eyes pinning her to the bed like a trapped butterfly.

'Don't be embarrassed,' he murmured, 'you're beautiful. I told you.'

He slid a hand over her swollen vulva, his fingertips spreading open her labia and probing the cream-filled tunnel of her vagina.

As his fingers played a magic tune upon her sex she could feel an intense heat spreading through her pelvis. It was more than she could create for herself, a far more poignant pleasure than her own probing and caressing could elicit.

'You do enjoy that, don't you?'

He delved inside her with a finger, then another and another. Twisting and turning them, scissoring them apart, seeking out the sensitive spot behind her pubic bone. As he filled her so she opened up more for him, holding her knees, spreading her thighs wider to display all her feminine charms.

'Mmm, baby, I can't get enough of you,' he groaned, his hands roaming over her hot, swollen flesh until she began to thrash her head from side to side, her mouth emitting tiny whimpers of pleasure. Then he lowered his mouth to drink her in and she found she was lost completely.

As they lay together afterwards, both of them panting and bathed in perspiration, his cock wilting inside her, the big question 'What now?' floated around in her mind. Strangely, she didn't want him to stay with her all night.

He looked up at her, his soft eyes full of apology. 'I'm afraid I'll have to go in a minute,' he said.

'That's okay,' she murmured, stroking a damp strand of hair away from his face, 'I really enjoyed that. Thank you.'

His face broke into a broad smile. 'I can't believe you're thanking me,' he said, laughing, 'you're the most delicious woman I've ever known.'

The words thrilled her and he looked as though he was about to say more but she silenced him by kissing him on the lips. 'Get dressed,' she ordered, 'go now, before I want you all over again.'

He was fully clothed in seconds which made her think he was an expert at such things. As she lay on the bed, naked and languorous in the afterglow of passion, he looked down at her.

'Can I see you again?'

She nodded. 'Yes, but I shall be away all next month.' The sudden reminder of what she was about to do coursed through her like a bolt of electricity. Then she realised he was still talking.

'We could make it the first Monday in September,' he suggested matter-of-factly, 'I'll come here straight from the station so you'll know roughly what time to expect me. Will that be okay?'

'Yes,' she nodded happily, 'I'll look forward to it.'

He kissed her again, his expression regretful. 'I wish I didn't have to go.'

'I know, but you do, so get lost,' she said. Reclining luxuriously against the pillow, her eyes already becoming heavy with drowsiness, she smiled at him. 'See yourself out.'

Two days later, Guy Ricard telephoned and asked if they could meet to go over the details of their arrangement. Feeling a little hesitant, Tara agreed, offering her own home as the venue in preference to the indiscreet impersonality of a restaurant or café – and as a safer alternative to his London docklands apartment. An apartment which, apparently, was not suitable for André and the reason why the boy had been staying with a distant relative who lived in the same village as herself.

For the entire day she was a bundle of nervous energy. First of all she cleaned the cottage from top to bottom, then spent hours weeding an already perfect garden. In the end she gave up trying to take her mind off the Frenchman and enjoyed a long soak in the bath where she gave free rein to her lustful thoughts.

By the time Guy Ricard arrived she was bathed, perfumed and perfectly made-up – her clothes a carefully chosen ensemble from her new wardrobe. She was just checking the temperature of the wine when the doorbell rang and she moved with indecent haste to answer it.

31

It seemed strange to see him standing there, his imposing dark-suited figure filling the narrow doorway.

'Please come in, Monsieur Ricard,' she gasped, shocked by the sudden nearness of him, 'make yourself at home.'

She hoped she appeared as gracious as she intended, it would hide the nervous shuddering inside her.

As he entered the cottage he glanced around the traditional interior, his inscrutable expression betraying no first impression of her much prized home. He accepted her offer of a glass of wine with the merest glimmer of a smile and chose to sit down in an armchair. He glanced at her bookshelf. 'I see you like to read Anaïs Nin,' he said with an approving nod at the collection of works by the French erotic writer.

'I've just discovered her,' Tara said, taking a seat on the sofa opposite him.

Her words were a gross understatement. For the past couple of days, anxious to fill in some gaps in her sexual knowledge, she had watching countless explicit videos and read every piece of erotic literature that she could get her hands on. The work of Anaïs Nin had only just been introduced to her the previous day by the local librarian, who had looked on in bemused silence as she stripped the relevant bookshelf bare.

The more she watched and the more she read, the

more she realised that the gaps in her experience were nothing short of gaping chasms. It was for that reason that she had decided at the last minute to renege on her agreement with Monsieur Ricard. The only difficulty was, she didn't know how to break it to him.

'I have missed André this week,' she offered conversationally, doing her best to appear relaxed and calm.

'He too has missed you, it says so in his diary,' he said. He leaned back in the chair and crossed one immaculately trousered leg over the other, his ankle resting casually on his knee.

'What does it say?' Despite herself, Tara was intrigued.

He studied her for a moment, his blue eyes assessing her unusually chic appearance the slim-fitting white dress, the high-heeled shoes, the red lips. The whole ensemble was very becoming, he decided with an inward smile. Ignoring his thoughts, he proceeded to answer Tara's question.

'It says he misses you desperately and that he yearns to be seated next to you,' he said. 'He mentions how he loves to feel your arm brush against his as you work together. He is determined to find the courage to accidentally touch your breast.' He paused to sip his drink, his stare unwavering as Tara felt the irritating flush of embarrassment creep up her throat. 'It says he has come countless times just by thinking about you.'

Tara gasped aloud at this last statement. 'I didn't realise his feelings were so strong,' she managed to croak out.

'Oh yes,' he said, his eyes sweeping over her body in frank appraisal, 'but it is not surprising. You are, after all, a very alluring woman.'

'Am I?'

She realised her response was less than sophisticated. If this were a film, she thought, she would simply smile knowingly, not blush and become as gauche and awkward as a schoolgirl.

He declined to answer. Instead his manner became businesslike. 'Enough of this idle chatter,' he said, 'now we must discuss the terms of our arrangement.'

Tara swallowed deeply. This was the moment when she was supposed to tell him of her decision to back out, before he started to go into the details. 'I . . . I . . .' she stammered.

'Yes?' He looked at her, his gaze overwhelming her, its intensity snatching the breath from her body.

She shook her head, unable to speak.

'Very well,' he continued, reaching for the briefcase at the side of his chair and extracting a manilla wallet. 'In here are all the documents you will need, tickets and so forth. Also, there is a map so that you can direct the taxi driver from the airport.' He took a deep breath and looked up at her again, mistaking her wide-eyed fear for rapt attention. 'This . . .' he said, tapping a white envelope with a perfectly manicured fingernail '. . . is your first cheque – half now and half at the end of the holiday when I am satisfied that, er, services have been properly rendered.'

'Oh!' she gasped.

She didn't know how to reply, his businesslike manner was disconcerting and his efficiency positively frightening. Draining her glass of wine rather too hastily, she stood up to fetch a refill and was surprised to find that her legs had apparently turned to water.

Clutching the arm of the sofa until she felt strength return to her lower limbs, she watched him as he checked and double-checked the contents of the wallet before placing it carefully on the table. His actions were so measured, so precise, she couldn't help wondering if he was like that in everything he did. She crossed the room and grabbed the wine bottle.

Apparently oblivious to her discomfort, he glanced up and accepted her offer to refill his glass. 'If you're a lover of wine you will certainly enjoy your holiday,' he said, smiling properly for the first time, 'there are many fine vineyards within driving distance of the house. I will, of course, provide you with the use of a car,' he added as an afterthought.

Despite her agitation, there were certain questions that Tara needed answers to. 'Did you have a timetable in mind for this seduction?' she asked. Her question was deliberately blatant, forced out quickly before she lost her courage and buried it.

His blue eyes stared at her without blinking. 'Not really,' he said as his steady gaze swept the length of her body, instantly setting her desires aflame. 'I would prefer it to seem natural and unhurried. But, on the other hand . . .' he paused and sipped his wine '. . . I would like André to be able to enjoy you at his leisure. At least for a little while before the holiday ends. If you can manage the initial seduction within the first week or two that would be perfect.'

'Oh,' she gasped, swallowing deeply, 'you didn't intend for it to be a one-off affair then?' She grimaced inwardly at her own appalling choice of words. 'I . . . I mean . . .'

He put up a hand to silence her. 'Please do not bother to explain,' he said, 'I know what you mean. No, I certainly did not envisage that the holiday would entail only one quick screw.' He stopped talking as she suddenly let out a burst of hysterical laughter. 'What is the matter?' he said, suddenly sounding very French. 'Did I say something wrong – is screw not the correct English word?'

Tara blushed, her whole body on fire. 'Yes. I mean no. I mean – oh God, this is so difficult!' she cried, running her hands through her hair, trying to regain some semblance of self-control. 'Look,' she said eventually, anxious to clear the air between them, 'I think I may have made a mistake. I'm certain that I'm not the right person for this. I'm not beautiful. I'm not sophisticated. I'm not terribly experienced. I'm not . . .'

'Stop, please!' he shouted, silencing her instantly. He grasped her hands and studied them thoughtfully as they lay, white and trembling, in his broad palms. 'I don't want to hear from you that which you believe you are not,' he said, lowering his voice, 'I know what you are. André knows what you are. That is why he desires you and I can honestly say I do not blame him.' To her shocked delight he spoke the final words with conviction, his eyes crinkling and sparkling like ocean waves as he allowed himself to smile properly for the first time.

'What am I then?' she felt tempted to ask.

'You are soft and warm,' he said, his fingertips smoothing the skin over the fragile bones of her hand, 'and you are also compassionate and sensuous. In short, you are the perfect woman to seduce my son.'

'I see.'

All at once she felt lost for words – stripped of her usual bravado. Her heart was thumping wildly and for a few anxious minutes all she could do was sip her wine and think about what he had said. She had to admit that if Guy Ricard took the boy to a prostitute for his first time, as she had heard some fathers did, he could end up with a very warped idea of what sex should be about. At least she hadn't had to sleep with countless men to know that compassion and sharing were key elements in any successful relationship. She had plenty to give André in that respect.

'I think you understand my motive for asking you,'

37

he said, judging her changing expression correctly. 'He has made it clear you are his dream woman. I simply want his dream to come true.'

'Yes. You're right. I do understand,' she murmured and swallowed the last of her wine.

She was just starting to relax when, to her dismay, he snapped his briefcase shut and rose abruptly to his feet. *'Bon,'* he said, 'now the details are agreed, André and I shall expect to see you in a couple of days in France.'

Too stunned to reply at first, Tara watched him walk toward the doorway. 'Wait!' she called out, jumping quickly to her feet, heedless of the way her head swam and her legs wobbled.

'Was there something else?'

His question hung suspended in the air. Now she must tell him of her decision to renege on her promise.

'No,' she answered, her shoulders sagging as she realised she couldn't bring herself to back out, 'no, nothing. Please allow me to see you out, monsieur.'

After he had gone, she sat for hours, heedless of the lengthening shadows, her eyes fixed hypnotically to the envelope that lay on the table in front of her. They hadn't actually discussed money, she realised, hadn't fixed her *price*. Suddenly, she couldn't bear the suspense any longer. She had to know how much Guy Ricard thought she was worth.

Whatever she had been expecting, it certainly hadn't been that much!

She gazed at the cheque in her hands, her attention missing nothing – the logo of the smart city bank, the stylish scrawl of Monsieur Ricard's signature in violet ink, the carefully typed amount in words and figures: fifty thousand pounds. The figure became a mantra in her head. Fifty thousand pounds. Fifty thousand pounds. And, that was just half the amount, In total, Guy Ricard valued her services at one hundred thousand pounds – not bad for a few day's work!

She paced the room in agitation. This whole thing was sheer madness, she thought. Glancing at the cheque again she realised she couldn't accept it. There was no way she could even think of going through with their arrangement. She had to call him now and back out of the deal.

With trembling fingers she thumbed through her address book until she found his home number. Checking her watch, she estimated that he should have arrived home ages ago. He answered the telephone on the third ring.

'*Oui!*' His tone was typically curt and business-like.

Now she had his attention she wavered and a sick knotted feeling in the pit of her stomach threatened to rise up her throat.

'*Oui!*' His voice spoke again, the tone sounding even more sharp. Then he added, 'Who is this please?'

'I . . . it's me . . . Tara Cochrane,' she gasped.

To her surprise, the voice on the other end of the telephone line softened immediately. 'Oh, yes. Madame Cochrane,' he said, 'what can I do for you?'

'I just looked at your cheque . . . my cheque . . . the one you left,' she stammered, forced to take a deep breath to control the wild beating of her heart. This was going to be even more difficult than she thought. When he didn't offer any reply she bravely attempted to fill the gap with her own voice. 'I can't . . . I can't . . .'

'. . . can't honour our agreement for such a paltry sum?' he interjected.

He sounded as though he was serious.

'No, that's not what I was going to say at all!' she exclaimed, her surprise making her coherent for the first time since she had dialled his number.

'Then what do you want to say, Madame Cochrane?' he said.

He didn't sound at all irritated and for a second she wondered if he was toying with her. At that moment she wished desperately that she could see his face, just to make sure. She took a deep breath. This was it. This was when she told him no. 'I was going to say that the amount is a pleasant surprise,' she found herself saying.

'Oh,' he responded, sounding genuinely amazed, 'but you are actually worth far more than that, it's simply all I can afford.'

Surely he wasn't serious, she thought with a

40

sudden surge of annoyance, surely he must be trying to undermine her in some way? Her reaction was swift and venomous. 'For that money, I'm surprised you didn't insist on checking the merchandise first,' she said acidly.

The silence from the other end of the telephone line was painful, a long-drawn-out agony. When he spoke, his reply completely floored her.

'Of course,' he said, 'you are quite right, Madame Cochrane, how very remiss of me. Please be at my office at three o'clock tomorrow afternoon. I will see to it then.'

He put down the receiver and left her speechless.

Just as she had sat for hours in her cosy living room staring at the envelope, now she sat staring at the telephone. As a result of one simple conversation, the square white object had been transformed into an instrument of torture. Of course, he couldn't possibly have taken her seriously. And she couldn't possibly go. There was no way she could reasonably be expected to keep an appointment to be – what? – examined by a complete stranger? The thought incited a rush of moisture between her legs. Oh God, she moaned quietly to herself. She already knew that she was going to call his bluff.

Chapter Three

It took her a long time to get to sleep that night and when she did her slumber was punctuated by horrific nightmares, all of them centred around the figure of a large black bull ... a fierce, unstoppable beast who lurked in corners and surprised her, who blocked her path, who chased her through fields and woodland and vineyards – a huge, dominating, terrifying monster with piercing blue eyes.

She didn't need a degree in dream analysis to recognise that her persecutor was none other than Guy Ricard and the consequence was that she awoke feeling far, far worse than she had the night before.

After she had bathed carefully, conscious of the fact that she may well be expected to put herself on display, she stood in front of the mirror and stared at her reflection. She looked almost serene, with no outward sign of her inner turmoil.

I should have been an actress, she thought, and decided she would treat this whole charade as if she were. Then things would be different, it would not be Tara Cochrane who was being ogled, nor Tara Cochrane carrying out the seduction of André Ricard, but herself acting a part. And for that part she would earn one hundred thousand pounds.

At last she felt happier about the whole thing. Humming quietly, she began to select an outfit to wear. She intended to take as much care with her appearance as she had the night before, more so in fact because this time she had to ensure that she looked as good out of her clothes as she did in them.

All the time she prepared her outer self, she didn't allow herself to dwell on the way she was feeling inside. During the train journey she had all the time in the world to do just that. She didn't dare to acknowledge her true reason for visiting Monsieur Ricard's office. Instead her mind played tricks on her. It was easier to handle the situation that way and much less scary. The other option – the reality – was too shocking for her even to contemplate.

As she glanced around the carriage she found herself wishing that she had Glen there beside her again. His presence would remind her of what real-life relationships were all about, not the fantasy scenario that was taking shape around her. Idly she thought about him, remembering the way he had looked at her, the way he held her and touched her, the way he had felt inside her.

Gradually she found herself becoming warm. Somehow, during the course of her reminiscences she had transposed Greg's face with that of Guy

Ricard. Oh God! The realisation brought her up short. She couldn't begin to imagine how it would feel to have *him* inside her, to hear him say he wanted her, to hear him plead with her to make love to him. In her ears she heard the dark, seductive tone of his voice, murmuring softly, whispering what he would like to do to her body. Then she imagined she could feel his eyes on her and his hands – looking, touching, feeling, exploring . . .

She pulled herself up with a start. That part of her daydream could come true that very afternoon. Whatever the outcome, something had been awakened within her now that she would never let go of again. She was a woman – a passionate, sensuous, vital woman and whether she liked to admit it or not she no longer had the luxury of believing endless youth was at her disposal. Sighing softly to herself she realised, with a pang of regret, how much time she had wasted already. Time when she could have been enjoying herself and enjoying sex. Silently she thanked her lucky stars that she hadn't left it too late. At least she still had the opportunity to learn – and to teach.

Holding Guy Ricard's business card in the palm of her hand, she read out the address to the taxi driver.

'Right, oh!' he said, looking straight ahead as he pulled into the stream of traffic, 'we'll have you there in no time. Lovely day isn't it, miss?'

His jolly, weatherbeaten face grinned at her and

she suddenly felt like screaming at him to shut up. It wasn't fair that he should be so happy, when she was feeling so wretched.

She glanced tremulously at her watch – a quarter to three. Suddenly she wished the driver wasn't quite so assertive or the London streets so uncharacteristically deserted. It seemed that, whether she wanted to or not, she was destined to arrive at her appointment on time.

Within minutes the taxi pulled to a halt outside a tall office building, its façade unwelcoming, its windows blocked by reflective glass. She paid the driver and, ignoring his cheery goodbye, glanced up at the building. Somewhere inside there sat Guy Ricard, waiting – waiting for her.

The business card indicated his office was on the eighth floor so she took the lift, holding onto the hand rail as if she might collapse from sheer panic. By the time the lift door opened she was trembling violently, her chest and stomach knotted lightly, her throat parched.

When she introduced herself in a hoarse croak the receptionist asked her to wait, indicating a range of low, functional seating that was typical of any commercial reception area in any office building. Too nervous to concentrate on her surroundings, Tara stared at her hands as they clenched and unclenched in her lap. A moment later she spread her fingers wide, unwound her tightly crossed legs and forced herself to relax.

As the minutes ticked by she convinced herself that Guy Ricard had only been joking about seeing her and at that very moment he would be staring at the intercom in amazement as the receptionist informed him that Tara was waiting for him in reception. A few seconds later he would emerge from his office, smiling sheepishly and offering his apologies for dragging her all the way to London on a wild goosechase; surprised that she had not recognised his feeble attempt at a joke.

'Monsieur Ricard will see you now,' the receptionist said, her clipped tones shattering Tara's train of thought.

Immediately her stomach started to churn again and her legs turned to water. 'Thank you,' she managed to murmur, 'which way should I go?'

'Straight down the corridor, last door on the right. You can't miss it,' the young girl instructed without looking up.

Conscious only of her pounding heart, Tara followed the girl's directions, pausing before a door which bore the gold engraved nameplate – G. Ricard. She knocked timidly at first and when there came no immediate reply she rapped her knuckles harder against the wood – much too hard, she realised as the sudden pain made her wince.

From the other side of the door his voice boomed, 'Entrez!'

Her fingers wound around the metal door handle and she lowered it, pushing the door open gently

47

with her arm. Hesitantly she stood in the doorway, her eyes scanning the room.

It was a large office, huge in fact. Across the wide expanse of pale cream carpet she could see a vast wooden desk, behind which sat Guy Ricard. He was writing, his head bent studiously over his work. To her left, stood a long, wide table, with six or seven chairs grouped around it. To her right was a small grouping of sofas and low tables. Other than that there was little furniture.

He glanced up, his expression and tone humourless. 'Don't just stand there,' he ordered. 'Come in. Take a seat.'

He pointed to the empty visitor's chair in front of his desk.

Feeling as though she was crossing something the size of the Sahara desert, she dragged her unwilling feet over the wide expanse of carpet and sat down, placing her handbag on the floor next to her and crossing her legs.

'I thought you'd be surprised to see me,' she said, laughing in her nervousness. Whatever happens, she thought, I mustn't forget that I am only acting a part.

He looked up at her. 'Why should I be surprised?' he said, 'I asked you to come.'

She leaned forward a little, her expression earnest. 'Yes, I know, but . . .' She realised she was floundering. Apparently it wasn't a joke after all.

At that moment they were disturbed by another

knock at the door. Guy Ricard bade the caller to enter just as he had done minutes earlier, but this time he stood up to greet the guest.

Tara turned around in her chair to get a better view. The visitor was a small, bald man wearing a nondescript dark brown suit. In his right hand he carried a large black briefcase which she eyed suspiciously.

'Welcome, *mon ami!*' Guy Ricard cried, his face wreathed in smiles as he stepped forward and clasped the man by the shoulders.

The visitor merely nodded his greeting with a sour expression and turned to look at Tara. 'Is this her?' he asked Guy, eyeing her dispassionately.

'I am forgetting my manners,' Guy Ricard responded, flashing a smile at her that did not quite reach his eyes, 'Madame Cochrane, this is Doctor Newell. I have asked him to carry out a proper medical examination of you.'

'What!' The single word exploded from her lips.

The Frenchman opened his mouth to reply but the doctor interrupted him. 'Please, Madame,' he said to Tara, 'do not be alarmed. It is perfectly reasonable in these, ah . . . circumstances, to ensure that you are not harbouring an infection of any kind.'

Despite her shock, she had to admit that what he said sounded perfectly reasonable.

'I can ask my secretary to be here during the examination if you are concerned about any impropriety.' Guy Ricard offered, 'It would be only natural for you to prefer another woman to be present.'

Tara thought about it for a moment before shaking her head. Under the circumstances, she thought, the fewer people who became involved the better. 'No. That's alright,' she muttered, 'I trust you.'

Her nervous glance first swept over Guy Ricard and then the doctor, who immediately became thoroughly businesslike and professional.

'In that case,' he said, 'please take off your clothes and, er . . .?' He waved his hand in the direction of the meeting table and looked enquiringly at Monsieur Ricard.

The other man faltered for a moment then jumped up and removed a pile of papers from the surface of the table. 'Yes, yes of course, *monsieur le docteur*,' he said with an apologetic shrug, 'I know it is not ideal but . . .'

The doctor silenced him by raising his hand. 'It is perfectly adequate,' he insisted before turning to Tara. 'Now then, madame?'

'Cochrane,' she murmured.

'Madame Cochrane. Please remove all your clothes and come over to the table.'

To her consternation he turned away from her, opened his briefcase and started to extract a few worrying-looking items.

For a moment she hesitated. She didn't want to do this. She couldn't possibly do this. Slowly she unzipped her dress.

All the time she was undressing neither the doctor nor Monsieur Ricard paid any attention to her. Guy was engrossed in some paperwork on his desk and the doctor still rummaged busily through his capacious briefcase. When she was completely naked the Frenchman chose that precise moment to look up, his eyes momentarily locking with hers.

For an instant she thought he looked startled to see her like that and his surprise helped to quell her feelings of shame. Eventually he tore his eyes away from her and glanced down at his paperwork once more.

If she had thought the short walk to his desk upon her arrival had been arduous, then the one to the table, where the doctor waited patiently, was like climbing the Andes. I can't do this, she thought, putting one foot slowly in front of the other, her cheeks flaming with mortification. I can't do this.

At the doctor's indication she used a chair to climb carefully onto the table, her naked skin reacting with displeasure to the cold hard wood. Quivering with shame, she sat bolt upright, her arms held stiffly by her sides as she struggled to prevent her shoulders from shaking.

Apparently unaware of her discomfort, the doctor examined her breasts, palpating the flesh gently, feeling under her armpits and peering carefully at the puckered skin around her nipples. At last he nodded with satisfaction and asked her to lie down flat.

Making sure that her head faced Monsieur Ricard, she did as he asked, shifting uncomfortably as her spine came into contact with the hard surface.

'I apologise, madame,' the doctor said, 'this won't take long, I assure you. Now please bend your legs and just let them drop open.'

At the sound of the doctor's voice, Guy Ricard raised his head again, his movement causing Tara to look around. Again their eyes locked and he looked away quickly, obviously sensing her humiliation.

Biting her bottom lip hard to stop it from trembling, Tara bent her knees, sliding the soles of her feet along the smooth, cold wood until the tight muscles in her calves met the softer flesh of her thighs. The whole thing was so shaming she had to will herself with all her might not to let tears betray her. Taking a deep breath, she opened her legs and stared at the ceiling, her eyes concentrating hard on one single spot of flaking paint as she endured the indignity of the doctor's examination.

Finally he told her she could sit up and he handed her a small bottle. 'Please be so kind as to provide me with a sample of your urine,' he said, 'then we are finished.'

He smiled at her for the first time and removed his latex gloves with a loud *snap-snap*.

Tara hesitated and Guy Ricard looked up, obviously trying hard not to stare at her nakedness. 'There is a small bathroom through that door there,' he said, pointing to his right, beyond the table. To her surprise his tone was much gentler than the one she was used to.

After the horror of the surprise medical examination, providing a sample of urine was easy. With a smile of triumph she presented the doctor with a full bottle.

'Just a few drops would have sufficed,' he murmured, his tone totally devoid of humour. Turning to Guy Ricard he added, 'I will rush the tests through and let you have the results tomorrow morning, first thing. As far as I can tell, however, I'm positive this young lady is in perfect health.'

The two men both smiled, firstly at each other and then at her. Tara tried to smile back but she was far too conscious of her nudity. As Guy Ricard saw the doctor to the door she started to tremble, wondering what on earth was going to happen next.

'I am so sorry about that, madame,' he said as he returned to stand before her, studiously avoiding her unclothed body with his eyes, 'but you understand my reasons, I hope?'

Tara nodded. 'Just about,' she muttered, shifting uncomfortably from one foot to the other, finding it difficult to maintain her stance – shoulders rounded, arms and hands desperately trying to conceal her breasts and the blonde tangle of curls at the apex of her thighs.

He stared directly into her eyes. 'Madame, forgive me, I am being thoughtless,' he said, 'no doubt you would appreciate a drink after your ordeal?'

For a brief moment she wondered if he was being sarcastic but his gaze was open and honest. In reply, she nodded. 'Yes, please. Vodka or gin, with tonic if you have it.'

He opened a mahogany cupboard to reveal an array of bottles and glasses. Noticing Tara's look of surprise, he explained, 'I often have to work late and a drink helps me to unwind.'

'Oh!' she murmured before adding in a louder voice, 'If it's all the same to you, I'd like to get dressed again now.'

He looked around, obviously surprised. 'Now?' he said. 'But we haven't finished.'

'Haven't we?'

She stared at the closed door, her feverish imagination conjuring up an army of doctors and nurses on the other side, all of them wielding a variety of instruments of torture and humiliation.

'No,' he said firmly and handed her a glass before motioning to her to resume her seat by his desk.

She felt her stomach tightening again, the soft, sick trembling sensation of nervousness creeping throughout her whole body. 'Who else is going to examine me?' she asked, her voice sounded strange to her own ears, as though she were swimming underwater.

'I am, of course,' he said.

Watching him recline in his sumptuous chair, his long legs stretched in front of him, crossed casually at the ankles, it struck her how truly arrogant he was and she inhaled sharply with anger. It was an unfortunate gesture for her to make. At once her generous breasts heaved and wobbled, immediately attracting his attention.

After a moment or two he tore his eyes away from them and looked deeply into her eyes. 'I'm sorry, I was distracted for a moment then,' he said. 'Now what were we talking about?'

She pretended to think for a minute, although she hadn't forgotten at all. Finally she said, 'You had just mentioned that you also wanted to examine me.'

He looked genuinely surprised at the way she stressed the word *examine*. 'But it was your suggestion,' he said, 'last night, on the telephone, remember?' He paused to sip his drink, then yawned slightly. 'It's been a tiring day,' he explained apologetically.

That was the last straw as far as Tara was concerned and she gave full vent to her anger. 'But of course!' she exclaimed in a tone heavy with sarcasm, her breasts rising and falling rapidly. 'It must have been absolutely exhausting for you, sitting there at your desk all day, plotting how many different ways you can humiliate me!'

She broke off and drank the whole of her drink in one go, grateful for the numbing warmth that spread instantly throughout her trembling body. Suddenly, she didn't care what he thought of her any more. She had endured enough, she wanted to go home, back to the haven of her quiet country cottage.

He relieved her of her empty glass, replenished it and handed it back to her. 'I have no idea what you are talking about,' he stated calmly.

She stared at him for a moment wondering if he really was telling the truth – that in all honesty he had believed her suggestion the previous night to be not only genuine but a sensible precaution. She took another gulp of her drink. A few more of these, she thought, and I'll be past caring.

'If you are quite recovered, shall we proceed?' he asked.

Tara stared wordlessly at him. He stood inches away from her, his tall, virile body immaculate in a stylishly cut navy pinstripe suit. All at once his presence hit her like a thunderbolt and she felt the telltale moisture surge from her sex. Without taking her eyes from his she rose to her feet, wobbling a little unsteadily so that she was forced to clutch at his arm for support. To her surprise he held her gently, one hand cupping her elbow, the other resting on her shoulder. His touch coursed through her body like an electric current, sending waves of molten desire crashing through her subconscious.

'Where would you like me?' she whispered, thinking he could interpret her question any way he chose.

He walked back to his chair and sat down, taking care not to crease his trousers. He reclined, glass in hand, one leg crossed on top of the other and the empty hand resting casually behind his head.

'Come here.'

She briefly considered disobeying him, after all, she could just put on her clothes and leave. But it wasn't in her nature to back down. Squaring her shoulders defiantly she stepped forward and placed her glass carefully on his desk.

'Come a little closer,' he ordered.

Aware that her breath was coming in short, shallow gasps she moved nearer to him, taking one tentative step at a time like a tightrope walker, only stopping when he raised his hand.

Slowly he ran his deep blue eyes over her body, starting with her hair, her face – which glowed crimson despite her false bravado – and her neck and shoulders which were tense and shuddering.

'Relax. I am not going to eat you,' he said.

Oh God! Her insides turned instantly to water. He obviously wasn't aware of the colloquial meaning of his words, his inadvertent *double-entendre*.

She shivered under his impassive gaze, the involuntary reaction causing her breasts to tremble slightly so that his line of vision shifted to that part of her, his eyes flicking over her nipples so blatantly that she could almost feel the physical impact upon them. Standing defiantly in front of him she watched as his gaze moved lower, lower, lower, right the way to her ankles before rising up her legs again and coming to rest at the top of her thighs where the soft blonde fleece hid the incessant pulsating of her sex.

He can see it, she thought wildly, even though my

thighs are pressed together very tightly he can see the way my body is reacting to him.

'Turn around,' he said.

She realised she was becoming used to obeying his commands and simply stared at a nondescript print on the opposite wall while he studied her back view.

Finally he exhaled, apparently satisfied. 'I must congratulate myself and André,' he said, 'we have chosen well.'

He didn't invite her to move, or to sit down but she sat anyway, retrieving her drink and taking another huge gulp. Her body relinquished a little more tension as the fiery liquid snaked down her throat. For the first time she realised she was becoming quite light-headed.

He stared hard at her. 'I didn't say you could sit down yet,' he said.

She looked back at him, her expression challenging, her attitude nonchalant. 'I know that,' she said, flicking her hair back from her face, 'but you've spent enough time looking at me. You've seen all there is to see.'

His arrogance seemed to increase as he shook his head slowly from side to side. He stared pointedly at the blonde vee of her pubis. '*Au contraire*, madame,' he said, a devious smile snaking about his lips, 'you have a great deal that I have not yet seen.'

'Oh, no!' Tara cried.

Despite her horror at his intention she felt a

strong burning sensation deep inside her pelvis and another rush of moisture soaked the seat beneath her.

'*Mais oui*,' he insisted, 'you must.'

He leaned forward, his eyes flicking from the top of her thighs, to her face, then back again.

In retaliation she shook her head. 'I don't have to do anything,' she insisted, hoping she sounded a lot more confident than she felt.

'But yes,' he said, his voice low and insistent, 'I have paid for you. You must do whatever I say.'

For a few shocked minutes she simply stared back at him. She wanted to reply that he had paid for her on behalf of his son, not himself, but then she realised that any argument would be pointless. At least now she knew where she stood. The lines of demarcation had been very firmly drawn.

'Very well.' She rose to her feet and began to walk toward him again.

Startled by her sudden volte face he put up his hand to stop her. 'Just a minute,' he said. Gathering his papers from his desk, he placed them on top of a low cupboard. Then he did the same with the rest of the items: a pen tray, the telephone and intercom, a photograph of André, until the desktop was completely cleared. When this was done he stood up, walked to the door and locked it.

While he did this Tara found her eyes drawn to the photograph of André, for some obscure reason its presence suddenly seemed to her to be obscene

59

and she let out a nervous laugh.

'You are amused, madame,' he said, 'why so?'

'Please stop calling me madame,' she sighed, ignoring his question, 'my name is Tara.'

'*D'accord*,' he agreed, and proceeded to repeat her name a couple of times, testing the sound of it, 'Tara, Tara.'

'Oh, please, you make me sound like a film title,' she commented drily, although one glance at his implacable expression told her that sarcasm was totally lost on him.

'Come and sit here, in front of me,' he said. He patted the covered portion of his desk.

I'll just have to go through with this, she thought with a frisson of anticipation and she began to squeeze awkwardly past his legs, nodding her thanks as he pushed his chair back a little to give her more room. When she reached the centre of the desk she placed her palms on it and jumped just a fraction so that her buttocks connected with the top, wriggling her hips until she was comfortable – or at least as comfortable as she could be in such peculiar circumstances.

Using his feet to propel his chair closer to the desk once again, he reached forward with both hands and slowly stroked his palms along the length of her thighs, his caress soft yet deliberate, stoking the embers of her mounting desire.

At his touch she began to tremble like a trapped animal, half of her wishing he would release her, the other half wishing desperately that he would make love to her there and then. It seemed to take a long time for the trembling to subside, her nervousness being replaced with profound arousal. Without thinking she let her head drop back and allowed a long, contented sigh to issue from her lips.

'You are not supposed to be enjoying this, Tara,' he commented, his tone and expression deadpan.

'Aren't I, monsieur?' she asked. She raised her head and looked straight at him.

Her stare held a challenge. It was about time she stopped thinking of herself as a victim, she decided, and allowing herself to be treated like one. With her heart thundering, its beat echoing in her eardrums, she edged forward a little on the desk and placed the soles of her feet on the edge of his chair. Ignoring his look of surprise, she insinuated them deliberately into the warm leather where it dipped slightly at either side of his thighs.

He stared back silently, moving his hands around so that the tips of his fingers pressed against her inner thighs where they were clenched tightly together. Using gentle pressure he prised them apart.

'I won't hurt you,' he said, 'I just want to look at you.' His voice was low, compelling her to give way and open her legs in front of his eyes.

She couldn't bear to watch him and closed her eyes and concentrated on the sensation of his touch. It was exquisite torture to feel his fingertips delicately prising her apart, the moist folds of her sex opening out for him like flower petals – a pink rose. He stroked her gently and began to run his fingers around the hard bud of her clitoris, exciting it with a skilful delicacy that made her want to scream aloud. Instead she gasped as his thumb pressed against the swollen nub of flesh.

'I'm sorry, did I hurt you?'

His voice broke through her thoughts and forced her eyes to open. This time she found the courage to look down at him and noticed how he gazed at the plump pouch of her sex, his expression almost reverent.

He loves women, she found herself thinking, here is a man who genuinely appreciates the appearance and the feel of the naked female form. In answer to his question she shook her head. 'Something amusing just crossed my mind,' she lied.

'Oh!' he said, apparently surprised by her reply. He reclined a little in his chair and added, 'So you are not concerned by this situation?'

Tara gazed at him. She desperately wanted to be able to lie again. To shake her head airily and say, 'Of course not, why should I be?' As though she did this sort of thing all the time, or at least as though she was accustomed to men looking so closely at her naked body. Instead she said. 'Of course I am. More than you will ever know.'

To her surprise the tears that had been threatening all afternoon suddenly welled up in her eyes.

'Get dressed.' His voice was soft as he backed his chair away from the desk and offered a helping hand for her to get down.

'Have you finished?' she said in a small voice, her fingertips brushing hastily at the salty droplets on her cheeks. His compassion shocked her and her voice trembled in response.

He shrugged, then he glanced at his watch. 'I did not realise it had become so late. I think I owe you some supper.'

'You don't owe me anything, you've already been more than generous,' she said, although she hoped he would insist.

He looked down, noticing with an expression almost of surprise that he was still holding her hand. Rather than let her go, he led her to the pile of her discarded clothes. 'I want to,' he said simply.

While she dressed he busied himself by replacing the items back on his desk, arranging papers and finally by making a telephone call to André.

Despite her intention to the contrary, Tara couldn't help eavesdropping on the short, one-sided conversation. She had to admit Guy Ricard sounded as though he was a loving father and, not for the first time, she wondered what it would be like to be on the receiving end of this softer side of him. As she sat on one of the low sofas clad in silky white camiknickers, just rolling the second stocking up her leg, he looked up from his paperwork and spoke.

'You certainly know how to dress like a woman.'

'Thank you,' she said, 'these things are new.'

She didn't know how to respond, although she glowed with pleasure at the compliment.

'Perhaps now you will be able to buy many more new clothes,' he said.

Suddenly she felt queasy, his innocent words reminding her with a jolt of their true relationship – that she was bought and paid for.

'I think I just lost my appetite,' she muttered grimly. Stepping into her dress she zipped it quickly but halfway up her back the zip became stuck. 'Damn!' she cried, feeling tears of frustration well up yet again. She struggled with the zip until she sensed rather than saw him rush to her aid.

In an instant he had sorted out the problem – his deft fingers unhooking the trapped fibres of material without tearing them.

She felt the heat of his body like a furnace and longed to simply relax against him, to feel his arms go around her and hold her, keeping her safe from harm.

'*C'est ça!*' He exclaimed as he released her, his expression one of satisfaction at a job well done, nothing more. 'Shall we go, Tara?'

He led her to a basement car park where he strode purposefully toward a black Renault. Of course, she should have known he would remain patriotic, even in his choice of car. His style of driving was like everything else he did, careful, efficient, resolute – his large, lightly tanned hands turning the wheel with confidence. As he changed gear she found herself following his action with her eyes, noticing the expensive watch on his wrist that just emerged from the cover of a pristine white cuff.

There and then she decided white cuffs against tanned wrists were a definite sexual turn on. With a longing bordering on desperation she wished the hand would leave the gearstick and move across to her thigh. Straight away she cursed herself for being so coy back there in his office, not to mention so illogical. When she'd had both his hands upon her she had wanted to escape his clutches, now she wanted nothing more than to be back in them again.

She was surprised that he didn't take her to a French restaurant. Although, on reflection, she realised that English French restaurants were probably more often than not an insult to the French. Instead they ate Italian, pizza for both of them — thin and crispy with lashings of tomato, fresh herbs and stringy mozzarella cheese. He had ordered first and she had to admit his choice had surprised her, having assumed he would automatically opt for something outlandishly gourmet. Unable to keep her thoughts to herself, she shared them with him.

In reply he laughed. 'Why would you think such a thing, Tara?' he said, 'I am a simple man. My pleasures are few.'

She didn't know what to say. She wished fervently that she could join the ranks of his few pleasures.

Her downfall that evening was the copious amount of wine they drank with their food – rich red wine, the sort she had no head for at the best of times.

'I think I'm becoming tipsy,' she giggled, knocking her fork onto the tiled floor with a loud clatter.

Far from looking annoyed at her display he merely smiled and glanced at his watch. 'I don't know what to do with you,' he said thoughtfully, 'I can't allow you to travel home alone on the train. Not at this time of night and in your ... er ... condition.'

Tara shrugged carelessly, dislodging one of her shoulder straps so that it fell down her arm, exposing the top of her breast. With a sigh he reached forward and repaired her modesty. 'I shall have to take you home with me,' he said, 'you can use my bed.'

She blushed and let out a nervous giggle, like a schoolgirl. 'I thought you'd never ask,' she said.

Silently he rose and helped her to her feet. Picking up her handbag, he placed it firmly under her arm and then, holding her by the waist, led her from the restaurant.

Outside on the street, she sagged against him, stumbling in her high heels. Looking up at his stern profile, she instantly regretted her over-indulgence.

'I'm sorry,' she said in a small voice.

'Whatever for?' he asked.

He led her to the car and almost folded her into the passenger seat, her limp body complying with his manipulations. As he sat behind the steering wheel and placed the key in the ignition, she said, 'Well, I'm not handling this properly, am I?'

'Are you not?' he replied, gazing at her with apparent amazement. 'Under the circumstances I think you have been quite astounding. I don't think I could have behaved any better – if I were a woman, I mean.'

She looked at him, wide-eyed. 'Your English is so good,' she murmured in a breathy voice that told of her genuine admiration. Suddenly she became aware of how heavy her head felt and she rested it against the back of the seat, her eyelids fluttering. 'I'm so glad you're not a woman,' she added with a sigh and drifted into oblivion.

Chapter Four

When she awoke, it was five fifteen the following morning and she was in a strange bed – alone. All at once she remembered the events of the previous day. She looked around the empty room then peeked under the maroon cotton duvet. She was still wearing the white satin body she had put on the day before but her dress, stockings and suspender belt had been removed. He must have undressed her.

For a moment she felt shocked. Then, with a sudden surge of humiliation, she remembered how he had already studied her naked body. In the circumstances, it could hardly be considered improper that he had stripped her to her underwear.

He must have heard her because he appeared in the doorway, dressed in a black bathrobe and looking cool, calm and collected as usual.

'You are okay?' he said, his voice husky.

She nodded and pulled the duvet up to her chin. 'I'm sorry about last night,' she began, her eyes wide.

'Don't be,' he said, 'there is no need.' He sat next

to her on the bed. 'I told you, I admire the way you handled things yesterday.'

She felt the mattress dip and relaxed a little. She let her hands drop to her lap and looked down at them, studying them as though she had never seen them before. Then she glanced back up at him.

'I thought perhaps you regretted your decision to pick me,' she murmured. 'I'll understand if you want to call the whole thing off.'

'Are you crazy?' The words shot from his lips like a peppering of machine-gun fire, richocheting against her throbbing eardrums.

'Please!' She put her hand to her head and winced a little.

Laughing softly, he stroked her shoulder. 'I am more certain than ever that you should be the one to seduce André,' he said in a voice as dark and thick as treacle. 'You possess very admirable qualities.'

'Like the ability to get drunk on a couple of glasses of wine?' Her lips moved but her mind and all her other senses were galvanised by the light pressure of his fingertips along the length of her collarbone and the sensual caress of his voice. She wondered if it was her imagination, or wishful thinking, but the atmosphere between them suddenly seemed heavy with unspoken thoughts.

'You know that is not what I meant at all,' he said. His fingers hooked the shoestring strap of her satin body and pulled it down her arm, uncovering her breast.

A gasp of surprise burst from her lips and she breathed deeply, her breasts rising and her nipples tightening under his gaze. She sat perfectly still, her heart pounding, waiting for his next move.

He slid his fingers tentatively up her arm, over her shoulder and down, the palm of his hand coming to rest on her breast.

'I think this would be a good time to complete the examination, don't you?' he whispered softly, circling her breast with the flat of his palm, rolling the hard bud of her nipple under it until the nub of flesh grew tighter and tighter.

With a huge sigh Tara nodded, unable to take her eyes from his face as he slid down the other strap and began to stimulate the other breast in exactly the same way.

'I believe André will not be disappointed with these,' he said. He bent his head and sucked first one nipple and then the other, his hands cupping her breasts, holding them tightly, squeezing them together as he flicked his tongue from side to side.

She felt a thrill of shock course through her at his words and actions. In her excitement, she had forgotten about André and she wondered briefly what sort of man could consider making love to the same woman as his son? There was no doubt in her mind that whatever might happen between herself and Guy, however intimate they might become, he would not go back on his intention. He would still want her – no, expect her – to seduce André.

As Guy continued to caress her breasts with maddening skill she arched her back, urging him to take more of her between his soft warm lips, to wrap his strong, insistent tongue around the swollen buds of her nipples. With one hand she stroked his hair, running her fingers absently through the thick dark strands in a rapidly hastening tempo as her desire for him circulated in the pit of her belly.

Tentatively she dropped her hand lower, sliding it down the back of his neck under the thick collar of his robe, running her palm across the expanse of his shoulders and feeling the hardness of the muscle beneath her fingertips.

Gently he pushed her back so that she reclined against the pillows, forcing her to release her hold on him for the moment. With a single movement he pulled the duvet off the bed, his eyes sweeping along the length of her as she lay shivering in the chill air of the early morning, half clad in the virginal white silk. With little regard for its delicacy, he pulled at the thin covering, tugging it down her legs and off her body. She lay naked and trembling, staring up at him wide-eyed with nervousness and excitement.

'*Fantastique!*' he murmured, running his hands down the length of her torso, kneading the pliant flesh of her waist and hips, his thumbs massaging the soft swell of her belly.

'Oh, Guy!' she cried.

It was the first time she had used his Christian name and he looked up. His eyes locked with hers for a second, surprise at hearing his name on her lips evident from the expression on his face. 'I would prefer it if you called me monsieur when André is around,' he said. His expression suddenly became serious again, although he didn't allow the rhythm of his caress to falter. 'At all costs he must not suspect that you and I have, or have had, a relationship of any kind. It is imperative for his own self-esteem,' he added.

Startled, Tara nodded but, as his words sunk in she began to see the wisdom of his request. 'Of course. You can rely on me to be discreet. Nor do I have any intention of discussing what takes place between André and myself.'

It was strange but as soon as she spoke about herself and André she realised her intention to seduce him was a reality.

'*D'accord*,' he nodded, 'I knew I could trust you.' He stroked his hands across her belly, then allowed them to drift across the light downy plain of her pubis.

Automatically her legs parted and she moaned.

'If I ask you to come to my bed whilst we are in France you must not mind about leaving before daybreak,' he murmured, his breath whispering across her thighs.

His words excited her. She hadn't considered the possibility of sleeping with Guy as well as his son while they were in France. With a giggle, she wondered if she should start building up her energy reserves. Then she realised it was probably already too late. This was their last day in England, by the following night they would all be together in France. Living under one roof. Playing happy families . . . and she was to be the lover of father *and* son.

He stroked his hands more firmly across her pubis, applying a little pressure with the heel of one hand so that her labia parted slightly and she felt the stimulation reach the sensitive bud of her clitoris.

She wriggled and parted her thighs further, opening up to him as he pressed more firmly, his palm sliding a fraction lower as she made way to accommodate him. Then, he turned his hand and slipped it between her legs, stroking the whole of her swollen vulva. He rubbed it back and forth over her heated flesh, until she began to moan and writhe beneath him.

His manipulation of her body was exquisite, as though he already knew her and knew exactly how to pleasure her. She wondered how many women he had enjoyed before her, and if he had been faithful to his wife. With a start of surprise she realised there was so much she didn't know about him. In reality they had hardly spoken at all.

With great finesse he slipped his fingers between her labia to stimulate the swollen bud that lay hidden beneath – the hot core of flesh that already throbbed and pulsed with mounting excitement. And he allowed a satisfied smile to snake around his lips as she ground herself shamelessly against his fingers. Then he took his fingers lower, delving into the hot, wet cavern of her vagina, guiding her skilfully towards orgasm.

'Guy, oh my God!'

Before she had the chance to prepare herself she felt her climax explode, taking her completely by surprise though not satisfying her by any means. It was as though he had just opened a channel of exquisite sensations that had never been available to her before. And, although she felt disloyal at the thought, she was certain her husband had not brought her to this level of arousal. Even Glen, although their brief encounter had been enjoyable, had not managed to lead her anywhere near this vale of pleasure.

Guy Ricard smiled down at her, enjoying her reaction, taking pleasure in the proof of his own skill. She pretended to be bold and brave and independent but he was able to see through her. He recognised how little experience she had of life, of men, and how much she had still to learn. By the end of the summer, if he had not lost his touch, she would eventually become a complete woman.

Not realising that she was, in fact, the seduced rather than the seducer, Tara gave herself willingly to the unique gratification of being loved by Guy Ricard. Heedless of her moans and wild gyrations, he continued to stroke and fondle her feverish body, taking her beyond the limits of her endurance.

'Please, Guy. I can't take any more,' she was forced to gasp at long last. She arched her back, almost senseless with pleasure as he cupped her buttocks and brought her toward his mouth, covering the throbbing tenderness of her clitoris with the warm wetness of his lips and tongue. Her hands groped in thin air, wanting desperately to push him away before she lost control completely.

Guy Ricard smiled to himself and deliberately ignored her pleas. He delved remorselessly into her with his tongue, using it like a small cock as he held her writhing hips fast in his large, strong hands. He liked to see her in the grip of so much pleasure and forced her to take it. He wanted to see how much she could bear, how long before she fell over the edge.

'Oh, God . . . Guy . . . I can't . . .!' Her breath was so shallow the words had to be almost torn from her body. She thought she would go mad from the incessant round of stimulation and release.

Eventually, he lowered her hips, stretching out full length beside her, calming her shuddering body with smooth strokes of his hands.

For a while she lay satiated, her arms thrown above her head, her legs carelessly splayed as she simply stared at nothing. Gradually she descended back into reality.

'I want you to fuck me now,' she said finally, her voice a whisper.

'No, Tara.' He continued to stroke her, his expression unsmiling.

'But . . . you must . . .' She wasn't prepared for his flat refusal. He had to enter her, to fill her with his throbbing cock and take his own pleasure, it was the next logical stage. Suddenly, she realised something and put out her hand to delve inside his robe.

'I'm sorry. I've been so selfish,' she said, her expression full of apology. She felt for his sex but he gripped her wrist firmly and removed her hand.

'You haven't been selfish,' he said, 'I don't want you to touch me.'

'But?' Now she was totally confused.

'Don't argue with me, Tara. Make no mistake, if and when I want you to stimulate me I will certainly let you know. And as for penetration . . .' he began.

'Yes?' She hated his choice of word.

'. . . I don't do that.'

Despite her fatigue she sat up quickly, dislodging his hand as it stroked her breast. 'What do you mean, you don't do that?' she exclaimed. 'What sort of thing is that to say?'

He shrugged. 'Since my wife died . . . well . . . I just don't.'

She stared at him, amazed. 'I don't believe it,' she said. 'Your wife's been dead for how long?' She was sure André had told her that he had never known his mother.

'Sixteen years,' he said, moving away from her and putting his feet to the floor. 'She was killed in a car crash when André was only a year old.' His voice was monotone, his expression blank. He yawned. 'I think I should be getting ready for work.'

Open-mouthed, she watched him rise from the bed. 'Is that it? Now you're going to go to the office as though it was just another day?'

For a second he hesitated, then he turned and looked stonily at the young woman who sat cross-legged on his bed, tousled and naked and confused. 'It *is* just another day, Tara,' he said calmly.

She wanted to go to him then, to hit him, to argue with him, to force him to show some emotion but instinctively she knew it would be useless. 'In that case I'd better get dressed too and go home,' she said, 'I have a lot of packing to do.' As she spoke the last part of her sentence she looked at him. 'I suppose I do still have a month in France to look forward to?'

He looked genuinely surprised by her question. 'Of course, why ever not?'

'No reason,' she said with a shrug.

As soon as he left the room she got up and started to pull on her clothes. She couldn't believe the events of the past few days, or even the past few hours. It was inconceivable that a gorgeous man such as Monsieur Guy Ricard had not had sex with a woman in sixteen years. She amended her thoughts to encompass his delightful terminology: had not had *penetrative* sex in sixteen years.

He returned to the bedroom just as she was slipping on her shoes. 'I forgot to mention, there is a bathroom through here,' he said, crossing the bedroom in a couple of strides and pushing open a door to a small en-suite room.

'I know,' she said dully, 'I already found it.'

She stared at him. Suddenly it seemed as though they were strangers again, as though everything that had gone before was part of a dream.

'Would you like some breakfast?' he suggested. 'Some coffee?'

Despite his offer she noticed how he glanced at his watch, making it clear that he would prefer not to delay their departure.

'No, thank you,' she said with a brief smile and shaking her head. All at once a thought occurred to her. 'Is there a station nearby?'

'I will drive you to Charing Cross.' He walked back into the living room with Tara close behind him.

'Guy?' She felt as though she had to say something about their situation.

'Yes, what is it?' His tone was so curt she almost recoiled. Then his face softened. 'Don't waste your time trying to analyse me, Tara,' he said firmly, 'and don't fool yourself into thinking you can change me. Many women, more experienced women than you, have tried and failed.' He smiled wistfully and added, 'I suppose, deep down, I don't want to change at all.'

She stared at him, wondering at his casual use of the term *many women*. She pictured him surrounded by a veritable harem – women of all shapes and sizes trying desperately to convert him to . . .

what . . . normality? She had to admit it was not too
awful from a woman's point of view to meet a man
whose only interest lay in pleasuring her. Still, she
would be spending a month with him, that was
plenty of time for her to change his mind.

'Point taken,' she said, 'shall we go?' She smiled
at him, her air deliberately casual, her mind made
up before they had even left the building. She could
never resist a challenge.

With perfect timing the doorbell rang just as she
finished her packing. She was not surprised to see
her neighbour, Ginny, standing on the doorstep,
although she was surprised that her friend hadn't
let herself in the back door as she usually did.

Tara raised an eyebrow. 'Why are you ringing the
doorbell?'

'I'm never sure if you're going to be alone these
days,' Ginny said drily. She pushed past her and
walked straight to the kitchen where she filled the
kettle and started to spoon coffee into a couple of
mugs as though she was on her own home.

'Ginny!' Tara exploded, she knew her friend was
referring to Glen. 'It was once. The first time in
over a year. I would hardly call that promiscuous.'
Suddenly she felt guilty, she hadn't told her friend
about her encounter with Guy Ricard.

'I know, just call me a jealous bitch.' The other
woman laughed, her plump shoulders shaking.

The kettle switched itself off and Tara squeezed

past Ginny's ample form to pour the boiling water onto the coffee granules, stirring them thoroughly, her mind elsewhere until a voice interrupted her.

'I think that will do,' Ginny said gently. She reached out and grasped a mug. Sipping her coffee, she regarded Tara thoughtfully. 'Are you all ready for your . . . er . . . trip? Is your packing all done?'

Tara nodded. 'I'd just finished when you arrived.' She walked through the open back door into the garden, inhaling the mixed scent of the fresh blooms. 'Will you water my garden while I'm away?'

Her friend nodded. 'Of course, what are friends for?' She sat down in a garden chair. 'Aren't you nervous?'

'About going to France?' Tara asked, knowing she was being deliberately pedantic.

'About what you're supposed to do when you get there?' Ginny said.

'I don't know. I suppose so.' Tara sat down heavily, suddenly feeling very tired, her hangover creeping back up on her. 'I nearly backed out,' she admitted finally.

'That doesn't surprise me,' Ginny said, 'I can't believe you're still planning to go through with it. Or . . .?' She broke off suddenly and took a long swallow of coffee.

'Or what?'

Ginny shrugged. 'Nothing.'

'Or what?' Tara persisted. She had to know what her friend had been about to say.

With a small sigh the other woman looked squarely at her friend. 'Or are you planning to go over there, stall them, then take the money and run?'

'No. Of course not.' Tara shook her head, shocked that her friend could believe her capable of such behaviour. 'Besides,' she said, staring into the depths of her cooling coffee, 'I've already been paid. Half of it, anyway.'

'Really?' Ginny was agog. 'How much?' Sometimes she could be very blunt, Tara thought.

Tara wavered, ashamed of the amount as though the actual sum but not the reason for its payment was obscene. 'A few thousand,' she said, choosing to be vague.

'Wow!' Her friend regarded her with wide eyes. 'What are you planning to do with the money?'

Tara shrugged. 'I don't know. Buy some clothes, maybe a car. I haven't really thought about it.' She hadn't thought about it because she had never intended that the situation should progress as far as it had.

In the end it was a relief when Ginny finally left. Tara looked at her watch, it was almost six o'clock and she found herself wondering where the day had gone. A light supper, a bath and then an early night seemed to be the best way to pass her last few hours in England.

If she had hoped to fall straight into a deep sleep she was to be disappointed. Despite her fatigue she couldn't stop tossing and turning, her mind churning over and over with the torment of thought. Eventually she got up, rifled through her bathroom cabinet until she found the sleeping pills that the doctor had prescribed for her after Lance's death, took just one and then tried to read. Within half an hour her eyelids were drooping, the drug mercifully pulling her into the deep, dark chasm of sleep.

The alarm clock almost rang itself out before she finally surfaced. Looking at the dial she saw it was half past eight. It didn't leave her with much time as she had arranged for a mini cab to collect her at ten o'clock. She deliberately forced herself to eat breakfast: two slices of wholemeal toast, a boiled egg and several cups of tea. Then she rose from the table, washed and dried the few dishes and moved to the mirror in the hallway to apply a coat of lipstick and check her hair.

Next to the front door stood her large suitcase and a smaller tote bag. Suddenly, she was startled by the insistent hooting of a car horn. She checked her watch, the minicab was dead on time. Feeling for all the world like a murderess going to the gallows, she opened the front door picked up her bags and stepped out into the sunshine, pausing for a moment to enjoy its warm glow on her face as if it were for the last time.

'Shall I take those?' The impatient tone of the minicab driver jolted her out of her reverie. He nodded at her twin burden.

'Yes, please,' she said. She handed her bags to him

and turned to shut the front door, pushing it hard to double-check that it was locked securely.

During the drive to the airport she forced herself to watch the passing scenery and not think about the purpose of her trip. During the check-in procedure she forced herself to stare at her fellow travellers and keep her mind blank. During the wait in the departure lounge she forced herself to flick through a magazine and contemplate nothing more than the fashions and beauty items. By the time she was seated comfortably on the plane she could no longer avoid thinking about her predicament.

Of course she couldn't go through with it. As soon as I get to France, she resolved, I'll telephone the house and tell them I'm not coming after all. Then I'll catch the next flight home again.

When the plane landed she found herself being hustled through the baggage claim and customs procedure and finally out into the French sunshine.

'Taxi, madame?' A driver stood in front of her, eyeing her bags. She almost giggled, he looked exactly the same as the minicab driver in England. '*Oui, merci,*' she said. She allowed him to open the door for her, a Gallic act of chivalry that was lost to English taxi drivers, she noted. As soon as he was seated behind the wheel she showed him the map Guy had given her.

'*Bon,*' he replied. He nodded and smiled, revealing a row of broken, nicotine-stained teeth.

Tara sat back in the seat, revolted by the sight.

They eased out of the airport, around the city ring road and along the main autoroute. Eventually, they turned off the main road and started to travel across country, along narrow country lanes lined with lush green vineyards. Finally the taxi pulled into a long driveway which terminated in front of a large stone house.

Tara reached for her bag. It had been a long journey, much longer than she had anticipated and consequently she was not surprised when the driver quoted a staggering amount of money for his fare. However, she reasoned, she had been paid more than enough to justify it.

As the car pulled away in a cloud of dust, Tara looked up at the house and then around the wide expanse of green and brown landscape that surrounded it. It seemed as though she had been abandoned in the middle of nowhere.

'Madame Cochrane, *bienvenu.*'

She turned automatically to the familiar and very welcome sound of André's voice.

'Good afternoon, André,' she said. Her clipped English served to remind him that she was there, at least as far as he was concerned, to ensure that he kept to his studies.

He blushed. 'I'm sorry. Good afternoon, Mrs Cochrane.'

She didn't know whether it was her imagination but he appeared to stress her title.

'Please, André. I think as we are on holiday you

should just call me Tara,' she said firmly.

'Oh no madame, I couldn't,' he said.

His protest was born of genuine good manners but she shook her head. 'I insist.' She smiled and glanced down at her suitcase. 'Would you mind, André?'

At once he rushed to her side and picked up the heavy case and also her tote bag, lifting them easily.

For a moment or two she allowed herself to study him. It had only been a week since she had last set eyes on him but already he seemed different – more grown-up, more masculine. Although she couldn't help wondering if her new perception of him was based on wishful thinking.

Inside the house she was struck by its luxury: the thick carpets, the elegant furniture, the paintings and the good quality antiques.

'This is not at all what I expected,' she murmured as he led her up a sweeping staircase and along a wide hallway.

Through each open doorway she could see a bedroom with a different colour scheme. It struck her that if it had been an English house they would have referred to as the 'blue room', the 'pink room' and so on.

As they neared the end of the hallway, André put down her bags. 'This is your room,' he said, then nodded at the next room along, 'and that's my room just there. So, if you should need anything . . .' He didn't finish the sentence but shrugged and blushed a little. She could see he was imagining her coming to his room in the middle of the night, anxious for comfort.

'Thank you, André,' she said. To her surprise she was finding it difficult to speak normally with him. Suddenly she wished that Guy would show up. 'Is your father here yet?'

To her disappointment, André shook his head. 'No. We were warned not to expect him until eight or nine and therefore to start supper without him.' He opened the bedroom door, picked up the cases and stepped inside.

Tara followed. 'We?'

André looked around. 'Yes, what?'

'Pardon?' She glanced at him quizzically, not knowing what he was talking about.

'You said *oui*,' he said, 'I replied, yes what?'

She stared at him for a second, nonplussed, then she realised they were talking at cross purposes.

'No. Oh, André.' She laughed lightly at the same time placing her hand on his shoulder in a friendly gesture. 'I meant *we*, in English. If you remember, you said *we* were warned . . .'

'Oh,' he laughed at the misunderstanding, then he glanced at her hand his expression immediately changing, casting a shadow over his smiling face.

Slowly she withdrew it.

'I meaned Lisette, our housekeeper. She is the other part of we.'

'I meant,' Tara replied, automatically correcting his English.

87

For the first time she looked around her bedroom. Decorated in shades of green, it seemed as though it was an extension of the rolling countryside visible from the window. It couldn't have been more perfect.

'There is a small bathroom with douche,' André explained, walking across the room and opening a small wooden door.

'In English it is a shower, André, not a douche. A douche is something else entirely.'

'What?' he said.

She was already gazing thoughtfully out of the open window and she missed his question. 'Mm?'

'What is a douche, Madame Cochrane? I ... I mean, Tara.'

She turned around to look at him. 'I told you, it means shower.'

'No!' His expression showed he was finding their incomprehension frustrating. 'You said douche meant something else.'

'Oh,' she said and sat down heavily on the bed, suddenly feeling exhausted, 'yes, I did, didn't I?'

'Well,' he persisted, 'what does it mean?'

She looked at him for a moment, wondering how to reply. In the end she decided the truth was her best option. 'A douche is something women use to ... er ... wash themselves with.'

'What, like a ... how you say ... flannel?' he asked.

'No, not quite.' She shook her head slowly. 'Some women use them to clean their vaginas.' She had decided the time had come to stop beating around the bush.

For a second he still looked confused so she pointed rather inelegantly between her legs.

'Oh.' His face and neck quickly became a deep shade of red and to Tara's amusement he suddenly seemed very anxious to change the subject. 'Can I get you a drink, Madame . . . Tara?'

'Yes, thank you, André,' she said, stifling a smile. 'Do you have any wine?'

At her question he laughed. 'We are surrounded by vineyards,' he said. 'Of course we have wine.'

He led the way downstairs again and into a large, stone-flagged kitchen. In the centre of the room stood a scrubbed oak table and on top of the table stood a large earthenware jug. Pausing to take a couple of glasses from a cupboard he sat down at the table, indicating that she should do the same. Then he poured two generous glasses of dark ruby wine from the jug.

'Santé!' he said, raising the glass to his lips.

'Cheers,' Tara murmured in reply.

She couldn't help thinking how strange it seemed to be sitting across the table from him drinking red wine instead of teaching him verbs and grammar. On his home territory, André seemed like a different person. As she sipped her wine she contemplated him, noticing how his hair had grown a little, how his top lip showed the distinct dark shadow of a moustache, how his biceps bulged perceptively under the short white sleeves of his T-shirt. Gradually she felt the warmth of the wine spread through her body. She reflected that she had missed lunch, having been uninspired by the fare offered by the airline.

'André, do you have a girlfriend?' she said, surprising herself with the out-of-the-blue question.

He too looked startled for a moment, then he blushed. 'One or two. Why?'

One or two, she thought, then surely he has already lost his virginity?

'Are they . . . serious, these girlfriends?'

For a moment he seemed not to understand her meaning, then he shook his head.

'Oh, no, Madame . . . Tara,' he corrected himself hastily, 'they are friends that is all. We dance, we go for walks, or to the cinema.' He didn't elaborate any further.

Without thinking she reclined in her chair and crossed her legs, her sarong skirt falling open.

His gaze automatically travelled the length of her legs, coming to rest on the place where her skirt joined her bare thighs. Despite his shyness it was obvious he couldn't tear his eyes away.

She thought his action reminded her of Guy. Like father like son. Just thinking of him took her back to the events of the previous two days. Deliberately she resisted the urge to cover her legs and instead she swung the foot of her top leg casually from side to side, ensuring that André's attention remained captive.

90

Eventually he spoke. 'Would you like me to show you around the grounds, Tara?'

She noticed it was the first time he had not called her Madame and realised the atmosphere between them had changed imperceptibly. And all she'd had to do was cross her legs.

Chapter Five

Following him through the open doorway into the garden, she was struck by the difference between this garden and her own. For a start, this one extended for some sixteen acres, or so André told her, forming a veritable estate which included a stream and woodland. As they rounded the corner of the house, she found that they were standing in a wide courtyard, surrounded on the other three sides by outbuildings. In front of them, in the centre of the courtyard, sparkled the enticing blue-green water of a swimming pool.

'Oh, how wonderful!' she exclaimed and stepped forward to peer into the clear depths. Squatting down beside it she put her hand in the water, waggling her fingers.

'Is it cold?' André asked.

'No, warm.' She looked up at him and then straightened. 'Do you think anyone would mind if I went for a swim?'

'No, of course not,' he said, 'I usually spend a lot

of time swimming.' He glanced around, frowning a little. 'To be honest there's not much else to do around here.'

'Really?' Tara almost shocked herself by her thoughts and quickly smothered a smile. 'I'll just go and get changed.' She found her room easily and emerged about ten minutes later wrapped in a bright yellow towelling robe. In the hallway she met André who wore only a brief pair of bathing trunks.

'Oh!' she exclaimed. His sudden appearance took her by surprise. Without thinking she glanced down at his trunks, her eyes automatically sweeping over his crotch. With a small tingle of amusement she noticed something stir.

'I need that swim,' he said, his voice thick as he pushed hastily past her and rushed down the stairs, taking them two at a time.

Feeling a little guilty, Tara scolded herself. She wasn't there to tease the poor boy. If anything, she was meant to relieve him. She too descended the stairs and, using the side door that André had shown her, stepped out into the strong sunlight once again. By the time she reached the pool, André was already immersed in the warm water and as soon as she appeared he began churning up and down, covering length after length in a frantic crawl.

For a moment she stood by the table at the edge of the pool, hesitating, her hand on her loosely knotted belt. Her costume was brief to say the least. In fact it had been a last minute, 'mad' purchase, made without concern about when she might actually wear it. Now, here she was, having hardly arrived at her destination and already she was flaunting her body. Taking a deep breath she opened her robe, slipped it from her shoulders and dropped it casually onto a chair. Of course André looked up.

She expected nothing less than the reaction she received. She had selected this bikini for its stark simplicity. Plain white, its top was boned and shaped like a brassiere, pushing her full breasts upward and together, whilst the bottom was a simple g-string. All in all, it left very little to the imagination. From the corner of her eye she could see André frantically treading water. He was struggling, choking almost, in his desperation not to look at her. To save his blushes she pretended not to notice. Instead she ambled casually over to the very edge and dived in.

For some time she swam up and down, covering the lengths easily and reminding herself of the pleasure of swimming – a pastime she had not enjoyed for quite a while. Eventually, feeling slightly breathless, she climbed up the steps, leaving the refreshing water behind, allowing it to drip freely from her body. As she rose from the water she could feel André's eyes on her back, his stare burning into her naked buttocks like a branding iron. Then she heard his voice cry out joyfully.

'Papa!'

She looked around, startled. From the side of the

house emerged the tall, besuited figure of Guy Ricard.

For a brief moment he stared at her as though he was surprised to see her there. Perhaps he had doubted that she would really go through with their arrangement, or perhaps it was her costume. Whatever the reason, she had obviously arrested his attention. Tearing his gaze away from her reluctantly, he smiled at his son who was already halfway out of the pool.

Father and son walked toward each other. Now that they were together Tara could see how very alike they were, a couple of inches in height the only real difference between them.

'I managed to get away early.' Guy Ricard spoke to his son in French and reached out to ruffle his hair. Then his gaze encompassed Tara and he smiled warmly. 'I hope you have been looking after Madame Cochrane?' he said to André.

She noticed how the boy blushed when his father asked the question and how he couldn't quite bring himself to look at her.

'*Oui*,' he said simply, nodding.

'*Bon*.' Guy Ricard walked over to Tara, with his back to André he could allow his eyes to roam freely over her body.

Now Tara felt herself blushing. 'Hello, monsieur, it's nice to see you again,' she said lightly. It was difficult to make casual conversation when all the time she was fighting an overwhelming urge to drag him away to somewhere secluded so that he could touch her again and make her come.

'Likewise.' He skimmed his eyes over her barely covered breasts and allowed his mouth to curve into a wicked smile that sent small darts of desire shooting through her whole body.

Glancing down she saw what he saw: the swell of her generous globes, the soft flesh lightly tanned, dusted with a few stray droplets of water. Without thinking, she shook her wet hair, her casual action precipitating a wave of movement that undulated throughout her whole body like the aftershock of an earth tremor.

'I shall expect you in my room tonight,' he said darkly. His statement was an aside, spoken so quietly that the words could reach no one's ears but Tara's. He turned back to his son who stood combing his fingers through his wet hair, slicking it back from his high forehead. 'Come, André,' he said, draping his arm around the boy's shoulders, 'I think it is time your poor, tired papa had a drink.'

As Guy and André Ricard turned and walked towards the house, she stared after their retreating figures. All at once she realised that she was not dealing with a man and a boy, but two men – two men who, although similar in looks, were very different in temperament. There and then she made a mental note never to allow herself to fall into the trap of confusing the two. Guy was Guy and André was André. And in each case her approach must be entirely different.

For a while she lounged in a chair by the poolside,

allowing father and son the opportunity to enjoy some time together alone. After about an hour she started to feel the drop in temperature as the day gave way to early evening and she belted her robe around her and walked back into the house.

As she stepped into the gloomy hallway, she noticed the two of them sitting opposite each other at the large kitchen table, glasses of wine in hand, just as she had sat with André a couple of hours earlier. She decided not to disturb them and went straight upstairs to shower and change.

The very presence of Guy in the house had brought her senses alive. To know that he was close, that he wanted her that very night made her feel almost unbearably excited. So much so that she briefly toyed with the idea of satisfying her own churning desire as she stood under the restorative spray of the shower. But she found the strength to resist, towelling herself dry quickly in case her hands should linger too long on her own body and she should succumb.

She moved briskly to her wardrobe, flinging open the walnut doors and surveying the capacious interior. Ignoring the urge to wear something vampish, and therefore totally inappropriate, she chose a short plain cotton skirt in a dusky rose colour and a cotton jumper in a paler pink. With hardly a glance at her deceptively casual appearance in the mirror, she slipped her feet into a pair of flat white espadrilles and made her way back down the stairs.

She noticed straight away that the men no longer sat in the kitchen. And, as she stood in the hallway, eyeing the range of closed doors, debating which room to try first, she was surprised by the sudden appearance of André.

'We're down here, in the dining room,' he said, inclining his head towards a long passageway leading off to the left.

She followed him until they reached a door at the end. Inside Guy was seated at the head of a long polished table, on either side of him places were set for a meal. André automatically took one place and indicated with his hand that she should take the other. White candles set into a plain candelabra flickered on the table between them.

'I'm sorry, I didn't realise I was keeping you waiting,' she said finally.

Her apologetic smile encompassed both men but Guy waved his hand dismissively. For the first time he looked totally relaxed.

'Do not concern yourself, madame,' he said, 'Lisette tells us supper is not quite ready.' He glanced at his watch. 'We don't usually eat until nine but as we have each had a long journey I thought an early night would be appropriate.'

His expression was entirely guileless but Tara found her cheeks colouring. To cover her embarrassment she picked up her wineglass and took a large sip. As usual, the power of the alcohol spread quickly through her body, going straight to her head. She glanced at her own watch. It was only seven o'clock and she wondered how much of an early night he had in mind.

'I didn't realise it was that late,' she murmured, lost for anything else to say.

Mercifully, at that moment they were interrupted by the arrival of a large, capable-looking woman dressed entirely in black. Obviously this was Lisette, she thought. For quite a while they were occupied with helping themselves from a selection of tempting dishes and tasting their choices.

'Lisette has excelled herself again, hasn't she Papa?' André paused to sip from his glass, his face wreathed in satisfied smiles.

Guy Ricard nodded. 'Indeed,' he said before turning to Tara. 'Is everything also to your liking?' For a brief second his eyes flicked to the loose vee-neck of her jumper as he spoke, it was obvious that she wasn't wearing a bra underneath the light cotton.

She felt her nipples harden automatically. 'Oh . . . um . . . yes. This is all so delicious,' she managed to gasp.

He smiled and pushed his plate away. 'I have no room for a heavy dessert,' he said. 'I think I shall just have a piece of fruit.'

At his words, André jumped up and crossed the room to a long mahogany sideboard, on top of which stood a large ornate glass fruit bowl. He picked it up and placed it on the table in front of them.

'Is that Lalique?' Tara asked. She was stunned to

see such a valuable object actually being used for the purpose it was intended.

'Mm.' Guy Ricard nodded, reaching forward to trace the air around the pile of fruit with a single perfectly manicured finger, pondering his choice.

Mesmerised, Tara watched his hand, her stomach tightening at the emergence of a white cuff from the sleeve of his dark blue jacket.

'I think I shall enjoy this nice ripe peach,' he said. He picked up the fruit and held it reverently, turning it between his fingers. André was already occupied with helping Lisette clear the dishes but Tara found herself being drawn into Guy Ricard's own private world.

'Look at it, Tara,' he said quietly as he eyed the fruit as though it was a work of art, 'it is so plump, so ripe, so juicy.'

Holding her breath she watched as he squeezed it gently between his fingers. She saw the flesh give slightly, then he ran the nail of his index finger delicately along the cleft in the soft, velvety skin.

An involuntary sigh escaped her lips, her gaze fixed enviously on the peach. With all her heart she wished it was her he caressed so tenderly. And one glance at him told her he could read her thoughts. With a wicked glint in his eye, he bit into the fruit, sliding his tongue along the soft inner flesh, lapping up the juice. His eyes spoke volumes, the sapphire blue of his irises sparkling in the soft candlelight.

She glanced around to make sure André was still

out of the room, presumably helping Lisette with the washing-up. 'Where is your room?' she said.

At her question he smiled, put down the remains of the peach and wiped his fingers on a napkin. 'At the opposite end of the house, a long way from André's so do not be concerned.' He reclined in his chair and smiled at her. 'Go there now and wait for me.'

For a brief moment she thought about refusing but he knew as well as she that her will was already lost to him.

'Alright,' she said. On trembling legs she left the room, crossed the wide hallway and climbed the staircase. She made her way along the landing in the opposite direction to her own room. It was not difficult to tell which room belonged to Guy.

She tried the door at the very end of the landing before any other. It opened into a room of such dark, luxurious opulence that she knew it had to be his and the many photographs of André confirmed her assumption. For a minute or two she browsed, feeling a rush of an emotion akin to maternal tenderness as she contemplated a baby picture of André. As she looked closer she saw how plump and dimpled he had been, with a shock of thick black hair and a cheeky, sparkling grin. In some ways he hadn't changed at all, in others he was unrecognisable as this charming infant.

On top of a tall walnut dresser she found another collection of photographs, framed in antique silver.

As she gazed at the frozen faces she wondered who they were, these people from Guy's past. She realised she still knew practically nothing about him at all, apart from his ability to pleasure a woman with his hands and mouth.

The face of one woman arrested her attention and her eyes were drawn to the unsmiling features like a magnet. Unlike the others in the photograph she did not stare at the camera with eyes fixed on the unforgiving lens. This woman's attention appeared to have been diverted by something much more interesting, her lips betrayed a knowing smile of amusement. For no apparent reason other than the woman's colouring, or something in her eyes perhaps, Tara recognised her as André's mother, Guy's long-dead wife.

Possessed by curiosity, she found herself picking up the photograph. She peered at it, somehow trying to define what it was about this woman who had managed to trap a vital part of Guy. To take it with her to her grave. The ability – no, the desire – to make love to another woman.

'Put that down.'

The suddenness of the voice behind her startled her so much that she almost dropped the photograph. 'I . . . I'm sorry,' she said, 'I was just looking at it.'

With shaking hands she moved to restore it but Guy took it from her and placed it face down in the top drawer of the dresser. Tara watched him for a moment, then turned and headed for the door.

'Where are you going?' he said, appearing genuinely surprised.

'I think it would be better if I left. I should never have come here in the first place,' she said. She wasn't sure if she just meant his room, the house, or the entire country.

'I'm sorry, I didn't mean to be so abrupt.'

Glancing at him she saw that his expression was genuine. 'Where's André?' she asked suddenly, deciding to change the subject.

'In bed,' he said. He walked to the tall window and drew the heavy drapes, cloaking the room in almost total darkness despite the fact that the sun still had not set. 'I took the precaution of locking your door from the outside so that if he should try it for any reason he would assume you are asleep,' he added.

'You think of everything, don't you?' Tara mused.

For a moment or two they were both silent, the sound of their breathing the only disturbance to the still, heavy atmosphere of the room. Tara could just make out his figure in the darkness, a slight chink in the curtains allowing her the luxury of partial vision. He was beyond arm's length.

'Do you think you will be able to comply with our arrangements?' he said suddenly. She saw him take a step towards her and then stop.

'Yes,' she said, 'in fact, I think it will turn out to be a lot easier than I expected.' It was the truth but in any case she was not going to give him the satisfaction of thinking she was still hesitant about their agreement.

'Good.' Suddenly he was in front of her, surprising her by his nearness when she had neither seen, nor heard, nor even sensed his approach. Deftly his fingers unfastened her skirt, allowing it to drop to her ankles.

Swaying slightly from the heady combination of fine wine and desire, Tara allowed him to guide her sweater over her head. Now she was just clad in a tiny pair of white lace panties. Although she could already feel her independence crumbling under his spell, she wanted desperately to take control. Playing on the element of surprise, she reached forward and unzipped his trousers, thrusting her hands inside and clasping his half-aroused penis and the velvety weight of his testicles.

Trying to dislodge her grasp, he stepped back but she followed him, not releasing her grip until his body was pinned against the wall. Then she dropped to her knees and fed the length of his stiffening cock between her wet, open lips, her tongue immediately trapping him against the roof of her mouth.

It was not a practice with which she was particularly familiar. Yet, kneeling there in front of him, she felt as though a primitive instinct was at work, guiding her, encouraging her to bring him alive by the power of her mouth alone.

At first he allowed her to fellate him, gripping

handfuls of her hair between his fingers as her head moved backwards and forwards in time with her hands, occasionally allowing a soft sigh to issue from his lips. Then he pushed her away, gently but firmly.

'I want to make you come,' she protested, her moist lips forming a slight moue as they were deprived of the hot throbbing muscle.

'Not yet,' he said.

She thought he sounded sincere. His hands stroked her hair, continuing their path down the sides of her face, and grasping her shoulders to raise her to her feet.

'We have plenty of time,' he added gruffly.

He kissed her intimately, his tongue probing deep inside her mouth as a prelude to other, more intimate explorations. And, as their mouths met, he held her close to his body, one strong, broad hand spanning her upper back, the other caressing her buttocks.

'I want you tonight,' she murmured but he ignored her, turning her around and forcing her back onto the bed, his fully dressed body covering hers.

For a moment she lay motionless under him, content just to feel the weight of him upon her. Then she felt the heat of his body, the citrus and musk scent of him filling her nostrils and she began to squirm and writhe, forcing her lace-covered mound to rub against his trousered leg in the agony of arousal.

Still kissing her, he clasped her hands in his,

drawing her arms up until they were fully stretched above her head, reminding her briefly of Glen. But, unlike her former lover, he moved on top of her, drawing her wrists together and fumbling with them, doing something with his hands that she could not discern. Gradually his kiss became less urgent and he allowed one hand to trace the length of her arm, her side, her waist, his touch as light as a feather. As he did so Tara flinched slightly, she always had been very ticklish. Almost unable to bear his torment she moved her hand to stop him. It was then she found that she was unable to move her arm.

His other hand was pinning her wrists above her head, she could feel it, yet she didn't believe he was so strong that he could hold her fast if she was really determined to escape his clutches.

'Guy?' She wriggled and tried in vain to tug her arms downwards.

'Is there something the matter, Tara? Whatever could it be?' his voice mocked her as he stroked her breasts thoughtfully with his free hand. Then he brought his other hand down and used it to prop up his head so that he could look at her properly.

'I just wanted you to let go of my arms,' she said with relief. Yet, even as she spoke the words, the realisation dawned on her that her wrists were still held fast despite the fact that both his hands were within her sight. Glancing up above her head, she saw that he had tied her wrists with a thin red cord, the other end of which was secured to a small brass eyelet in the wooden headboard. Using all the dignity she could muster she asked him to untie her.

'It's not funny, Guy,' she said, 'I'm not into playing those sort of games.' She pulled hard but the delicate-looking brass fixing would not budge.

'Perhaps not yet,' he mused.

'Perhaps not ever. Let me go!'

Tara was angry now. Determined to free herself, she bucked her hips and lashed out wildly with her legs. She wanted to hurt him, she wanted to make him untie her. To her extreme annoyance he simply began to laugh.

'You will only tire yourself out if you keep up that behaviour,' he said. Moving swiftly away from her flailing legs he climbed on top of her and sat astride her thighs, effectively limiting her movements.

To his amusement, Tara lost her cool. 'I hate you, Guy Ricard. I hate you and your games. Tomorrow I'm going home!'

She couldn't ever remember feeling so totally bereft of control, so completely at the mercy of another human being. She was easygoing, up to a point, but it certainly wasn't in her nature to be subservient to any one. 'I won't ask you again,' she said through clenched teeth, 'now let me go.' She used what she had always believed to be her firmest, iciest tone, the one guaranteed to bring the most unruly pupil to heel, or to reduce the most insolent waiter or shopkeeper to grovelling acquiescence.

'*Merde* . . . silence!' His command arrested her speech. 'I will let you go when *I* am ready and not before. Now be quiet.'

The sheer arrogance of his response shocked her into silence, wide-eyed she stared at him as he loomed over her. 'Have you finished?' he said, his tone and expression softening.

She nodded, not trusting herself to speak because she knew to do so would result in another tirade. She decided to wait until his defences were down.

'Will you kick out again if I move?' he asked. He rose to his knees but hovered over her thighs, waiting to see if she would react.

She shook her head and, when he was convinced, laid beside her again, his head propped on his hand.

'I know I should remind you that I have paid for you,' he said, glancing at her face, noting the way her lips pursed at his words, 'but . . .' he added hastily, '. . . whatever happens between us I want you always to enjoy it.' He stroked his hand across her breasts again, teasing her nipples into life, gazing into her eyes. 'Believe me, Tara, my pleasure is tied with your own. If I am not bringing you the gift of glorious rapture then how can I possibly derive my own gratification – do you comprehend?'

'Yes. I think so.' She moved voluptuously under his caress and beneath the promise his words held for her. Although she hardly knew him she felt as though she trusted him – trusted that he would never seek to cause her harm. If he wanted to teach her the ways of pleasure, who was she to argue? No-one here knew her, she had no ties to anyone other than to him because he had bought and paid for her, therefore she could be anyone she wanted, play any part she wanted – even that of the high-class call girl. Who, other than herself and the two men in this house, who were already her *clients*, would ever be able to dispute her chosen persona?

Suddenly she felt free, liberated from far stronger bindings than the loose cord that held her wrists. Now she could let her mind and body fly.

'Touch me, Guy!' she cried. The strength of her own voice surprised her almost as much as the way she spread her thighs and bucked her pelvis to draw his attention to her meaning. 'Make me come until I scream for mercy.'

He needed no further encouragement. With a smile of secret understanding, as though he knew he had just unlocked the last reserves of her subconscious, he pulled off her knickers and forced her legs wide apart, burying his face into the soft, musky sweetness of her sex, his tongue forcing her labia apart.

'Ooh . . . yes!' In no time she was grinding herself against his mouth, desperate for release from the surging heat that threatened to engulf her. No sooner had she ridden the first peak than he brought his fingers into play, guiding her into a second wave of orgasm and a third, his expert manipulation of her body so delicious that all she could do was take it . . . and take it. Finally, she begged for mercy.

'Please, Guy, let me touch you!' She beseeched him with her eyes, her gaze transmitting her desperate yearning for his thick, hard cock. 'Please.' She didn't care that she was begging, didn't care that he refused to use his throbbing hardness to pleasure her, all she wanted was to return the gift he had given to her.

'*D'accord*,' he said finally, 'but I shall only release one hand. That and your mouth will have to suffice.'

She nodded her agreement and waited with bated breath until he reached for the cord and loosened the knot. Then he slipped one of her wrists from the binding before tying it tight again.

She reached for him, her eager fingers closing around his shaft. Briefly she licked her lips then brought him to her, enfolding his glans in the warm wet cavern of her mouth. With a skill that she was sure any self-respecting call girl would possess, she sucked and licked and caressed him, stopping only when she felt the first droplet of his virility ooze from the tip of his glans and coat her tongue. For a moment she stared up at him, expecting him to be watching her. But his eyes were closed, his head thrown back, lips moving silently, speaking the mute language of ecstasy.

Galvanised by his pleasure and by her skill at arousing him, Tara covered him once again with her lips, sliding them up and down his shaft, her wet tongue and lips moving around and around his glans. Her hand gripped him tightly as she fellated him, her whole mouth simulating the yet-to-be-explored pleasure of her vagina, loving him with rhythmic deliberation until he conceded his pleasure into the willing vessel of her mouth.

Afterwards he stared at her, his expression unfathomable as she licked the last of him from her lips like a victorious predator that had just enjoyed its prey. Softly, he stroked her hair and her belly, eventually releasing her other wrist so that he could enfold her in his arms, as the insidious fingers of drowsiness plucked at their satiated bodies.

At six-thirty he awoke to find her gently stroking herself, her expression dreamy.

'*Bonjour, ma chérie,*' he said softly. He dropped a kiss on her nipple, teasing it awake with the tip of his tongue before repeating the delicious action on the tip of her other breast. 'I did not pleasure you enough last night?' He glanced at her hand, still moving gently between her legs.

Turning her head, she smiled at him, her blue-green eyes still dreamy. 'Yes you did, you know you did. I was just exploring and thinking how swollen I feel down there.'

'Let me see,' he said. Sliding down the bed until his face was level with the top of her thighs, he moved her hand and parted her legs before running his fingertips tentatively over the tender flesh.

'Is it bad?' She smiled, moving her legs further

apart, enjoying his attention.

Covering her sex with his palm he moved back up the bed, his expression serious as he gazed at her. 'I should not have done this.'

'Why ever not?' she said. She stared at him, amazed. They had done nothing that two consenting adults should be ashamed of.

'Because I should not spoil your flesh for André,' he replied gently. 'It is only right that you go to him fresh and untouched.'

'Then I would have to reapply for my virginity,' she commented wryly, adding, 'and besides, I do intend to bathe, you know.'

He nodded. 'Of course, I realise that.' He lay back against the pillows and stared at the ceiling. 'My God, how awful it would be for you to go to him with my scent still upon your body.'

Tara was nonplussed. He displayed such a strange set of values, she thought. To him it was not a problem to arrange for a woman to seduce his son, or to pay her and indulge in her himself. But heaven forbid that she should go straight from one man to the other. 'I think I ought to go back to my own room,' she said, sitting up and glancing at her watch. It was a quarter past seven and no doubt André would be stirring soon, if not already.

'Yes. You are right.' Guy Ricard sat up and, pulling her to him, kissed her briefly. 'I shall be out most of the day,' he said, 'please feel free to use the facilities.' He rose from the bed and walked to the dresser, from the top drawer he extracted a set of keys. 'These are your own keys to the house, front, side and back doors, your bedroom and the garage.' He pointed out which keys were which. 'And this is the key to your car,' he added with a smile that she couldn't fathom, 'you will find it is the only other one apart from mine in the garage.'

'Thank you.' She walked up to him and took the grey leather fob from his hand. 'I'll see you later, won't I?' she said.

To her relief, he nodded. 'Of course. Have a good day.'

He checked the corridor outside, frowning as Tara sprinted to the other end of the house wearing nothing but her espadrilles. With a brief wave she unlocked her own door and entered the room.

Once inside the sanctuary of her bedroom she sank onto the bed, craving another hour or so of sleep. She lay flat on her back, stretching her limbs and torso, remembering how it had felt to have her arms tied above her head, to be helpless at Guy Ricard's mercy. She shivered as her instinct told her that he had so much more to offer her in the way of physical pleasure, that they had barely skimmed the surface of carnal delight. The one stumbling block, of course, was his refusal to penetrate her but she felt up to the challenge. If anyone was capable of making him succumb it was her, she didn't doubt it for a second.

But she wanted more than simply to trap him,

she wanted to bring him to the point where he desperately needed to make love to her, where he pleaded to be granted the pleasure. Then and only then would she be satisfied that she had properly conquered Monsieur Guy Ricard.

Chapter Six

She awoke for the second time that morning to the soft caress of the summer sun streaming through her window onto her naked skin. For a moment or two she luxuriated in it, knowing that she had nothing more to think about than pleasure. Stretching languorously she glanced at the clock on the wall, it was eleven thirty.

With a gasp of surprise that she should have been quite so lazy, she rose from the bed and made straight for the shower. Feeling the restorative spray bringing her properly awake, she began to contemplate her timetable for the rest of the day. Some breakfast certainly, suddenly she felt ravenous. Then swimming and sunbathing. She didn't feel up to anything more adventurous or energetic than that . . . except sex of course.

Thinking of sex made her think about Guy, until she swiftly replaced him in her mind with the image of André. It was not fair to the poor boy to be always thinking about his father. After all, he was the real reason that she was there.

She dried herself and then picked up the white bikini that she had worn the day before. It was as dry as a bone and she slipped it on beneath a short, sarong-style skirt. With the addition of a little waterproof make up, she felt ready to face the world. She made straight for the kitchen, thinking how empty the house seemed without Guy's presence. She found the disconcerting figure of Lisette bustling around the large, homely room, obviously creating a masterpiece for lunch.

'*Voulez-vous quelque chose pour le petit dejeuner, madame?*' The Frenchwoman's offer of breakfast was made with a pleasant smile but as she said the words she also looked pointedly at her wristwatch.

Tara winced, noticing how the metal strap bit unkindly into her plump, freckled flesh. She nodded enthusiastically. '*Oui*, Lisette. *Merci beaucoup.*' She sat down at the table and gazed around her inquisitively until Lisette presented her with a tray.

'Madame.'

Tara took the tray out into the garden and set it on the table by the pool. In no time she had finished the small basket of petit pain and apricot conserve and was enjoying a second cup of coffee when André appeared, also dressed for swimming.

'*Bonjour, André, il fait chaud aujhourd hui, n'est ce pas?*'

Blushing slightly, he nodded. 'It is indeed a very hot day today, madame.'

'I told you to call me Tara, remember?' she said, before adding, 'I think swimming and sunbathing are the perfect solution to a day such as today, don't you agree, André?' Without waiting for him to answer, she put down her coffee cup and reclined on the padded wooden lounger, closing her eyes to the cruelty of the sun's rays.

André stared at her in silence for a moment before clearing his throat nervously. 'Um . . . madame . . . I mean, Tara, you will burn in this sun.'

At his words she opened one eye and looked at him. 'You are absolutely right, André,' she said with a smile, 'and I have no protective lotion. Oh well, I shall either have to sit in the shade, or go out and buy some.'

'We . . . I mean . . . I have it,' he said. He jumped up from his chair and went inside the house. A few minutes later he returned, triumphantly bearing a plastic bottle.

Shielding her eyes from the glare of the sun, Tara looked up and smiled. 'Thank you, André.'

She got up and removed her skirt before sitting down again, aware the whole time that he was trying in vain not to look at her. She anointed her skin with deliberate care and began to massage the cream into her flesh with smooth, careful strokes, the palms of her hands sliding easily over the glistening skin. All at once she was struck by an idea. It was an obvious one, admittedly, but certain to have the desired effect.

'Could you put some of the cream on my back and shoulders please, André?' she asked. She turned over and stretched out full length on her stomach, wriggling into a comfortable position. A ploy, she noticed from the corner of her eye, that was not wasted on him for a moment. Just when she sensed he had almost galvanised himself to begin, she reached behind her back and unfastened her bikini top, whipping it away from under her body in a deliberately careless gesture. 'There. Now I won't get any nasty white lines.'

She smiled at him, then closed her eyes and waited . . . waited for him to touch her for the first time. She had expected his touch to be tentative but she could hardly feel the featherlight pat of his fingertips as he dabbed the cream onto her skin. 'You will need to rub it in, André,' she urged.

This time his touch was a little more definite, growing more assured as she made no further comment other than a slight moan of contentment. Eventually she spoke out again. 'That's wonderful, André. You should think about becoming a masseur.'

Without thinking, she turned around to smile at him only to see him staring at her with a strange look on his face – an equal mixture of shock and disbelief and pleasure. The expressions manifested themselves one after the other as he looked, not at her face, but at her naked breasts. It had been an uncontrived action but one that she could not have executed better if she had planned it. Deciding it was too soon to turn over completely, she lay face down again.

'Please continue, André,' she said.

She felt his touch again, hesitant at first but quickly becoming more confident. She could imagine the thoughts that were going through his mind. He wanted her. She knew beyond a shadow of a doubt that it would be easy for her to seduce him now. But she wanted it to be right. If she was going to make his dream come true then the circumstances and her actions would have to be as perfect as in a dream.

Therefore, instead of pouncing on him, she let him continue with his massage. He was getting bolder now anyway, his touch more insistent as he started to bring the whole of his hands into play, not just his fingertips. Perhaps he imagined she was some-one else, a girl of his own age perhaps. As he covered her with the thin film of protective cream, she encouraged him to speak about himself.

'Do you have many friends here, André?' she asked casually.

'Mm,' he said, sliding the palms of his hands over her shoulders and the tops of her arms, 'there are one or two who live in the town.'

She smiled. 'Is there a girl amongst them, one you especially like?'

'*Oui.*' He nodded but she couldn't see him do it, only feel the vibration of his action.

'Her name?' She was determined to get him to open up a little. They needed some common ground to work on.

'Eloise Le Fevre.'

The magical sounding name caressed the nape of her neck as he let it issue from his lips in a long slow breath.

She shivered as goosebumps rose on her skin. 'That's a pretty name. Is she pretty too?'

All at once, it was as though she had unlocked a secret door. In a mixture of halting English and French he told her all about Eloise: her long red hair, her pretty face and perfect figure. He finished by telling her about Eloise's forbidding father.

'But fathers are like that, André,' she said, 'they are protective of their children. It is only natural. And,' she added, 'if Eloise is as pretty as you say, he must be afraid for her . . .' She had been about to say, 'afraid for her virtue' but she thought it sounded a bit old-fashioned so she simply added the word, 'safety.'

'I know what you mean.' André was massaging her skin much harder now, his passion as he thought of Eloise becoming evident through the pressure of his finger tips.

'Ouch! Oh, stop please, André,' she called out, anxious to call a halt to the massage. She turned around to look at him, worried that she might end up covered in bruises but instead of resuming her face-down position when he took his hands away, she turned around completely and reclined on her elbows. She forced herself to appear totally unself-conscious as she gazed at the boy's rapt expression. 'Surely you have seen a woman's breasts before,

André?' Her voice was soft but not mocking, her words simply a statement to which he replied by shaking his head.

'On television, yes,' he admitted, 'and on the top-less beaches. But not like this. Not so close up.' He couldn't stop staring at her and made no attempt to hide his interest.

Conscious of his fascination she began to stroke the smooth round globes, the skin slick with perspir-ation and the layer of cream. With slow deliberation she ran her fingertips lightly around the darkened skin that surrounded her nipples and then touched the pink buds themselves.

A long sigh issued from the young man's lips as her nipples sprang eagerly to attention and she smiled at him.

'Would you like to touch them for yourself, André?' she said. 'I don't mind.'

Without waiting for his reply, she reached out and took his hand. She placed it squarely on her breast and held her breath with anticipation as he struggled to gain some self-control.

Then, tremulously and wide-eyed with wonder, he squeezed her pliant flesh, moulding it in his hand for a few minutes before stroking his fingers around and around both globes.

She breathed a sigh of encouragement. The way he touched her felt wonderful and he was already starting to arouse her in earnest.

Encouraged by her response, he allowed his eyes

to flicker briefly to her face before returning to the sight which captivated him the most. His lips curved into a smile which, she realised with a pang of desire, was strangely reminiscent of his father. Bringing his other hand into play he ran his fingertips across her nipples, delighting in their response like a baby delighting in its own hands and feet.

'I can't believe it,' he murmured, 'I can't believe the way they feel. They are so . . . so . . .' It was obvious that he was lost for words.

'Don't speak, André,' Tara said gently, 'just touch me. Enjoy my body.' She gave a sensuous wriggle and he moved forwards, leaving his own chair to perch on the edge of hers – eager to be closer to her, to feel more of her.

Minute heaped upon blissful minute as she lay, eyes closed to the strong heat of the sun, her half-naked body a glistening offering to the eager hands of the young boy beside her. For a split second she allowed her eyelids to flicker open and as she did so she thought she could make out a figure watching them from a first-floor balcony.

She couldn't stifle a gasp of surprise, she could have sworn it was Guy Ricard. He'd told her he was going to be out all day.

'What's the matter, did I hurt you?' André asked anxiously.

'No. No, of course not,' she said.

She patted his hand absently but to her dismay he followed her gaze. Noticing the retreating figure of his father, he pulled his hands away from her as if she were on fire.

'*Mon Dieu, c'est terrible!*' he cried, looking genuinely frightened.

'What is it? What's wrong?' She put her hand out and touched his arm, noticing how he jumped as though he had been stung.

'My father. He saw us,' André said.

His eyes were full of panic but she managed to soothe him.

'I'm sure he didn't,' she lied, 'but even if he did, so what?'

He looked at her, his amazement obvious. 'Do you mean that – so what?'

She nodded. 'I am a grown woman, you are a grown man, there is nothing wrong with what we were doing.' It was absolutely the best thing she could have possibly said.

For a few moments he pondered her words, then he looked at her, his expression suddenly older somehow.

'I am a man, aren't I?' he said.

'Of course, look at yourself in the mirror sometime if you don't believe me,' she said and laughed aloud as she traced the faint outline of his moustache with her fingertip. Then she ran her hands approvingly over his shoulder and arm muscles. 'Have you been working out?'

He looked at her, his expression quizzical. 'Working out?'

'Yes. With weights.' She mimed the action with her own arms, causing her breasts to swell and heave as she did so.

'Yes, every day,' he said, 'perhaps you would like to join me, Tara?' He stared blatantly at her breasts and smiled a knowing smile.

'André!' She was pleasantly shocked by his cheek. She smacked the palm of her hand against his upper arm in a playful gesture and then jumped up, running away from him to dive into the clear blue water of the pool.

In an instant he was behind her, catching up with her as she surfaced halfway down the pool, her eyes sparkling with the exertion and with merriment.

'I've got you, I've got you!' He called out triumphantly and grabbed her around the waist with surprisingly strong hands to lift her off her feet.

As she looked down at his handsome, laughing face and noticed the way his dark sloe eyes crinkled at the corners and how firm his grasp was around her waist, she couldn't help thinking, at long last, that she had made the right decision.

'Yes, André, you've got me,' she said, almost under her breath.

She could have kissed him then. It would have been so easy and so natural. Yet for some unfathomable reason she felt reluctant, as though the timing still wasn't quite right. If a thing's worth doing, it's worth doing well, she told herself. Instead she wriggled from his grasp and swam away, hoping that he would join in the game and chase her. She was not disappointed. Eventually, she stopped trying to escape from him and gripped the handrail at the end of the pool, gasping a little for breath. Apart from her head and neck, her whole body was completely submerged.

André slipped one arm around her waist, pulling her towards him a little. She didn't resist and allowed her body to float naturally against his torso.

'I like you, Tara,' he said.

She smiled at him in return. 'I like you too, André,' she said, 'and I think we're going to have great fun this holiday, you and I.'

His eyes held hope but then he looked downcast for a second. 'But you are here to make me study. My father will not allow me to . . . to . . .' he struggled for the most appropriate English words.

'I know,' she said, pressing a finger to his lips. 'In England we have a saying, "All work and no play makes Jack a dull boy." Do you understand what it means?'

He shook his head slowly. 'No. I think . . . no.' He shook his head in frustration.

'It means . . .' she began and stopped to think for a moment, realising all of a sudden what a stupid expression it was – like so many other English sayings. Instead she said, 'It means that we are going to have some fun while we are studying.' She smiled and made a wide sweeping motion with her arm. 'Look around us, André. Tell me what you see, tell me in English.'

'I don't . . .' he began, but she interrupted him.

'Tell me what you see,' she repeated, her tone insistent. '*La piscine* ... pool, *l'eau* ... water, *l'arbre* ... tree, *les fleurs* ... flowers. I know that's all basic stuff but, don't you see, we can go around together and learn so much in the process? There's shopping and the cinema and restaurants and ...' she stopped, believing she had finally got her message across. Of course, his education would not be complete without learning the parts of the body but first things first. She smiled and added, 'Do you understand now?'

To her relief, André nodded enthusiastically. '*Oui, Dieu merci*. I thought my father was being most cruel when he said I had to study even during our holiday, now it will be fun.'

They smiled at each other for a moment. It was a turning point, she felt. Somehow, the ice had been broken between them and their relationship now felt a little more equal. She didn't realise how uncomfortable she had felt before, playing the heavy-handed teacher to his pupil. At that moment they were disturbed by the appearance of Lisette on the patio, she waved her arm and, even from that distance, Tara could see her disapproving expression as she eyed the pair of them together in the pool, their bodies so close.

'I think that means lunch is ready,' André said, his voice already displaying a newfound confidence as he enunciated the English words. He heaved himself out of the water, then reached down to help her.

'Thanks,' she said. She stood at the edge of the pool, unselfconsciously squeezing the water from her hair as he watched her.

'You look like a . . . a . . .' he struggled for the word, '. . . *une sirène.*'

'*Une sirène?*' She murmured and pondered the French word for a moment until she remembered its meaning. 'Oh, a mermaid!' She laughed aloud. 'Do I? Thank you.'

'Yes,' André said. He gave her a long, thoughtful appraisal which she found strangely compelling. 'You look like a beautiful mermaid . . . a goddess of the sea.'

Lost for words at his unexpected eloquence and the depth of emotion in his voice, she simply stared at him, her breath catching in her throat. Countless responses jostled in her head but none of them seemed fitting. All too fleetingly, the moment passed them by and they turned to go inside the house for lunch.

André hovered as she paused to don her skirt and bikini top, his expression regretful as she covered the damp globes of her breasts.

'Don't worry, it's only for Lisette's benefit,' Tara hastened to reassure him. 'They can come out and play again after lunch.' She laughed lightly at her own little joke but André exploded with mirth.

'You are a crazy woman,' he said. He shook his head in disbelief and was still chuckling to himself as they entered the cool, shaded sanctuary of the kitchen.

Having eaten breakfast less than a couple of hours earlier, Tara only picked at the delicious spread of salads, meats and cheeses but André tucked in heartily whilst carrying on a conversation with Lisette. At first Tara eavesdropped but eventually she became tired of having to concentrate so hard on their rapid French and frankly boring subject matter. She excused herself, taking her glass of wine to wander along the hallway, exploring the ground floor of the house.

Peeking through various doorways, she found a couple of small sitting rooms lined with bookshelves and a large lounge with a TV. Eventually she came to a games room. Dominated by a full-sized snooker table, it also boasted a jukebox and several card tables set up with different board games, chess, backgammon and so forth.

She wandered from one game to the other, picking up a chess piece, examining it, putting it down, shaking a pair of dice and throwing a double six. As she gazed around the room it wasn't difficult to imagine Guy and a few male friends playing snooker and other games, discussing business and the price of stocks and shares and, of course, women. Then she imagined he and André sitting there on a darkened summer's evening, their dark heads bent thoughtfully over a game of chess. Suddenly, her stomach contracted with longing. The sound of a light tread behind her made her turn and she saw André hovering in the doorway.

'Do you play?' he said. He walked over to the snooker table and began placing the coloured balls on their spots.

'Not very well,' she admitted, 'but I wouldn't mind a game.' She selected a cue, gazing along the length of it like a true professional to check that it wasn't warped in any way.

'You look as though you know what you're doing,' André said as he selected a cue for himself and covered the tip with a liberal dusting of blue chalk.

'Good,' she said, 'then perhaps I'll unnerve you. Shall I break?' She walked to the far end of the table and placed the white ball in the position she considered most advantageous. As she bent forward slightly to take her shot André gasped.

'*Merde*!' The expletive shot from his lips and he added, 'if your intention is to put me off my game, you are doing it well.'

She followed his eyes as they travelled from her face to her breasts, which strained for escape from the scant covering of her bikini top. With a knowing smirk she wriggled her hips and shoulders, pretending to seek a more comfortable position from which to take her shot. Deliberately, she held the cue in an awkward way and fluffed the shot.

'That is no good,' André said, immediately taking charge. Putting down his own cue he walked around behind her and placed the cue correctly in her hands, standing so closely behind her that she could feel the rapid beat of his heart and the soft whisper of his breath upon her shoulder.

Suddenly she turned around in his grasp so that she was facing him, her back arched slightly over the rounded edge of the table. From that position it was the most natural thing in the world to kiss him. Softly, the pressure of her lips no more than an undertone, she brought him completely under her spell. There was no going back now, the die had been cast.

'Tara!' His attempt at a protest was feeble. Already he was desperate to kiss her harder, she could feel the excitement in his response.

'Shh, *tais-toi*, André,' she said softly as she wound her arms around his neck and kissed him deeply. With gentle deliberation she prised his mouth open with her tongue and began to explore the mysterious cavern. At the same time she insinuated her body against his, feeling his flesh grow warmer and his limbs tremble. In no time at all she could sense his growing arousal.

As though she had unblocked a dam he ground against her, kissing her fervently, running his hands over her back and shoulders.

She realised his passion was becoming uncontrollable. If she wasn't careful he would soon lose the battle where he stood, in the middle of the games room. That was not how she wanted to conduct his seduction. Gently she pushed him away from her, pulling her head away so she could speak.

'Let's go to my room, André,' she said gently. 'We

will be much more comfortable there and more private.'

She couldn't help wondering about the insidious presence of Lisette. The same thing had obviously crossed André's mind because he immediately stopped, letting her go reluctantly.

Despite the fact that the dark figure of the housekeeper was nowhere in sight, they moved quietly along the passageway and up the stairs, hardly daring to breathe until they were locked in the privacy of her bedroom. As soon as they were alone, he fell on her, his mouth hungry for hers.

'Oh, Tara! Oh, Tara!' He couldn't hide the strength of his passion and for a few minutes she allowed him to take control. Then she stopped him gently.

'Slow down, André,' she said, smoothing her hands along the width of his broad shoulders and down the length of his arms before taking his hands in hers. 'There is no rush. We have all the time in the world.'

Her tone calmed him. By slowing down his actions she allowed his mind to dwell on the magic of the situation. For a few minutes he stared at her, his expression unreadable, then he reached forward and, with tentative fingers, traced the curve of her breasts.

Holding his eyes with her own steady gaze, she unfastened the bikini top and allowed it to drop to the floor. Her skirt followed and she stood before him once more clad only in the brief white bikini bottoms.

His gaze covered her exposed body, warming her skin far more thoroughly than the midday sun. Then she took his breath away completely by pulling down the bikini bottoms, bending forward from the waist as she slid them down her legs and stepping out of them completely.

'*Oh, mon Dieu! Je ne crois . . .!*' he cried out.

He stared at her, his eyes transfixed by the glossy triangle of blond curls at the apex of her thighs.

'Come, André, lie down with me,' she said softly. She put out a hand and led him to the bed, pushing him back until he fell against the soft coverlet as powerless as a rag doll.

Laying down beside him, she began to stroke his chest and stomach, trailing her fingertips across his quivering torso and teasing his nipples with the lightest of touches. She bent her head and kissed him, her hair covering their faces like a golden veil while her naked breasts pressed against the smooth skin of his ribcage.

Eventually he began to lose his fear. His limbs became less rigid and his body stared to relax. He brought his arms up and around her and began to trail the length of her spine with his hands, running his palms over the sleek expanse of her back and shoulders.

As he explored her she felt her own desire growing, small sparks igniting within her, leaping into flame as his fingertips accidentally stimulated one of her many erogenous zones. She released his lips for a moment and began to investigate the length of his body with her tongue, her eyes flicking downwards. As she suspected, his swimming trunks could barely conceal the insistent bulk of his erection.

Tara decided it would be better to give him the gift of release sooner rather than later, then she could begin to teach him the myriad secrets of sexual pleasure. Gently she pulled down the garment, taking him so much by surprise that she was concerned he might ejaculate there and then. Somehow though he managed to control himself as she slipped the trunks over his feet and dropped them onto the carpet.

She couldn't resist simply looking at him for a moment, amazed that he had now lost all resemblance to the gauche student who had sat at the dining table in her small cottage. As she gazed at the beauty of his powerfully erect manhood, she realised that here lay a man – a handsome, vital, virile human being with the power and capability of satisfying her as much as she intended to satisfy him.

Without taking her eyes from him she reached for the packet of condoms that lay ready and waiting on the table by the side of her bed, the packet that Guy had no use for. Shaking away the unwelcome image of his father from her head, she looked at André and smiled, watching him watching her as she tore open the packet and extracted the small piece of latex.

'I don't want to sound like your teacher again, André but these are very important. Don't ever forget that. When you sleep with a girl, any girl at all, you must use one of these. Is that understood?'

'Yes, madame,' he said, his tone depicting more than a little amused sarcasm.

'*Bon. D'accord.*' She played up to him by becoming artificially brusque. 'You put it on like so . . .' deftly she unrolled the thin covering over his erection, noticing with a smile how it jerked wildly when she touched it, '. . . then you use it like so.' Without giving him the opportunity to think about what she was doing she climbed astride him and took him deep inside her.

He came immediately. 'Oh, my God. I am so sorry.' He looked and sounded so angry with himself that she had to stifle a smile.

She climbed quickly off him and lay down beside him again, pulling his head to her breast. 'It's okay, I expected that,' she said.

'Really?' He looked up at her in wonder, his face suddenly becoming young again.

She nodded and smiled. 'Really,' she said and added, 'now that is out of the way we can start to enjoy ourselves properly. The next time you will be able to last longer.'

He shook his head slowly from side to side. 'I don't believe this is happening to me. It is like a dream come true.'

His words touched her, justifying her actions and

136

her reasons for being there. 'I know, André,' she said gently, 'it is for me too.' For a moment or two she allowed him to lay there, basking in the afterglow and his own thoughts. Eventually, she removed the condom and cleaned him delicately with a tissue. 'There, as good as new.' She smiled and without thinking, dropped a kiss on the very tip of his cock. Instantly he sprang back into life.

'I want to make love to you, Tara,' he said, 'properly, I mean.' His tone and expression were so earnest that she smiled indulgently until he surprised her by sitting up and cupping her breasts in his hands. He slid his thumbs over her nipples, stimulating them so expertly it was as if he had been born to it.

Sighing softly, she rose to her knees and pulled his body closer. His solid body felt so good she did not hesitate to slide her hand down, over the flat plain of his stomach and belly, until her fingers could wrap themselves around the length of his cock. Loving the feel of him, she moved her hand up and down the shaft until he began to groan.

Releasing one breast, he mirrored her action, insinuating his palm between their bodies until his fingertips brushed her pubis and then lower still, slipping his hand between her legs as she parted her thighs for him. Again he was entranced by the heady experience of discovering unchartered territory.

'Oh ... oh ... C'est incroyable!' He cried as he investigated the hot, moist crevice of her sex, his fingertips discovering her with the tenderness of a blind man. After a hesitant pause, he slipped a finger inside her and then another and another.

Tara felt a sudden rush of desire that made her arch her back with pleasure and grind herself against him. She began to moan softly.

'Do you like this?' he asked unnecessarily.

'Mm . . . yes. Oh God, yes!' she groaned. Caught up in the violence of her own lust she released his penis and ran her hands over his buttocks, gripping them firmly.

Without bothering to ask first, he reached with his spare hand for a second condom, ripped open the packet with his teeth and slid the rubber covering expertly over his throbbing erection, then he withdrew his fingers and pulled her on top of him once more.

This time she had to ride him, he made sure of that. He was determined to delay his own release until he could no longer stand the torment. It delighted him to feel her tightness holding him fast as she rose and fell, her breasts bouncing tantalisingly out of reach. Wanting to touch them, he sat up and cupped his hands around them, trapping the aching globes as she kept up the rhythm of her mounting passion.

For Tara the act was a revelation, like nothing she had experienced before. It was as though he were her instrument of pleasure – a living, moving, life-size doll that she could mould and temper any way she wished. Slowing down her movements a little, she covered his hands with her own and lifted her breasts higher, bringing them to his lips.

'Kiss them,' she said.

Her tone was soft but as she ordered so he complied, wordlessly and skilfully, taking each nipple between his lips, sucking them until she thought they would explode from the exquisite pleasure of his caresses.

Then she began to ride him again, more deliberately this time, raising and lowering her pelvis in a continuous flow, and taking care not to disturb his mouth upon her breasts. Without thinking, she moved a hand between her legs and began to stroke her clitoris, desperate to relieve the agonising throbbing in that tender region.

'What are you doing?' André stopped suckling her and looked down, his eyes fixed on the hand between her legs.

'I'm pleasuring myself, André,' she said with a small sigh. Shaking her hair back from her face, she added, 'Women are so lucky, they have many pleasure zones.'

His expression showed that he didn't quite understand her.

'Look at me, André,' she said. She moved her hand to one side and shamelessly spread her labia, exposing the hard pulsating core of her desire to his stunned gaze. Then she took his hand and placed one of his fingertips upon it, recoiling slightly from the direct pressure as she did so. 'It is called the clitoris ... I believe you have the same word in French? It is very, very sensitive and the centre of a woman's desire.'

He didn't realise it but his exploratory actions were driving her crazy and in a matter of seconds she felt the warmth of orgasm overtake her, driving her over the edge of delirium. If her response surprised André he didn't show it.

'You like that then?' he commented dryly, his eyes twinkling with amusement and the sudden realisation that sex was not all one way.

She nodded, needing a few moments to find her voice again. 'Oh yes, André. I really like that.' Then she laughed aloud, pushed him onto his back and rode him mercilessly until he too cried out with pleasure.

Chapter Seven

Heedless of the outside world, they remained locked in her room, André eager to explore every part of her and for her to arouse every part of him. As the clock struck five, he lay on his stomach between her outstretched legs, minutely examining every part of her sex as he had been for hours.

'This is so, so fascinating,' he said and shook his head slowly from side to side in amazement, repeating a phrase that had almost become a litany. Gently, he parted her labia for the umpteenth time, his fingertips gently unfolding each soft fold of flesh as though they were flower petals. Each time he slid his thumb over the pulsating bud of her clitoris as it emerged from its protective hood of skin, smiling as she flinched and writhed at his touch. 'I love it when you do that.'

'And I love it when *you* do that,' she countered, sighing from the bliss of having someone so enthusiastic about pleasuring her.

Suddenly he gave a deep sigh.

'What's the matter, André, I thought you were happy?' She propped herself on her elbows and looked at him, her face full of concern.

He nodded and turned his huge, dark eyes up to her face. 'I am,' he said, 'very happy. That's why I feel so sorry for my father all of a sudden. Now I realise what he has missed all these years.'

At the mention of Guy she felt the colour drain from her face. For a few hours she had forgotten about his very existence. 'I'm sure he has . . . er . . . lady friends?' she ventured finally. 'He probably just believes in being discreet.'

'Oh, *mais oui*,' he agreed, a bit too readily for her liking. 'He has brought one or two of them here but I still feel sorry for him.'

She felt her stomach tighten at his words, although it seemed ludicrous considering the conditions of their 'relationship' that she should feel pangs of jealousy at the merest mention of Guy Ricard's other women.

'I expect he misses your mother terribly?' she mused, opening her arms to him so that he could snuggle against her. Inexplicably she felt the need to supply comfort rather than arousal.

'*Non. Certainement pas!*' His tone was almost vehement and he shook his head, his dark hair brushing her face. 'He has always been so very angry with my mother but he will never tell me why. For all these years he has held his anger inside him.'

It was a long outburst for him and she resisted the

urge to congratulate his use of the English language.

'Why?' she asked.

Her question was simple but André shook his head, obviously perplexed. 'I don't know. He would never tell me. Just that she did something very bad before she died, that is all.' He shrugged and looked downcast.

Suddenly, outside the bedroom door came a noise, as though someone was directly outside the room, listening to their conversation. They both looked startled and, before she could stop him, André called out. A scuffling sound told Tara that whoever had been listening had now been frightened away. It was probably that strange woman, Lisette, she mused. Oh well, too bad.

For a while they lay together, thinking and dozing, the gentle rays of the evening sun washing over their naked bodies. They must have fallen asleep completely because when Tara next opened her eyes and looked at the clock it was almost eight thirty.

'*Mon Dieu!*' Despite her agitation, her exclamation made her laugh, now she was truly becoming immersed in the French way of life. Gently she touched her lips against the corner of André's mouth, smiling at the way he came awake, startled to see her there for a second, his eyes widening with recollection.

'What time is it?' His eyes flew to the clock and immediately he looked aghast.

She got up from the bed and stretched. 'I suppose

Lisette will be fuming if we appear late for supper?'
she said.

'It is not Lisette who worries me,' André muttered
as his eyes searched the bedroom floor for his discarded swimming trunks. 'My father will be furious
if I am not there to greet him before we dine.'

'Well, we won't be late if we hurry.' Tara walked
to the wardrobe and flicked through its contents,
wondering what to wear.

'I will go now, Tara.' André murmured. Moving
silently, he came up behind her and slid one hand
over her breasts and stomach, his other hand caressing her buttocks before insinuating itself between
her legs.

'I will *come* now if you don't stop that!' she said,
turning her head and kissing him on the lips. What
a shame they had to stop when she was truly beginning to enjoy him. She confessed her thought to him.

'Can we continue tonight, after my father goes to
bed?'

She pondered his request, wondering if Guy
expected her himself. Too bad, she decided.

'Of course.' She smiled and kissed him again, then
wriggled away from him. 'Go now,' she said, a giggle
trembling inside her, 'before I decide to keep you
here as my prisoner.'

'Ah non, ce serait terrible!'

His sarcasm made her smile and, as she watched
him leave, she realised a lot of things about him
brought a smile to her face. Seducing André hadn't

been so difficult after all. With a pang of premonition, she realised the hardest part might be letting him go.

It was just after nine when she entered the dining room. Seated once again at the head of the table was Guy Ricard but André's place was still empty. As she sat down he looked pointedly at his son's empty chair and then raised his eyebrows questioningly. Silently she nodded, a slight blush covering her cheeks. If she had expected him to look pleased, or satisfied even, then she was disappointed. In fact, to her intense surprise his face darkened.

'What?' She spoke sharply, the single word ricocheting around the walls.

Just as Guy opened his mouth to speak, André appeared. Looking from Tara to his father, he too blushed slightly and Guy Richard's expression became even blacker.

Wondering why he should seem so angry when the seduction had been at his request, she picked at her meal and drank rather more wine than she should. Consequently, when they all rose to go to the sitting room she swayed and stumbled slightly in her high heels.

With a faint sigh of annoyance, Guy Ricard caught her and held her around the waist until she regained her balance.

'*Merci, monsieur,*' she whispered, turning her head to smile at him she found herself falling headlong

into his deep blue gaze, forgetting for a moment that
André was still present.

'*Ce n'est rien.*' His expression was inscrutable as
he released her, rigidly leading the way to the larger
and more comfortably appointed of the sitting
rooms.

Despite the fact that she had enjoyed cavorting
with André all afternoon, she felt an immediate
flush of desire as Guy touched her. Perhaps it was
because he was older and more experienced, she
mused. Or perhaps it was because he refused to take
her completely. Whatever the reason, she felt almost
overcome by the strength of her attraction to him.

When he wasn't around it was possible to put
him to the back of her mind, but in his presence she
felt compelled to be with him, totally. Against her
better judgement she accepted his offer of cognac,
instantly bending her head forward to inhale the
smooth, luxurious aroma as he placed a heavy crys-
tal glass in her hand, his fingers closing around hers
for a fraction of a second.

For a while all three of them watched television,
a comedy show that would have been mindless and
inane in any language but André appeared to be
enjoying it. Then, when it ended, he announced that
he felt like going for a walk into the local town to
see his friends.

He seemed surprised when Tara declined his offer
to go with him but she explained, with a careless
wave of her brandy glass, that she had drunk too

much to go for a walk and he would probably end up having to carry her. Her explanation was obviously a convincing one because he nodded happily and left straight away.

Alone with Guy, she wondered if her decision to stay behind had been wise. For a while both of them sat in silence, Tara sipping her drink, her eyes fixed unseeingly on the images that flickered across the TV screen. The tall English grandfather clock ticked away the minutes of her discomfort.

Eventually he spoke. 'You have done it then?' His gravelly voice sounded ominous in the oppressive silence.

She nodded, unable to find her own voice. He made it sound as though she had committed a murder not a seduction.

Guy Ricard moved to sit next to her, reclining comfortably against the back of the leather sofa, his legs stretched out in front of him.

'And, was it good?'

At that Tara laughed, laughed until tears sprang to her eyes. 'Yes, as a matter of fact it *was* good, very good.' She turned to him, her eyes full of anger and confusion. 'What kind of question is that? What sort of man are you?'

The violence of her response obviously stunned him as he fell silent, his head bent in contemplation over his glass of cognac.

'You didn't think I would actually do it, did you?' she said. Her voice was soft, her question incisive.

'No.' He shook his head and glanced at her, his deep blue eyes arresting hers. 'As a matter of fact, I did not. I thought you would avoid the issue for a couple of weeks and then admit defeat.'

'But why?' she said, almost plaintively, 'I don't know why you even asked me to in the first place if you honestly believed that I wouldn't go through with it!' She thought for a moment then continued, 'My God, you even paid me fifty thousand pounds. What sort of person pays a complete stranger fifty thousand pounds for a job they don't expect them to carry out?' She stopped, almost breathless, and gulped down the last of her drink. The strength of the alcohol almost took the rest of her breath away.

'I was testing you,' he said simply. 'I wanted to see how far you would go.'

'Oh. I see,' she said in an ironic tone. 'That explains everything then.'

'I wish you would be quiet,' he said with a sigh, 'sarcasm is not an attractive trait.'

His patient, condescending tone only served to increase her anger.

'I don't give a fuck what you think, or what you want!' She sank back into the sofa, wishing it would swallow her up completely.

Suddenly he was seated astride her, his hands gripping her wrists, making her drop her empty glass. 'Don't you dare use that language with me, you whore!'

His reaction stunned her, thankfully desensitising

her to the force of his words. They stared at each other, their expressions furious, their eyes locked in combat.

Then she spoke. 'I shall say and do exactly as I please.' Her tone was glacial, her words carefully chosen and spoken in such a clipped English way that they were a double insult to him. 'You might have paid for me but you don't own me. And if you think that makes me a whore, I shall damn well act like one if I feel so inclined.'

'*Mon Dieu!* I could ... I could ...'

He shook with fury but her anger was greater, giving her the power to wound him beyond belief.

'You could what?' she said scathingly, 'hit me ... kill me ... rape me?' She held on to the word *rape*, suspended in the air like a sword. Then she laughed, shaking her head in derision. 'I don't think that's very likely, do you?'

With a look of pure hatred, Guy Ricard rose to his feet and stormed out of the room, throwing his brandy glass into the empty fireplace with such force that it shattered into a million tiny shards. As she watched his retreating figure, Tara realised that he had left her feeling equally as crushed.

Moving back to the realm of normality had not been easy but she felt as though she had accomplished it by the time André arrived home. He found her sitting where he had left her – alone, in the dark, an old black-and-white movie playing out its final drama on the television screen.

'Has my father gone to bed?' His voice was a whisper, although the house was so large no one could have overheard him.

Tara nodded, finding it difficult to even think about Guy. The less her mind had to dwell on him the better. Suddenly, André's appearance was very welcome and she held out her arms to him.

'Come here, André. Did you have a good time?'

'Uh, huh,' he said with a nod. He sat down beside her and pulled her onto his knee. 'I . . .' he started to speak, then blushed and became silent.

'What is it? You were going to say something.' Her tone and expression were persistent. With a proprietory air she ran her fingers through his thick dark hair, moving it out of his eyes so that she could look into them. 'Tell me what you were about to say, André.'

He shook his head. 'I cannot. I feel ashamed.'

'Why?' She continued to stroke his hair, wondering what on earth could be bothering him so much.

With a deep sigh he spoke, his speech hesitant. 'I have a friend. A best friend – Gaston.' He looked at her and even though the room was dark she could see he was blushing.

'Go on,' she urged.

'I told him, Tara . . . about us. I didn't mean to. I just . . . I was just so happy I wanted to share it.' He dropped his gaze.

'And?'

He raised his eyes to hers in confusion. 'And what?'

'And what else?' she persisted. 'You told Gaston about us and what else?' Tara realised she was becoming a little weary of having to push him so hard to reveal his terrible secret.

To her surprise, he shook his head. 'There is no "what else." That is it. I told Gaston about us.'

'Oh!' She pretended to look serious for a moment before her face broke into a smile. 'So what?' she said. 'You have just lost your virginity. Of course you want to tell your best friend about it.'

He shook his head slowly in amazement. 'I cannot believe you are not angry,' he said. He kissed her on the lips, very quickly. 'You are so understanding. So wonderful.' He kissed her again but this time the kiss went on for longer, rekindling her passion for him and his for her. Finally he broke away, almost gasping for breath.

'Let's go to bed, André.' Tara said. She smiled gently and rose from his lap, pulling him up by the hand. Pausing only to switch off the TV, she led him out of the room and up the stairs.

Although they had only known each other intimately for a few hours, their lovemaking was already more familiar, more leisurely. André undressed her slowly, covering each new part of her with kisses, then she did the same with him. Finally, as she knelt before him, she lingered, cupping his testicles in one hand, taking the shaft of his penis in the other and guiding the glans between her lips.

'Oh!' he cried.

She felt him shudder, his hands caressing the back of her head as she slowly engulfed him, winding her tongue round and round him like ribbons around a maypole. Eventually, she felt his passion increase and wondered briefly whether to stop but instead she continued, licking and sucking him until he spurted into her mouth. Afterwards he apologised again.

'Don't,' she said, laughing lightly and licking her lips, 'you haven't done anything wrong. I like it.'

He shook his head slowly. 'You are always surprising me, Tara. I thought you had already taught me everything I should know.'

'Oh no, André.' She rose to her feet and kissed him on the lips, wondering if he could taste himself on her. 'Sex is always about discovery. That is what makes it so marvellous. There are so many new things to experience.'

Briefly she allowed her thoughts to dwell on Guy. Was that what drew her to him, the hidden knowledge that he had a lot to teach her? She shivered, scared to admit to herself that she wanted to find out, wanted to meet his every challenge.

When she and André finally appeared in the kitchen for breakfast the following morning she found a note from Guy. As soon as André was temporarily occupied, she slid the sheet of notepaper out of the envel-

ope and looked at it, her eyes skimming quickly over
the words. She could tell by the curt tone of the
message that he was still angry. 'Meet me at Le
Reynard, a bar in the centre of town, at twelve
o'clock. Come alone and don't be late. Guy.'

After reading it a second time, she tore the note
into quarters and crumpled the pieces in her hand.
Damn his arrogance! Part of her was tempted to
ignore his command altogether. The other part knew
she would be there.

'What are your plans for today, André?' she said.
She broke open a warm croissant and spread it with
raspberry conserve, inhaling the sweet aroma with a
sigh of ecstasy before biting into it.

He picked up the bowl of hot chocolate that Lisette
had set down in his place.

'I don't know.'

To her amusement he shrugged and glanced at
the ceiling with a knowing smile.

Despite her trepidation about meeting his father
she laughed. 'We can't do that all the time, André.
You have a life and so have I.'

'Oh!' He pretended to pout, his full lips suddenly
looking infinitely kissable. 'Do you have plans for
today then?'

'Mm.' She tried to be noncommittal but he pressed
her.

'Do they include me?'

She paused to wipe her fingers on the white linen
napkin beside her plate. 'Maybe later but I have to

go into town this morning. Some business,' she added, sipping her coffee and ignoring his downcast expression. 'It shouldn't take too long though. I should be back by three, or four at the latest. We could have a swim.'

He brightened visibly at the thought of her semi-naked body. 'Okay. I think I'll go and see Gaston for a little while then.' He finished his chocolate and wiped his mouth on a napkin. 'Could you drop me in town?'

'Oh . . . er . . . yes, I suppose so,' she said. The last thing she wanted was for André to witness her business with his father. Still, there was no reason for him to know where she was planning to go, or who she would see there.

Bearing in mind she would be going into the town, she decided to change. Excusing herself, she went up to her bedroom and considered her choices. She decided upon a short-skirted strapless sundress, in black with a white polka dot, which she wore with a pair of high-heeled sandals. Hopefully she would be able to park the car close to Le Reynard so that she wouldn't have to walk too far.

André was waiting for her at the bottom of the stairs when she appeared, her short skirt displaying almost the full length of her tanned legs as she walked down the staircase. As he glanced up at her, he let out a low whistle.

'Now why don't you dress up like that for me?'

At the last step Tara paused and smiled

flirtatiously, pleased with his comment.

'I didn't think you were interested in my clothes, they hardly seem to stay on for long when you're around.'

He laughed at her response, pulling her off the step and into his arms. He ran his hands down the sides of her body and up her skirt.

'I don't think anyone could blame me for that,' he said. Cupping her buttocks through the fragile lace of her knickers he pulled her to him and kissed her hard.

Much as she was enjoying his attention, Tara was only too aware that she had an appointment to keep and she wasn't sure how long the journey to town would take. She broke away from him and glanced at her watch.

'How long will it take us to get to the town?' she asked, removing his hands and smoothing the creases from her dress.

'It only takes half an hour or so on my bicycle, so in a car . . .?' He shrugged.

From that Tara estimated about fifteen minutes depending on the traffic. It was already ten past eleven, so she told André she thought they ought to make a move. Inside the vast garage that could easily have held six cars she found only one – a Mercedes sports car, its bodywork painted a sleek and shining metallic green.

Her surprise was evident. 'I thought your father would leave me a small Renault or Fiat,' she said,

'I had no idea this was waiting for me.' She stroked her palm lovingly along the wing, almost regretting that she hadn't investigated the garage the day before.

'My father likes luxury,' André stated. *'Un vieux tacot n'est pas son genre.'*

Tara laughed. 'No. I can't see your father in an old banger somehow. Come on, let's try her out.'

There was no time to waste but fortunately the car was so fast and the roads so clear that they arrived in the town just after twenty minutes to twelve. At his request, she dropped André off in the outskirts then drove into the centre to look for Le Reynard. After stopping to ask a couple of people for directions, she found it in a back street – a tiny bar with hardly enough room to accommodate the dozen small wooden tables and the juke box that were its only furnishings. A quick glance around told her that Guy Ricard had not yet arrived so she went straight to the bar.

'Oui madame?' The bar keeper almost made her laugh aloud. He seemed to her so typically French. With his leathery brown face and his garb of off-white shirt, brown trousers and braces, he was like a caricature.

'Une boisson gazeuse, s'il vous plaît,' she said absently as she found her eyes wandering to the door, anxious for her appointment to begin. She nodded her thanks and picked up the glass of cold sparkling mineral water that the barman set in

front of her. After a moment's hesitation she took it over to a table by the small, grimy window next to the open door. Outside the sun looked very inviting, the pavement and the surrounding shops and houses shimmering in the heat haze. After a while she glanced at her watch again, noticing with a frown that it was a couple of minutes past twelve. How dare he be late when he had made a point of ordering her to be on time!

Eventually, the door opened and he entered, looking surprisingly casual and relaxed, she noticed with a flicker of desire. Without glancing in her direction he walked straight to the bar and ordered a bottle of wine and two glasses, then he turned around and stared at her. At least she assumed he was staring at her for he wore sunglasses.

As an act of defiance she stared back at him, refusing to look away. Her stomach contracted at the sight of him leaning casually against the bar in a pair of white cotton trousers and matching shirt, the rolled up sleeves exposing his deeply tanned arms. After he had paid he came up to her table, his long legs moving in easy strides.

'You're late.' She couldn't resist the barb as he placed the wine bottle and glasses on the table.

In response he leant back in his chair, his hands linked comfortably behind his head.

'We are a little touchy today, *n'est ce pas?*'

Her immediate reaction was to explode with anger but she refused to allow him to rile her so easily.

'What do you want?'

He shrugged. 'I wanted to see you, to talk to you.'

'Not to apologise? I suppose that would be too much to ask,' she said and immediately cursed herself for her impulsive retort.

'Apologise? Now that is an interesting assumption. Why on earth should I need to apologise to you?'

'You know damn well why.' She spoke through gritted teeth. Without waiting for him to offer she picked up the bottle of wine, poured a glass for herself and drank half of it. Then she looked at him, hating him anew.

'I hope you are not planning on becoming drunk again,' he said laconically, 'it is so unbecoming in a woman.' He raised his sunglasses, stared at her, then lowered them again.

She decided not to dignify his remark with a response, instead she sipped her wine, wanting him to get to the point quickly so that she could go. Without realising it, she started to tap one foot impatiently on the dirty linoleum.

'Would you like some lunch?' The normality of his question took her by surprise.

'No,' she said, 'I want to know why you asked me to meet you here?' She poured a second glass of wine and sat back in her own chair, trying to look as relaxed as he.

'I told you. I wanted to see you. Away from the house. Away from André.'

At last, she thought, they were getting to the point.

'Okay, Guy, you're seeing me. Now what?'

He took off his glasses, placed them carefully on the table, poured himself some wine and held his glass to hers.

'*Santé, chérie!*' He smiled a genuine smile which she couldn't help responding to. Leaning forward he clasped the glass between his hands, looking deeply into her eyes: 'I am sorry about yesterday. I should not have said the things I did.'

'No, you shouldn't,' she agreed, shaking her head before adding, 'I think I should go home.'

'Home? But what would André do if you left, what would *I* do?'

His surprise was apparent.

Nevertheless, Tara sighed in exasperation. 'I don't know, Guy. You would both do what you normally do every other year I suppose. You certainly don't need me around to come between the two of you.'

'You are not coming between us,' he said. 'This whole thing, it is my fault!' He sipped his wine, not taking his eyes from her face. 'I want you to stay, Tara.'

Shaking her head in confusion, she tried to make sense of his words and actions. One minute he acted as though he detested her and the next . . .?

'I can't handle your mood swings Guy,' she said, her expression earnest. 'I never know where I stand with you from one minute to the next.' She hoped he would appreciate her honesty and not throw it back in her face.

'Ah! But, Tara, isn't that one of the main reasons you are attracted to me?'

His mouth curved into a satisfied smile.

'Who said . . .?' She began, then realised denial would be pointless.

'Come back with me now,' he said urgently, 'let me make it up to you.' He leaned towards her so closely that his breath caressed her face.

Despite her annoyance with him she felt herself weakening. 'We can't. André . . .?'

He nodded, understanding her reticence, then rose from his chair. 'There is a hotel around the corner, we will go there.'

Wordlessly, she stood up and followed him – out of the bar and up the narrow, winding street to the very top. Just when she had begun to wish that she had worn flatter shoes they reached a small hotel, the dilapidated establishment little more than a pension.

He pushed open the door and held it so that she could enter. The entrance hall was tiny, with only a wrought-iron table to serve as a reception desk. At that moment an old woman emerged from a dark wooden door opposite them, her face as red and wrinkled as a dried tomato skin. Guy spoke rapidly with her for a couple of seconds, then she handed him a key and pointed with one gnarled old finger towards the staircase.

Guy went first this time, pausing at the top of the staircase as he tried to decide whether to turn left or right down the narrow hallway.

'This must be it.' He stopped in front of a door marked with the number five and tried the key in the lock. It swung open with the squeak of rusty hinges.

As hotel rooms went it was not luxurious by any means. But then neither of them could care less about creature comforts. It was private, it had a bed and that was all that mattered.

As soon as Guy had locked the door they fell upon each other. Stumbling backwards they fell on the bed, Guy's hands reaching under her dress, pulling away her knickers and ripping them in the process.

Tara couldn't stop herself from crying out. As though a touchpaper had just been lit, she felt the heat surging within her, boiling and bubbling away like a cauldron. Her fingers hastily sought his zipper, her pelvis writhing against his hand as he plunged his fingers deep inside her.

With little finesse he used his free hand to pull down the top of her dress, exposing her breasts. She gasped as his mouth covered them, kissing . . . sucking . . . licking . . . And in the next instant he started to nip them gently with his teeth and pull at her nipples with his lips.

It was wonderful yet unbearable, the pain and torment exquisite. Tara moved her head from side to side, her mouth making unintelligible sounds of pleasure as her climax overtook her and carried her away. But, as always with Guy, the enjoyment didn't stop, each sensation being topped by the next, each wave of bliss surging then gathering new strength until she cried out for mercy.

'Stop! *Oh, mon Dieu,* I can't take any more. *Ça suffit!'*

'I don't believe you are asking me to stop.' He shook his head and smiled, slowing the manipulation of his fingers inside her but not stopping completely.

'I . . . just needed . . . a . . .' She barely had the breath to reply.

'So?' He lay on his side, head propped in the palm of his hand, looking down at her, 'Do you still want to go home?'

'Pardon?' She had forgotten her earlier outburst and, as she realised what he was talking about, she shook her head. 'Oh, no. You know very well that I don't. Anyway . . .' she added, assuming a stern expression, '. . . I wouldn't give you the satisfaction of defeating me.'

'Aha!' He used his hand to part her thighs a little further and to insinuate his fingers between her labia, the sensitive tips stroking the quivering flesh there until she began to moan anew. 'You think you are stronger than me. Perhaps you want to make this a challenge?'

'I thought it already was,' she said. She stared up at him, working by touch alone to unfasten his trousers completely and clasp his stiff manhood in

162

her eager hands. 'Will you please put this inside me today?'

To her frustration, he shook his head. 'You already know the answer to that.'

'But why not – why won't you – is it just me?' she cried. She struggled to sit up but he pushed her down with the palm of his hand against her breasts.

'No, it is not just you. Please learn to be content with what I give you.'

'I can't be content!' She knew she was starting to lose control again. She could feel it, the anger and bewilderment, all welling up inside her ready to explode.

'Then I shall have to find another way,' he said simply, his expression an enigma.

However angry he made her she couldn't resist the power of his hands and the way he managed to bring her to the brink of ecstasy so quickly and so surely. She stayed with him in the hotel room until the sun began to drop in the sky.

'Oh, look at the time!' she said, catching sight of her watch, 'I promised André I would be back hours ago.' She felt instantly guilty. Guilty at disappointing André and guilty at mentioning it at all to Guy.

He surprised her by showing he understood her dilemma but, with a note of caution in his voice, he added, 'Be there for André by all means but do not allow him to try and rule your life. He has his friends. He always managed perfectly well without you before.'

She knew his words weren't intended to be hurtful

and nodded. 'I know, it's just that at the moment it's like I'm his new plaything.'

'And what a gorgeous plaything you are.' He laughed and slapped her naked buttocks.

It was an innocent gesture but she came the instant he did it. She looked at him with surprise but he gave a knowing smile.

'There is obviously much you still have to discover about yourself, Madame Cochrane.'

Chapter Eight

It was almost nine by the time she arrived at the house, her return carefully orchestrated to be a good half hour after Guy's. The instant she walked through the front door André was at her side.

'Where were you? I was late but you are later still.'

'You don't own me, André!' she exclaimed, feeling slightly annoyed. Then she relented a little. 'I was tied up.'

Just as she spoke the words, Guy passed by in the hallway and flashed her a look that almost made her laugh aloud. She had indeed been tied up for several hours.

'I didn't mean to anger you,' André said, 'I was worried, that is all.' He looked downcast, reminding her that he was too young to appreciate anything less than absolute honesty, or at least a palatable version of the truth.

'I met a friend. He . . . she is staying locally and we arranged to meet. We talked and ate and lost track of time. I'm sorry, André.'

Before either of them could continue, Lisette bustled past with a huge tureen, her stony silence commanding them to supper. The food, as usual, was delicious and Tara found herself eating rather a lot of it.

'You cannot have eaten much lunch,' André said, staring pointedly at her empty plate.

'No. Well . . . you know what it's like when you're talking,' she muttered.

Thankfully, Guy interrupted, his attention directed at his son.

'I spoke to your grandparents today. They are anxious to see you, so I said you would spend the weekend with them.' He made a point of not looking at Tara but she could feel the excitement building within her at the thought of a whole weekend alone with him.

André was not as ecstatic. 'Oh. But, Papa!'

Guy held up his hand to silence his son. 'No buts, they are expecting you on Friday. You must go.' The obvious finality in his tone and expression brooked no further argument.

When supper was over and all potential pitfalls of their conversation successfully avoided, André suggested a game of snooker. His offer took in both Tara and his father, although he could only play with one of them at a time.

'Do you play?' Guy looked surprised when Tara nodded enthusiastically.

'A little,' she said, her secret smile extending to André this time, who immediately blushed and made an excuse to leave the room ahead of them.

Noticing the exchange, Guy raised an eyebrow but said nothing. Once inside the games room, he offered to let André play Tara first. As she chose her cue and chalked the end he poured them both a glass of cognac. His fingers deliberately brushed hers as she accepted the glass and his smile, as knowing as his touch, sent an electric shock of desire zinging through her. Afterwards, he sat down in one of the comfortable leather armchairs at the backgammon table and prepared to watch them.

Bending over the table, Tara was only too aware of her short skirt. And she didn't have to look at him to know that Guy was watching her every movement. Even when she was facing him, she could feel his eyes on her cleavage, her breasts straining to escape the strapless top of her dress as she reached to take a shot. Despite his offputting attention, she managed to beat André and glowed happily as the young man circled the table and held out his hand.

He leaned forward as he took her hand in his. 'Can I come to your room again tonight?' he said quietly. His question caught her off guard, trapping her in the heady moment of victory.

Thankfully, the telephone rang at that moment and Guy left the room to take the call in private.

Even with him out of the way, Tara was still hesitant. 'Yes. Er . . . yes of course, André.'

Half of her wanted to refuse him. Guy had left her feeling so sore, not to mention exhausted. Even so, she couldn't resist the thought of André's eager cock inside her. A proper fuck was, of course, the vital activity that her afternoon had lacked!

By the time Guy returned they were well into their second game and this time André was winning. A few shots later, he potted the black with a flourish and it was all over.

'Bravo, *mon fils!*' Guy slapped his son on the shoulder. 'Are you ready, perhaps, to take on a real challenge?'

Smiling at their closeness, Tara replaced her cue in the rack on the wall and helped herself to another measure of cognac. Then she sat in the same seat that Guy had vacated and proceeded to watch the two of them play. It seemed so strange to see the pair of them together like that. Close and loving. Father and son. Yet there was nothing juvenile about André. They were both men. She of all people could testify to that.

When the game was over she declined to play Guy and made no secret of the fact that she intended to spend the night with his son, although André was blissfully unaware of the silent messages that passed between them.

As soon as they were locked away in the privacy of her room, André reached under her dress and pulled down the lacy g-string that she had changed into, to replace the pair Guy had ruined earlier. To her surprise he dropped to his knees in front of her, clasped his arms around her thighs and rested his cheek against her belly.

'You do still like me, don't you?' he said, gazing up at her.

'Of course, André,' she replied softly, 'you know I do.' She stroked her fingers through his hair, her gesture soothing. 'Stop worrying all the time,' she added, 'just live for the moment.'

She dreaded that he would become too attached to her. It was one thing to seduce him and to make his first foray into sex a pleasant, possibly even a memorable experience, but she had no intention of allowing things to develop beyond that point.

He was silent for a moment, then he sat back on his heels and began to massage her buttocks, his manipulations of her flesh firm and rhythmic.

'If I . . .' he paused and took a deep breath, as though he regretted opening his mouth to speak.

'Yes, André,' she urged quietly.

'If I slept with another girl, would you be angry?'

'No,' she answered quickly and honestly, her reply obviously surprising him.

'Why not?'

'I told you before, André. We are both free agents. If you want to have sex with someone else, girl or boy, it's fine with me.'

'Oh . . . no, never a boy!' His horrified tone made her laugh aloud.

'I thought only people as old as me were supposed to be prudish?'

'You're not old!' He was shocked by her remark.

'I am twelve years older than you André.'

He stared at her for a second. 'Are you? You don't look it.' Clearly he had thought she was younger. Then he grinned up at her. 'You certainly don't look it from here.' With a cheeky smile he lifted the front of her dress.

'Why . . . you!'

She burst out laughing and squatted down in front of him, intending to kiss him. But his hand went instantly between her legs, his fingers exploring as he reminded himself of her particular territory. With his other hand he pushed her dress roughly up her thighs, exposing as much of her as possible to his hungry gaze.

Tara gasped aloud as she felt a rush of heat course through her. It immediately weakened her legs so that she sat back on the floor with a bump, her thighs spreading wide. She could feel him look at her and feel his eyes and hands grazing her sex. Simply knowing how she must look to him, made her desire mount almost to bursting point.

'Take me, André. I need to feel you inside me, now!' She reached out to him, loving the way he was so eager to oblige her every whim and always so ready, physically, to satisfy her.

In the swiftest of moments he was on top of her and inside her – his hard, avid cock driving into her deeply and rhythmically. His movements sent her over the edge, never slowing, never letting up as she felt herself falling into delirium. This was what she needed from André, his youthful enthusiasm for her body and the joy he derived from giving her pleasure.

Through heavy-lidded eyes she watched his expression change from one of lustful determination to rapture, his eyes closing in ecstasy. Eventually, he slumped on top of her and rolled to the side, spent but happy.

'I can't imagine finding someone else as fantastic as you anyway,' he gasped, picking up the thread of their earlier conversation.

'Don't be silly, André,' she said, 'there are lots of women like me out there.' She smiled dreamily and reached with her hand to stroke his wilting manhood. Almost instantly it started to become erect again.

'Turn over, I want to take you from behind,' he said, his words making Tara tremble. Suddenly he sounded so masterful and sure of himself – not unlike his father.

With a tremor of excitement she did as he asked, raising her hips obligingly as he entered her. She gasped again. Thanks to André, she was starting to believe the actual moment of penetration was one of the most blissful sensations a woman could ever experience.

He pushed her dress up to her waist and pulled her hips towards him, spreading her buttocks apart at the same time. 'My God, you look fantastic from this angle!' he groaned, plunging deeper and deeper inside her until she was panting for breath.

She could not believe the passion he unleashed that evening. It was as though he had finally realised what sex was all about, as if each of their previous encounters had merely been an appetiser for the real thing. She pushed herself up on her hands, arching her back, urging her pelvis to meet his thrusts.

'Oh, yes. Please . . .!' She wanted all of him, every last centimetre.

Just when she thought he must be tiring he pulled her upright, so that she was sitting on his knees. Unzipping her dress, he pulled it over her head. Now that she was naked he could touch her properly, all of her. With one hand he caressed her breasts, moulding them feverishly and with the other he felt between her legs, his fingers delving between her labia, breaking down her last reserve as he tantalised her.

'André! Oh, yes . . .!'

Another wave of rapture crashed through her and another. And still he didn't let up or give into his own temptation for release until he was satisfied that she had come properly. Then he withdrew from her and turned her around, impaling her straight away on his rock-hard cock and immediately resuming the intensity of his previous movements.

It was incredible, Tara thought during a brief, lucid moment. The sex was incredible. He was incredible. His stamina was incredible. Tonight, she thought, she would have to beg for sleep. But so what? She had nothing to do the following day but relax and in the afternoon he would be going to his grandparents' house. For three whole nights she would lose him. The realisation gave her the impetus to ride him harder and eventually force him to lose control.

Later, as they lay together in the comfort of her bed, he bemoaned the fact that his grandparents wanted to see him.

'But your father told me you always see them when you come here, that it was the main reason he bought this house,' she said as she smiled down at him, stroking her fingertips lightly across his nipples and teasing them into hardness.

'I didn't know you and my father had spoken that much.'

His comment was innocent but Tara felt the first suspicion that they were edging into dangerous territory. Her response was cautious.

'I think he mentioned it the other day.'

To distract him she slid her body lower down the bed and took his cock in her mouth, teasing it back into life yet again with the skill of her tongue and lips.

'I have not done this to you as yet,' André said, stroking her hair.

She looked up at him. 'Do you know something, you are absolutely right?' She pretended to look shocked. 'To think I could have allowed such a vital part of your education to remain untaught.'

He shook his head. 'I did not understand all of that.'

'It doesn't matter.' She climbed astride him and began to inch up his body, not stopping until her thighs gripped his shoulders.

Of course, André couldn't resist looking at her, touching her, opening her up to his view.

'Now this is a very interesting angle, Tara.' He spread her labia and stroked a fingertip across her clitoris, his lips curving into a smile as she flinched.

'Use your tongue, André,' she said, her tone gentle but insistent.

Still holding her apart with his fingers, he stroked the tip of his tongue across the same delicate morsel of flesh, repeating his action again and again. His enthusiasm was galvanised by her obvious enjoyment. As though he had been born to pleasuring women, he flicked his tongue over her before plunging it into the moist chasm of her vagina.

'Oh, my God!'

Her gratification was instant and all-encompassing – a non-stop surge of sensuality that overtook her whole body with the force of a tidal wave. Holding on to the bedstead for support, she ground herself against the blissful gift of his tongue and lips, wondering how she could continue to accept such pleasure without losing her mind completely.

In the next instant he surprised her by throwing her back and immediately burying his face between her legs once more, pinning her pelvis to the bed by the force of his hands as he drove her mad with desire.

'Fuck me, André,' she managed to gasp at long last.

'*Je ne comprends . . .*' he began, deliberately teasing her but the time for niceties was past.

'I said, fuck me. Now!' She reached down and pulled him up so that he was lying on top of her. She tried to grasp his penis so that she could guide it herself but he wouldn't let her take charge.

Grabbing her by the wrists he watched as she writhed in frustration.

'I want it, André.'

'I know.' He continued to hold her and watch her, a smile playing about his lips.

At that point, in the starkest moment of sheer passion, she almost accused him of being like his father – of deliberately withholding himself from her. Oh, my God, she thought, this is becoming too scary.

'André, please.' She urged her hips upwards, the soft down of her pubis grazing the tip of his penis.

Conceding defeat, he entered her. This time he did it slowly, not giving in to her demands completely, still maintaining control. Laying within her, he released her wrists.

'If you want it, you fuck me, Tara,' he said.

She didn't need to be asked twice.

The following morning after breakfast she and André went for a walk. He wanted to show her a little of the grounds, not least so that his father would think he had honoured his promise to show Tara around and look after her.

'I can't get over how amazing this place is,' she said, shaking her head in amazement as she looked up at the canopy of trees overhead. They had just walked across what seemed like acres of open scrub and pasture land, now they had entered some woodland and yet they were still within the bounds of the property.

'Are you tired?' André sat down on a tree stump and pulled her onto his knee.

'Mmm, a bit,' she said, 'that sun is so hot, at least amongst these trees it's a little cooler.' She draped her arm around his shoulder and allowed her head to drop back while she closed her eyes for a few blissful seconds.

André looked at her, noticing with a flicker of arousal the way her T-shirt strained over her breasts as she arched her back. He couldn't resist touching her, running the palm of his hand over each generous mound and feeling her nipples come to life beneath the thin layer of cotton.

'Mm,' she sighed again. She felt so contented, so relaxed. Their surroundings were delightfully cool and tranquil and she couldn't help feeling glad that André was there with her to share the moment. Impulsively she reached for the hem of her T-shirt and pulled it off over her head, enjoying the soft caress of the temperate breeze upon her naked skin.

'Mon Dieu! I cannot get enough of you, Tara, you know that don't you?' André covered her breasts with his hand again, gently stroking and squeezing until she felt the familiar warmth of passion catch alight low down in her belly and spread like wildfire through her whole body. 'I am dreading being away from you for so long,' he said.

She knew he meant it. He had said it so many times now. On at least half a dozen occasions the night before he had cursed his 'duty visit' and now the moment of his departure was drawing ever closer he seemed to be worrying about it even more.

'Believe me, André,' she assured him, 'you will have a lovely time.' She turned slightly so that she was facing him, her hands gently holding the sides of his face as she transfixed him with her eyes. 'You will make them happy and I will be waiting for you when you get back.'

'I suppose you will be desperate for me by then?' He spoke from a point of innocence, not intending his statement to be as arrogant as it sounded.

She smothered a smile. 'Absolutely.'

She bent her head and kissed him, hoping that she was able to quell some of his doubts. With an inward sigh she wished someone could do the same for her. For some reason she viewed the prospect of a whole weekend alone with Guy Ricard as a potential ordeal which must be endured. Perhaps it was simply a case of women's intuition but she felt convinced that he would plan something that would test her.

She gave herself a mental shake. It hadn't escaped her attention that André was becoming more aroused. As he kissed her, he was trying to unzip her jeans and put his hand inside them but they were not the most accommodating of garments.

'I don't know why you had to wear these things,' he grumbled, managing to pull the zipper completely down at last.

'If you had your way, I would have to walk around stark naked all the time,' she said and laughed but the very idea turned her on. Instantly she felt a rush of moisture flow from her.

Obviously, the prospect had the same effect on him. Standing up suddenly he forced her to stand too, her breasts brushing lightly against his chest.

'Take them off,' he said, meaning her jeans.

'What, here?' She looked around nervously then realised how unlikely it was that anyone could see them, the place was deserted and they had come across no other human being during their walk.

Without bothering to reassure her he pulled them down swiftly, taking her knickers with them. With a little trepidation she stepped out of them and looked around once again.

'No one will see us, Tara.' André's voice was low, urgent. He removed his own clothes and then pulled her gently down to the ground to lie on the thick green carpet of moss and ferns.

With no pretence at foreplay he entered her, pushing her knees back so that he could drive himself into her as deeply as possible.

'*C'est incroyable!*' he cried into the stillness.

Tara didn't know it but for the past two or three summers it had been his fantasy to lay a girl down in these woods and take her as he was taking Tara now. Except that Tara was surely much better than any local girl could possibly be.

'Mm. Harder, André. Harder!' She bucked against him, thrusting her pelvis up to meet his, urging herself to take more of him. She felt so free, so wonderfully uninhibited. It was as though they were a vital part of nature, striving together to contribute to the natural tide of life and doing what came naturally to all God's creatures.

They came together, absolutely together for the very first time and afterwards André stayed inside her, not moving, not talking, simply being.

As they walked back to the house he thanked her.

'What for?' Tara said with a smile, 'I should be the one thanking you.'

'You have made this the most memorable summer of my whole life.'

He looked so serious that she wanted to pull him to her and kiss him but she was aware of Lisette hovering on the patio, sweeping up non-existent debris with persistent diligence.

'André, it has hardly been a few days, you talk as though this was the end.' She walked to the edge of the pool and sat down at one of the tables there, patting the seat next to her.

'I feel as though it is,' he said, 'I'm going away, aren't I?' He stared morosely at the water. 'I don't suppose you could come with me?'

His question astounded her and caught her off guard. 'No, of course not. What would your grandparents think? What would your father say? No.' She couldn't be more definite than that.

Despite his unwillingness to go. Despite his entreaties for her to accompany him, the time came for him to leave and he left – alone. From an upstairs window, Tara watched him climb into the old Citröen that his grandparents had sent to collect him. Suddenly, and from that distance, he looked very young again. All too soon the car was gone in a cloud of dust and she turned from the window, sighing deeply and wondering what she would do in his absence.

At first she thought she would have a nap but her room was so hot and stuffy she just found herself tossing and turning in discomfort. Eventually, she decided the best remedy for the heat and for her mood would be a swim. A restorative dip in the cool water would no doubt do the trick. This time she bothered with nothing more than a brief pair of black bikini bottoms and a loose white chiffon shirt as a cover-up against the harsh rays of the sun. Ignoring Lisette's baleful stare as she passed her in the hallway, Tara walked out into the sunshine. She noticed straight away how quiet the place seemed without André or Guy.

She dropped the shirt on the seat of a chair and dived straight into the clear water, her breath catching in her chest at the sudden iciness on her skin after the burning heat of the sun. After a few lengths she began to feel better. Her head started to clear and she looked forward to the weekend as a time for herself, a time to recoup some of her lost energy. Eventually, she tired of swimming up and down and went to lay on one of the thickly padded loungers, pulling it slightly into the shade so that the sun would not give her a headache. Lulled by the unaccustomed exertion and the soporific warmth of the summer's day she drifted off to sleep.

As was so often the case these days, her dreams were largely erotic in content, played out by silent men with large cocks and featureless faces. Slowly, she started to awaken, aware that her clitoris throbbed with dreamy stimulation. Something cold touched her breast, an icicle against her nipple! She didn't want to wake up just yet and brushed her hand distractedly against the intrusive sensation. It moved, then touched her other breast.

'No,' she murmured in irritation, her eyelids reluctant to open.

The sensation persisted until her fingers came into contact with something cold and hard, it was the base of a glass. Opening her eyelids halfway she saw that a tall, fluted glass was being held against her nipples, first one and then the other. For a while she simply observed it. It was not unpleasant by any means and she felt the throbbing in her clitoris grow in direct proportion to the movements of the glass. Then she came awake completely and wondered who was doing this to her.

'Champagne?'

Her startled gaze was swallowed up instantly, the crinkly deep blue pools of Guy's eyes drawing her down and submerging her in erotic promise.

'Thank you,' she murmured. Unable to take her eyes from his, she wrapped her fingers around the stem of the glass, carrying the rim to her lips, tasting the sparkling acidity of the wine.

He had been leaning over her but now he came to sit beside her, the narrow confines of the lounger making it necessary for his thigh to rest against hers.

'I take it your dreams were good?' He hadn't released her from his stare yet and now she saw that he smiled the knowing smile of someone who shares a secret.

'Why do you say that?' She sipped her wine again, blushing at her own fragmented recollection of her dreamtime.

'Because you were becoming aroused.' He touched his champagne flute against her nipples again, smiling at the way they reacted pleasurably to the cold glass.

'Yes, I was,' she said. There was no point in denying it, she was still aroused and becoming more so with each passing second.

He moved his glass to his lips then brought it

back towards her body. Instead of holding it against her breasts again he tipped it slightly and allowed a small trickle of the chilled wine to run down the length of her torso.

'Ooh!' She couldn't help reacting to it, the deed was so unexpected and the sensation so pleasurable.

Lazily, he gathered the drops on his finger, following the trail it made. Time and again he repeated the act, the amount of wine he spilt increasing by the merest fraction each time until finally his fingers could not stem the flow and he was forced to use his lips and tongue to clean her skin.

Feeling as though she was on fire, Tara arched her body to meet his mouth, abandoning herself to the deliberate torment.

Putting down his glass, he ran his palms across her stomach. The pressure of his hands was insistent as he kneaded the pliant flesh beneath. Gripping her around the waist he brought her body to him, manipulating her like a rag doll as he buried his face in the heaving swell of her breasts.

'You want me, don't you?' he asked, needlessly. He already knew the answer to that.

'Oh yes,' she breathed, desperate for him to touch her sex, to release the lust that surged inside her. She knew it was pointless to expect any more than that from him.

'Then let us go to your room.' He stood up and pulled her from the chair, clasping her to him for a moment to kiss her, his tongue probing her mouth as though they had never kissed before.

'Okay. But why not your own?' She always thought he preferred to be on home territory.

'A change, that is all.' He shrugged nonchalantly, his hands never leaving her body as they walked across the patio, into the house and up the stairs.

As soon as they reached the seclusion of her room they came together, as always, like wild beasts. Hastily he pulled the thin shirt from her shoulders and cupped her naked breasts, lowering his mouth to them to suck her nipples greedily.

Was it possible that this time was even better than the times before? She grappled with his belt and zipper, almost ripping open the buttons on his shirt, her hands desperate to feel his flesh and to press her scorching body against his.

As he licked her nipples into a state of swollen agitation he thrust his hands into the back of her bikini, clasping her buttocks, insinuating his fingertips into the cleft between, probing her anus.

Feeling another rush of desire overtake her she cried out. She desperately sought his penis with her hands, clasping it gratefully and enjoying the sensation of firm muscle underneath her fingers.

'Oh, you're so big,' she said.

Her appreciation didn't go unrewarded. Hurriedly, inelegantly he pushed her back towards the bed, lifting her onto it and pulling down her bikini bottoms in one swift movement. Then, rising between her legs to spread them wide, he held her thighs apart with his hands as he dived into the moist heat of her sex with his tongue, bringing her instantly to orgasm.

'Oh, Guy!' She tried to spread her legs wider, wanting to give all of herself to him.

'*Un moment.*' He pinned her to the bed with one hand, although she had no intention of going anywhere, and removed his clothes with the other. After which, he ran his fingers over her sex, discovering her anew as he opened her up to his appreciative gaze. 'I think you will not forget this,' he said darkly.

To her amazement and with a force that surprised her, he plunged his cock deep inside her.

Chapter Nine

When he entered her she thought she would explode. The sensations he created were so powerful, so all-encompassing, that she thought she might die.

'Yes, you are indeed a hot one,' he said. Without withdrawing his cock completely, he pushed her further onto the bed and propped himself on his hands so that he could watch her changing expressions.

'You know how much I've wanted you, Guy,' she gasped, meeting his thrusts.

'Hm,' he murmured, looking at her quizzically, 'after your session with André in the wood this morning I am surprised you are quite so ... so ...'

She stopped moving for a second, stunned by his words. 'You saw us?'

'Yes.' He shrugged, his smile wicked. 'It was very entertaining.'

Her stomach tightened at the thought of Guy watching her make love to André. Part of her found it disturbing, almost incestuous, but she also found it highly arousing. At least it had urged him to take her himself. But now was no time for thought. Guy Ricard was actually inside her at long last, and she bucked her hips, encouraging him to resume their rhythm. He didn't disappoint her.

All too soon she came, violently and protractedly. Waves of ecstasy ripping through her, causing her to cry out. Minutes later he came too, also violently but silently, his expression hardly betraying his pleasure. When he withdrew she was relieved to notice that he had been wearing a condom, at the height of passion she hadn't thought to mention it, nor had she been aware of his thoughtfulness.

'You like the idea of being watched, don't you?' he asked, smiling lazily as his hand played between her legs.

She nodded guiltily. 'That was good,' she said at last, stretching luxuriously and taking the opportunity to spread her legs a little more as encouragement.

'*Oui*. You were, I think, so hot, er . . .?'

She looked at him and frowned, unable to believe that he would have difficulty remembering her name. Not now, not after everything they had shared.

Suddenly a disturbing thought began to formulate in her mind. She shook her head trying to clear it. The notion was too ludicrous even to contemplate.

'Do you remember our cosy chat the other evening, the one we enjoyed as we watched television with André?' she said lightly.

188

'Oh yes, what a pleasant evening that was.' He smiled easily and thrust his fingers inside her.

His response took a few seconds to register with her. Then she stared at him, her eyes wide with amazement.

'You're not Guy!' She sat up, pulling herself away from him, edging backward.

'How do you know?' he said, shocking her by the fact that he didn't try to deny it. Instead he reclined against the pillows, quite unconcerned.

'Get out!'

She tried to make her tone as menacing as possible, wishing desperately that she had something she could use as a weapon against him.

'I think it is a little late for that, *chérie*,' he said.

He moved forward and reached for her but she climbed off the bed and grabbed her robe. Quickly she wrapped it around her naked body and belted it tightly.

'I think it is a little late for that also,' he added, his arrogant smile infuriating her. Whoever he was, he was certainly from the same mould as Guy Ricard.

'I said get out, whoever you are!'

Tara was starting to feel slightly hysterical and to her relief there was a knock at the door. It opened slowly and there stood Guy himself, dressed smartly but casually in light-coloured trousers and shirt. Glancing from one man to the other, she could now see the subtle physical differences between them: a variation in the length of hair, one or two slight facial discrepancies. My God, she thought, I can't believe I was so easily taken in.

With his customary air of *sang froid*, Guy looked at her and then at the naked man on her bed. After a moment's deliberation he said:

'Xavier! When did you arrive?'

Suddenly the two men's faces were wreathed in smiles and they began to speak in rapid French. The other man, Xavier, stood up and began to dress as they talked. Then Guy clasped him by the shoulders and they kissed each other on both cheeks.

'Would someone mind telling me what the hell is going on here?' Tara cried. Having overcome her initial shock, she was now furious.

'Of course.' Guy's smile encompassed them both. 'Tara, please meet my twin brother, Xavier. Xavier . . . Madame Tara Cochrane.' Then he added with a laugh, 'Oh, how silly of me, you have already met.'

Xavier joined in his laughter, infuriating Tara even more.

'How dare you!' She wanted to kill them both.

At her outburst Xavier turned to her, his eyes twinkling as they raked her satin-clad form.

'*Dites-moi*, Madame Cochrane, did you not enjoy our introduction?'

She wanted to shout at him, to deny that she felt anything but fury.

'Yes.' She smiled eventually, her face relaxing in defeat. 'You know I did. I enjoyed it very much.'

'Then imagine how good it will be when we get to know each other better,' he said cheekily.

She couldn't believe he actually winked at her and then at Guy. And Guy smiled back as though she and his brother had just enjoyed nothing more than an innocent game of cards. Xavier said something to Guy that she didn't catch but whatever it was Guy nodded in agreement.

'By the way, Tara,' Guy said, glancing back at her as he and his twin left the room together, 'supper will be served early this evening – in half an hour.'

The last thing she felt like doing was pretending to enjoy a convivial supper with Guy and Xavier but her stomach got the better of her. Determined to appear as cool and unconcerned as possible she chose her outfit carefully: a closely fitting black dress which, as she left it unadorned, only served to enhance her every curve. With it she wore sheer black stockings and plain black suede high-heels.

There! She looked in the mirror, satisfied with her reflection. All at once she looked both sophisticated and seductive. Now it was up to her who she chose to be tonight. She couldn't help feeling pleased by the reaction of the two men as she stalked into the dining room. Immediately, Xavier rose to pull back her chair while Guy stepped forward to pour her a glass of wine.

'Thank you,' she said as her gracious smile took in both of them. She could afford to be pleasant.

After all, it was not that much of an ordeal to have two attractive men to herself.

Although she and Guy sat at their customary places, Xavier did not take André's place but chose the seat next to her. As soon as she sat down he slid his palm along the length of her stocking clad leg, his fingertips palpating exposed flesh near the top of her thigh. Guy did not appear to notice his brother's actions.

Despite her determination to remain cool, Tara could feel herself responding – not simply to Xavier's touch upon her leg but to the presence of the two men. They were both so incredibly handsome. And despite their arrogance, or perhaps because of it, she found the situation unbelievably arousing. Somehow, she managed to eat the food placed in front of her and make polite conversation. She was grateful that, for most of the time, the two men spoke only to each other.

As they caught up on old times and business news, Tara was content simply to listen, her capacity for understanding colloquial French improving rapidly by the minute.

Finally, when they had eaten their fill, Xavier suggested that they adjourn to the games room, saying he hadn't enjoyed a good game of snooker in ages.

'Tara plays,' Guy said, smiling in her direction and causing her to blush.

'But not very well.' She shook her head modestly.

Xavier winked at Guy. 'Then we will not make the stakes too high, eh *mon frère?*'

Deep inside, Tara felt a tremor of disquiet. Lisette had gone to her own quarters and she felt more than a little anxious about being left alone with the two men. To quell her nerves she accepted a glass of cognac and drank it down.

Guy raised a questioning eyebrow and took her empty glass. As he handed her a fresh drink, he whispered to her in a low voice. 'What is the matter?'

'Nothing,' she muttered, shaking her head, 'nothing at all.'

For a second he allowed his hand to linger on her shoulder. 'Good. Xavier and I are not rapists you know.' He laughed then and called to his brother to take the opening break.

As Tara watched them play she began to feel a little calmer. Their game was over quickly with Xavier just winning by a few points.

'Now Tara must play me,' Xavier said and his eyes twinkled devilishly as he held out a cue to her, 'you break.'

Conscious of the tightness of her dress, she lined up her shot and managed to dislodge a single red from the pack.

'Aha, I see you are not going to make this easy for me!' Xavier walked around the table, running his hand briefly over her buttocks on his second circuit. Before she had the opportunity to say anything he moved away and took his shot.

When her turn came again she could see the possibility of sinking a red ball. Stretching forward over the table, she took careful aim.

'Bravo!' Guy and Xavier both clapped, their pleasure at her success genuine.

Encouraged, she managed to sink the blue but then missed a second red. As Xavier moved to the table she walked back to Guy and picked up her glass.

'You look fantastic,' Guy whispered, his fierce gaze stripping her naked.

'Thank you,' she said, feeling unsteady all of a sudden. Their praise and their presence was really beginning to get to her. Between her legs, her sex moistened and throbbed. She clenched her thighs to try to quell the sensations that threatened to get the better of her. Xavier was playing well, she noticed, racking up point upon point.

'Winner gets a . . . how you say . . . a blow job?' he said. Eyeing the scoreboard, he grinned.

'Okay,' Tara met his challenge with a bold stare. If he wanted to make a game of it, then a game he would get.

With a look of surprise Xavier shrugged and motioned for her to continue.

She deliberately pretended to waver over her decision for the next shot, although in reality there were two easy balls awaiting her. She giggled to herself at the thought .

The cue ball connected with the red with a decisive *click* and she watched it roll smoothly into the pocket, her expression impassive. Similarly she sank the black, then another red and so on until she had overtaken Xavier's score. Finally, it was his turn once more.

'You have not left me much to work with,' he grumbled, obviously rattled by her performance. She walked over to the side table to retrieve her drink and was rewarded by a surreptitious wink from Guy. Xavier missed his shot.

'My turn, I believe,' she said and strode around the table, enjoying her moment of glory. The rest of the table was ridiculously easy to clear.

'*Mon Dieu*. I have to give you credit for that game,' Xavier said, as she potted the black ball for the last time.

'You owe me a lot more than credit, m'sieur.' She smiled but her eyes held his. Surely he would not have released her from the wager if the game had gone in his favour?

'I see.' His mouth curved into a smile. 'So when and where would you like me to meet my . . . obligation?'

She hesitated for a moment, thinking that perhaps she had backed herself into a corner. But it wasn't in her nature to play the shrinking violet.

'Here. Now,' she said firmly. Walking over to the snooker table, she placed the palms of her hands on the edge and jumped up so that she was seated on it. She swung her legs backwards and forwards casually and added, 'I'm waiting.'

Xavier and Guy looked at her and exchanged surprised glances but Guy shrugged and indicated with his hand that the next move was up to his brother.

'Very well,' Xavier said.

As he walked towards her, she felt her stomach tighten in anticipation and realised that he was going to call her bluff. Standing in front of her he pushed up her dress roughly, exposing the tops of her thighs.

'Oh!' She felt the breath catch in her throat at his action, then it caught again as he slid his hands underneath her buttocks and pulled down her black lacy g-string.

'*Bon.*' He smiled briefly then he turned. 'Pass me that chair please, Guy.' Clasping her buttocks, he pulled her right to the edge of the table, spread her legs wide and sat down between them. His eyes flicked up to her shocked face and he looked entirely innocent as he said, 'I see no reason not to enjoy a little comfort while I execute this terrible deed.'

She trembled as he stared blatantly at her quivering sex. Just behind him she could see Guy, also looking at her, waiting to see what would happen next.

For a moment or two Xavier simply looked at her. Then he began to stroke his fingers along her thighs, taking them up the smooth silky stretch of stocking to the soft flesh above and describing small circles on her exposed skin.

From somewhere far away Tara could hear a soft moaning sound and was surprised to realise that it came from her own lips. The ecstasy of his caress gathered within her and vibrated at the back of her throat before being expelled in long, sensuous breaths. Arching her back and spreading her thighs wider, she urged herself towards him, offering her most intimate secrets for his delight. His fingertips moved slowly across her thighs until they finally grazed her sex. Spreading the labia apart, he entered her with his tongue.

'I . . . Oh, yes!' she cried.

The pleasure was indescribable. She felt so wanton, spread out in front of him with her buttocks clenching and unclenching rhythmically against the polished wood and soft baize of the snooker table. Through heavy-lidded eyes she saw Guy step forward to stand directly behind his brother's shoulder, his gaze transfixed as Xavier's mouth carried her over the threshold of carnality.

'Guy?' Xavier turned briefly to glance at his brother, his eyes conveying a silent message.

Guy smiled and nodded and, before Tara realised what was happening, the two men had exchanged places. Now Guy's mouth and hands were upon her. She thought she should resist but she was too far gone to care, her senses transported faraway, almost into oblivion. Eventually, she came again, and Guy sat back with a look of satisfaction on his face.

'I think that fulfils the conditions of the wager,

don't you?' Xavier said, to which Guy nodded.

To Tara's disappointment, Guy stood up and replaced the chair against the table. He picked up her glass of cognac.

'You need a little fortification, *n'est-ce pas?*'

She nodded weakly. With an air of chivalry he held out his hand so that she could climb down from the table.

'*Merci,*' she said, smoothing down her dress and glancing absently around for her missing panties. To her surprise she noticed Guy was setting up the balls for another game.

'Now it is my turn to play you,' he said. 'What shall *our* wager be?'

This time she felt more hesitant. She had seen Guy play both André and Xavier and she recognised him as a formidable opponent. With a smile of cunning she picked a stake which, even if she lost, would represent a personal victory for her.

'The loser makes love to the winner – however they wish.'

Guy glanced at her sharply, recognising her artfulness. '*D'accord,*' he said and nodded gravely.

With a surge of excitement, Tara picked up her cue and twisted it around and around in her hands. This would surely be a worthwhile victory.

The battle was hard fought and it was obvious from the outset that neither of them intended to lose. Despite her determination Tara felt her ability waning and her confidence slipping away. The multiple orgasms she had won from Xavier and Guy after the last game had left her feeling drowsy. Combined with the effect of the cognac, she was starting to feel a good deal less than alert.

Notwithstanding her best efforts, Guy pulled steadily into the lead. Finally, he sank the last four colours in quick succession, guaranteeing his win.

'Aha!' His smile was wicked as he toyed with his cue, eyeing her with interest.

Despite her irritation at losing the game, Tara had to force herself not to return his smile. At last he was going to penetrate her.

'Get back onto the table please,' he said and kicked the chair towards her. With only a moment's hesitation, she climbed up, using the chair as a step. Guy and Xavier exchanged a knowing smile. 'Lie down and spread your legs,' he ordered.

'What about the baize?' Tara couldn't help being concerned.

His response was swift. 'Fuck the baize!'

He climbed onto the table and lay alongside her, his hand immediately delving between her outspread thighs.

Quivering with excitement Tara opened herself eagerly to his touch and moved her hand casually between their bodies to unfasten his trousers.

'No, leave it.' He moved her hand and held it above her head, immediately she moved her other arm up to meet it, wondering with a rush of wantonness if he might tie her wrists again.

As his other hand worked between her legs she felt herself becoming moist for him. The heat within her was building quickly to bursting point and she closed her eyes. His fingers were inside her, making her ready. Now it was only a matter of time.

His body shifted beside her and she felt both his hands between her legs. Allowing her eyelids to flicker open for a second, she saw Xavier standing at the other side of her, simply watching. She smiled, feeling relieved because she had thought Guy might have opted to pass the honours to his brother.

Suddenly she felt an insistent hardness touching the edge of her vagina and she eagerly opened herself to him, spreading her thighs as far as they would go.

It was incredible – at long last he was inside her! In a rush of pleasure she came but still Guy did not let up. She marvelled at the way he felt inside her – so big and so hard. Casually, she reached down with her hand, stroking the soft curls of her pubis before allowing her fingers to slip further between her legs. Her eyes snapped open. Guy was above her but now she knew he was not inside her and neither was Xavier. Beneath her fingers she felt the smooth shaft of a snooker cue.

'You bastard, Guy!' she yelled, trying desperately to get away from him. But she couldn't move. He had her impaled by his hands and the cue.

'You said however I wish,' he said, 'this is how I wish.'

She could have torn the supercilious smile from his face with her bare hands.

'Take it out of me,' she demanded.

'Are you sure? I thought you were enjoying it.' He smiled and glanced at Xavier. 'Did she not look to you as though she was enjoying it?'

Xavier smiled at his brother and nodded. He stroked his hand across her breasts. 'Would you like that I replace it, *chérie?*'

She wavered for a moment, then found her voice. 'No, I would not like. I don't like either of you,' she said angrily.

Still smiling arrogantly, Guy slowly withdrew the snooker cue, the polished wood glistening under a thin veneer of her juices.

Xavier eyed it and laughed. 'It seems she does not appreciate us men any more. Now she prefers something a little longer and a little harder.'

Tara lashed out with her response.

'That's hardly surprising when you consider some people won't . . . or can't . . . even get it up!' She flashed a look of pure contempt at Guy, immediately regretting her words when she saw his startled expression.

'I think it is time we stopped playing games,' he said, his voice low and controlled.

Suddenly subdued and wishing with all her heart she had not been so thoughtless, Tara climbed down from the table and walked to the door.

'Please excuse me. I've also had enough of playing

games. I'm going to bed. Good night.'

'*Bonne nuit,*' Guy spoke in monotone and Xavier merely nodded.

As she reached the top of the stairs Xavier caught up with her. 'Do not pay any attention to my brother,' he said, 'he likes you more than you think.'

'Does he?' She found it difficult to believe but she felt no sense of achievement at having wounded him with her words.

Xavier nodded. 'The trouble is he likes to play games. Marie, his wife, hurt him badly and now he takes it out on all women.'

She wanted to ask Xavier more about Guy but she could hear his footsteps just below them.

'Would you like me to comfort you tonight?' Xavier offered. He winked cheekily, lightening the mood between them.

Part of her was sorely tempted, another part of her was simply sore. 'No, thank you all the same,' she said, shaking her head.

Xavier shrugged and when they reached one of the bedrooms he said, 'I am just here if you change your mind.' Then he leaned forward and kissed her on the lips.

Left alone on the landing she wavered. There was no way she could simply go to bed. She wanted the opportunity to clear the air between herself and Guy and was relieved when she heard his tread on the staircase. She was waiting for him when he reached the top stair.

'What do you want?' His tone was flat.

'I want to apologise.'

'There was no need for your remark.'

'I know,' she glanced down. 'I'm sorry.'

For a moment both of them were lost in their own thoughts.

'Come, Tara,' Guy said gently and put out his hand.

She wavered, all she wanted was his forgiveness. At least that was all she thought she wanted.

Ignoring her indecision, Guy stretched his hand out to her, his fingertips touching hers. Wordlessly, she let him lead her to his room.

As soon as he shut the door behind them he pulled her to him, holding her so tightly that she could feel his heart beating rapidly beneath his shirt.

'You cannot win with me, Tara. I do not know why you bother to try.'

'Are you talking about snooker, or something else?'

'Both.'

He ran his hands over her dress, tracing the tightly encased curves of her body, feeling the way she trembled beneath his touch. She sighed, wishing she had the strength to resist him.

'All I want is for you to make love to me properly, Guy. Surely that's not too much to expect – I'm not that unattractive to you, am I?'

He laughed outright at her words. 'Oh, Tara. I do believe you are seeking a compliment,' he said. 'You already know I am incredibly attracted to you.'

'Then why?'

Her question was lost as he silenced her with a deep, intimate kiss.

'*Tais-toi*, Tara. I have told you not to keep on with this. I shall become tired of it eventually.'

He released her abruptly and she felt the withdrawal of his presence and of his affection as keenly as a bereavement. Her first instinct was to apologise yet again but instead she walked to his bed and sat down, crossing her legs. For a while they stared at each other, neither of them spoke.

'You enjoyed yourself with Xavier,' he said. It was a statement rather than a question.

She nodded silently, wondering where this was leading.

'And you enjoyed yourself with André this morning by all accounts?'

This time his tone was more questioning.

'Yes, I did,' she burst out, almost adding that she would have swapped either of them, both of them, to have been with him. But she thought better of it and kept her words to herself.

'*Bon*,' he said. He crossed the room and stood in front of her. 'Do you feel more complete as a woman?'

She thought about his question. 'What, here in France you mean?'

He nodded, his expression inscrutable as he stared down at her.

Tara looked up and met his gaze. 'Yes but I don't think the location has much to do with it.' She

laughed then and so did he. All at once the release
of tension, both in her own body and between the
two of them, seemed almost visible.

'My wife thought she knew everything,' he said,
his face softening.

'Oh?' Her stomach tightened at his sudden revelation but she resisted the urge to press him to
continue.

'She was having an affair at the time of her death,
you see.' He knelt in front of her and pulled her
down onto his knee so that she sat astride him,
her back resting against the side of the bed. She
wound her arms gently around his neck and kissed
him.

'You don't have to tell me this,' she said, her voice
almost a whisper.

He nodded. 'I know that. Believe me, I will tell
you only what I want you to know.' He looked into
her eyes, captivating her and holding her fast with
his gaze as he started to stroke his hands over her
body. His palms slid easily down her back, over
her buttocks and along her thighs before moving up,
over her stomach and breasts. 'She tried to taunt
me one day,' he said, continuing with his story
although his caress didn't falter. 'She told me André
was not my child.'

'But he is. You only have to look at him to see he
is the image of you!' Tara couldn't help but speak
out. The idea that André had been fathered by any
other man was too ludicrous.

'Thank you. I would like to believe that.'

'Believe it, Guy.' She began to unbutton his shirt.

'I shall not make love to you the way you want, Tara,' he warned as she removed his shirt completely and began to kiss his chest and throat.

'I know,' she said, 'it doesn't matter, I just want to be with you.'

She ran the tip of her tongue across his nipples, nipping at the taut buds as they hardened under her caress.

He gasped with delight. 'Ah, *mon Dieu*, Tara. I cannot let you win.'

She smiled up at him, her fingers reaching to unzip his trousers as she did so.

'So you say. But one of these days, *chéri*, you may find you have no choice.'

She didn't stay with him all night but returned to her own room at about four in the morning. As soon as her head touched the pillow she fell asleep. For once her slumber was dreamless and when she finally awoke eight hours later she felt completely restored. After a leisurely bath she dressed in a loose, white cotton sundress and wandered downstairs to look for Guy. She found him sitting on the patio by the poolside. When he saw her he smiled and gestured to the chair next to him.

'Coffee?' he enquired, holding up a silver pot.

'Mm, yes please.' She stretched sensuously, shading her eyes with her hand so that she could look at the pool glistening and sparkling under the hot sun.

'It looks inviting, doesn't it?' he said affably. 'Will you join me for a swim later?'

'I'd love to.' She accepted the cup of coffee from him and sipped it before adding, 'Is Xavier still asleep?'

Guy shook his head. 'Ah, *non*. He has gone into the town to collect his girlfriend.'

'Oh.' Tara was surprised, although she didn't doubt Guy's brother's success with the opposite sex – not if his performance the previous day was anything to go by.

'I know what you are thinking.' Guy's voice startled her, bringing her out of her reverie.

'I'm sure you don't.' Tara was confident but he surprised her, as always.

'You were remembering yourself with Xavier yesterday,' he said. 'Perhaps you feel a little guilty?'

'Guilty!' She looked at him for a moment and then laughed.

'The Tara I met in England would have felt remorse for sleeping with another woman's man,' he pointed out, although there was no censure in his tone.

'We didn't sleep,' she said, grinning wickedly, 'and I'm not the Tara you met in England.'

'I know.' He reclined in his chair and slid a pair of sunglasses over his eyes. 'I'm so glad.'

For a moment she stared at him, allowing his

words to sink in. 'What is Xavier's girlfriend like? Have you met her?'

'Only once. She is very pretty and extremely sexy.'

Her stomach contracted with jealousy as he allowed the casual comment to slide from his lips.

'Have you . . . have you . . .?'

She didn't know how to describe what it was that Guy did exactly.

'No.' He interrupted her, his mouth curving into a smile. 'Would it bother you Tara?'

'Of course not,' she lied. 'Why should it?' She sipped her coffee again. 'Are you intending to . . .?'

'Look, Tara,' he interrupted. She could just make out his eyes staring hard at her through the dark lenses.

'Yes, Guy.'

'Do not pressure me, okay?'

'*D'accord*.' She put down her cup, deciding on a change of tactics. 'I think I may go into the town tonight. Can you recommend a good bar or a club where a lone woman is not too conspicuous?'

He sat up instantly. 'I planned to take you into town tonight. Xavier and I intended to take you and Maxine.'

Ignoring his frown, she shrugged. 'Perhaps I shall go with you, perhaps not.' She did not try to hide her smile of satisfaction.

Chapter Ten

Fortunately they were disturbed by the return of Xavier and a small, dark-haired girl who Tara assumed to be Maxine. The girl sat down at the opposite side of the table and placed an overnight bag beside her on the patio. Tara thought that she was probably about her own age.

As soon as Maxine arrived, Guy stood up. 'I'll go and ask Lisette to make some fresh coffee,' he said.

They all watched his retreating figure for a moment or two, then Xavier introduced the two women. Maxine nodded at Tara and smiled.

'Maxine doesn't speak much English,' Xavier explained. 'Do you mind if we talk in French today?'

'Of course not.' Tara said, returning the other woman's smile. It would do her good to use the language properly. She had been very lazy in that respect since her arrival in France.

At that moment Guy returned with instructions from the formidable Lisette to go into the house for lunch.

'Thank God. I'm starving,' Maxine said as she placed her palm against her stomach and grimaced.

Xavier laughed and patted her bottom in a familiar gesture. 'You're always starving, my darling,' he said, and added with a wink, 'for one thing or another.'

Tara was surprised to find her own stomach contract. Not with hunger but with envy at their easy familiarity. Despite all she had been through so far with Guy, she hardly felt as though they could be counted as lovers. At least, not in the same sense as Xavier and Maxine. Maybe she would enjoy herself more by going out alone that evening after all.

Her mood improved as lunch progressed, thanks in no small way to all the wine they drank. After a couple of glasses the four of them soon relaxed in each other's company and Tara found it surprisingly easy to keep up with the conversation.

As they ate Maxine had no hesitation in telling them her life story – from the time she had been seduced at thirteen, through her career as a night-club dancer and then a call girl, up to the present day. As she outlined her history Tara could sense Guy's growing interest in the other woman.

Trust Guy to find a call girl interesting, she thought. Perhaps Maxine and I should have a frank discussion, maybe she could tell me where I'm going wrong with him.

After the meal Xavier took Maxine upstairs, ostensibly to show her to her room, and Tara and

Guy went into the large sitting room.

'I don't know about you but it's a little too hot for me out there at the moment.' He nodded towards the window and Tara followed his gaze. Outside on the flag-stoned patio a heat haze shimmered. As she nodded her agreement he pulled her down next to him on the sofa. 'Let's play at being teenagers,' he suggested, his mood uncharacteristically light-hearted.

'I suppose that means I have to keep my legs clamped together and say no whenever you try to touch me?' she said laughing.

His expression of mock horror made her laugh even more and she pretended to fight him off. Their game became increasingly physical and they ended up on the carpet with him on top of her, one knee trapped between hers.

'No, no!' She screamed as he used his knee to try to force her legs apart. Suddenly she caught a movement out of the corner of her eye and looked up.

Maxine stood in the doorway watching them, a look of envy on her face. 'God, I wouldn't be saying no if it was me,' she said breathlessly, her eyes hazy with desire.

Tara tried to sit up but Guy held her down, his eyes fixed on Maxine.

'She doesn't mean it,' he said to her.

From where she lay Tara couldn't see Guy's face but he sounded as though he was treating the other woman to what she termed his lazy smile, the one that turned her insides to water in an instant. To her intense humiliation Guy suddenly pushed up her dress, exposing the tiny g-string underneath — a thin wisp of lace that hardly covered her at all.

'Guy!' Her voice held a warning note but he continued to hold her flat to the floor, his legs forcing their way between hers. She fought to win his attention with her eyes but he ignored her, gazing instead at the girl in the doorway.

Unwillingly, Tara followed his eyes and was surprised to see how rapt Maxine's expression was. She seemed rooted to the spot, watching them and waiting to see what Guy would do next.

A long moment passed during which everyone present seemed to hold their breath. Guy looked meaningfully at Tara, his eyes catching hers for a split second before he ripped the g-string completely from her body.

The thick walls of the old stone house almost trembled with the force of expelled breath. Tara couldn't be sure if it had simply been herself who gasped aloud, or if Maxine was sharing in her surprised arousal. Although she had been exposed rather a lot during the past week, nothing measured up to the shameful eroticism of this moment. To have strange men ogling her was one thing but for this attractive and disturbing woman to be staring so blatantly between her parted thighs was quite another.

'Guy, let me go.' She tried to keep her voice under control. 'Guy!'

The second time she spoke his name he looked at her, his blue eyes drawing her into his own private world of danger and fantasy. He pushed her arms above her head, holding both her wrists easily with his left hand while, with his right, he unbuttoned the bodice of her dress and urged the loosened fabric over the heaving swell of her breasts.

'Tell me you don't like this,' he said huskily as he bent his head and kissed her nipples before circling them with his tongue.

'Guy . . .'

He raised his head and looked at her again. 'Tell me honestly that you're not enjoying this and I will stop, Tara. It is that simple.'

With that he stroked his fingers across the top of her thighs, skimming the delicate purse of flesh that hid a remorseless throbbing.

Tara glanced up at Maxine. The girl stood in the doorway but her eyes were glazed, her body sagging against the wooden frame. With one hand she was stroking her own breasts through her black cotton T-shirt, her nipples straining to break through the thin material. Tara realised that, given the opportunity, Maxine would take her place in an instant. Suddenly, Tara felt a fresh rush of desire, the surge of heat causing her to moan gently, her thighs twitching under the weight of Guy's legs.

'Tell me to stop, Tara,' he said, his voice entering

her subconscious from a long way off.

'No. Please don't,' she gasped. She arched her back, straining her body toward him, making sure he realised that her meaning was *don't stop*.

'That is better, *ma chérie*.' He kissed her on the lips. And, with his face still close to hers, he turned her head so that she could see Maxine. 'Look at her, Tara,' he murmured darkly, 'she wishes she could be here with us.'

Tara trembled, knowing only too well that she wouldn't be able to handle it if Guy asked Maxine to join them. To her relief he made no such suggestion. Instead he kissed her again, more deeply this time, his hand massaging her breasts as his tongue investigated her mouth. From the corner of her eye she watched the French girl. She dreaded what he might do next although deep down she knew and the certainty drew her to even greater heights of arousal. The moments seemed interminably long. If he was going to touch her in this woman's presence then she wished he would just do it and not torment her.

He was building up to it, she could feel it. The message transmitted via the subtle pressure of his hands and mouth, the way his knees forced her legs apart just that little bit wider.

'Aha!' he said softly. His fingers grazed her inner thighs, walking them tantalisingly toward her waiting sex.

A glance from the corner of her eye once more showed her that Maxine was mimicking his actions.

Her skirt was rucked up, revealing that she wore no knickers and her long manicured nails brushed against a thick, glossy thatch of pubic hair peeking out from under her hemline.

Tara didn't know quite what it was that intensified her reaction to Guy's caress but it was so acute she came the instant he touched his fingertip against the throbbing bud of her clitoris. But, as she floated away into the muted realm of ecstasy, she found her mind transfixed by the image of Maxine. From far away she could hear sounds, moaning sounds that signalled orgasmic pleasure unleashed. Were they coming from herself alone, or also from the figure in the doorway? All too soon she rose on the crest of the last wave and sank back into blurred reality.

'Is this a private party or can anyone join in?' It was Xavier's voice, breaking the thread of eroticism that joined the three of them.

She opened her eyes. Guy was kneeling between her legs, no longer holding them down and Maxine leant against the door frame. She was panting, her hair plastered to her face with perspiration. Xavier stepped into Tara's line of vision and, for some reason, she tried to conceal herself.

'I wondered where you had disappeared to,' he said to Maxine. 'I'm sorry I fell asleep so quickly, it must have been the wine.' He pulled the other woman to him, stroking her hair back from her face and smiling at her dreamy expression.

Guy rose to his feet and offered his hand to Tara. 'We all became a little distracted,' he explained, smiling lazily at his brother, 'especially when your lady friend caught us in flagrante.'

Xavier grinned back in exactly the same way, disorienting Tara for a moment by displaying such an acute likeness to his brother. She wondered what it would be like to have them both together. One brother was wonderful, so add his twin and surely the pleasure would be doubled at least. Except that she could only be certain of Xavier's cock inside her.

'I was going to suggest we all went for a swim but now that seems a little tame,' Xavier said.

'A swim would be lovely but I didn't bring a costume,' Maxine said. She pouted at Guy.

He responded predictably. 'Why bother with costumes? We are all above the age of consent.'

Tara's heart sank. She was sure that by the end of the evening she would have lost him to this predatory woman. And, with her professional skills, Maxine was bound to find the way to coax him back into proper fucking. She wondered whether to retaliate by making an overt play for Xavier but deep down she was certain that Maxine would easily forego her loyalty to him in order to win the unattainable.

'I'm game,' Tara said, surprising herself. It seemed she was constantly being forced into one competitive situation after another. But if Maxine wanted to challenge her for Guy's affections then she would fight damn hard to win.

Her response won a look of admiration from him which she held inside her all the way to the pool. Under the hot summer sun she found it a lot easier to dispense with her clothes than she had with her earlier inhibitions. Basking for a brief moment in the joint appreciation of the two men she ran to the edge of the pool and dived in.

Maxine was quick to follow. 'Come on, you cowards,' she shouted to Guy and Xavier as she trod water, 'what are you waiting for?'

Tara swam determinedly for a couple of lengths and was surprised when Maxine surfaced beside her at the shallow end, her small tanned breasts emerging from the water as she stood upright. Curiosity overcame her mistrust and Tara found she couldn't take her eyes off her.

'You are not used to displaying your body in front of other women?' Maxine said. She shook the excess water from her long dark tresses and glanced sideways, catching Tara out.

'No.' Tara looked down into the water, desperate to hide her embarrassment, 'I'm not used to displaying my body at all.'

'But you are so gorgeous,' Maxine insisted, 'those tits, that arse — surely you cannot be ashamed of them?'

Tara tried to absorb her words. She wondered whether she had been a little hasty in her assumptions about the woman. Of course, it helped that this was the first time they had been alone without the men to distract them. She glanced toward the other end of the pool. Still fully dressed, they were seated at a table, drinking wine.

'I think they changed their minds,' she said, smiling properly at Maxine for the first time.

'*I* think they would like us to become better acquainted,' said Maxine.

'Are you planning to stay here tonight?' Tara asked. 'Guy mentioned something about us all going to a club later.'

She floated on her stomach and kicked her legs lazily, sending a fine spray of cool water over her burning shoulders.

'Mm,' Maxine murmured, copying Tara, 'I brought some things with me just in case but Xavier has already assumed that I will stay. He has even given me a bedroom all to myself.' She laughed as though the idea of sleeping alone was totally preposterous.

'Have you known Xavier for very long?' Tara was curious about this woman. She was beginning to like her.

Maxine's eyes drifted to Xavier for a moment. 'He is a nice man. We have been sometime lovers for about six months but I live in the south, near Nice . . .' Her voice trailed off.

'Are you still a prostitute?' Tara asked, shocking herself with the unintentional bluntness of a question that had been fermenting in her mind ever since they had sat down to lunch.

'Call girl, *ma chérie*, call girl,' Maxine said lightly, 'and no. I became "respectable" about four years ago.

218

Now I own a couple of beauty salons which are very successful.'

'Oh.' Tara looked at her in admiration. 'Are you planning to make a play for Guy?' Again the unintended directness of her own question surprised her.

'Perhaps,' Maxine said, glancing sideways at her again, 'would it bother you?'

Tara fell silent for a moment. 'I should say no,' she said eventually, 'and in all honesty I have no claim to him. But . . .' she paused, feeling embarrassed. Then she found herself pouring out all her problems with Guy.

'Wow, that is a dilemma,' Maxine said, looking amazed. 'I must admit, I too am excited by the thought of such a challenge but if it would be a problem for you I wouldn't dream of straying onto your territory.'

'Oh God, that sounds so awful,' Tara groaned, '*my territory.*' She laughed aloud. 'But thank you anyway. I feel a lot better now.'

Just as she spoke they were startled to hear a sudden splash and moments later Guy and Xavier surfaced in front of them. Naked and wet, it was difficult to tell the difference between the brothers. Tara glanced at Maxine and realised that she too was wondering which was which.

'I can't tell you two boys apart,' Maxine said. The ends of her dark hair flicked water at them as she looked quickly from one to the other and then back again.

'That could be handy.' They spoke in unison, their voices identical as well.

'Stop it!' Tara laughed. 'Which one is which?'

'Well, I'm Xavier and he's Guy,' said one.

'No, don't listen to him. I'm Xavier and *he's* Guy,' said the other.

'I'm sure we have ways of distinguishing one man from another, don't we, Tara?' Maxine said. She smiled confidently and thrust her head under the water.

Tara copied her. Beneath the shimmering water she clasped a waiting cock, then swapped with Maxine, each of them working by touch alone to stake their own particular claim.

Finally Tara shook her head in defeat and looked at Maxine. 'I can't tell which one's which,' she said.

'Nor can I,' the other woman admitted.

Oblivious to them both the two men looked at each other and winked.

To Tara, it seemed as though Maxine's arrival had served to dissipate the air of latent unease that had hung over the old French house. Suddenly Guy and Xavier were transformed into naughty boys intent on tormenting herself and Maxine as much as possible – grabbing, tickling and chasing them up and down the pool until they were all gasping for breath.

'Stop. Oh, please stop,' Tara pleaded. They had been cavorting around in the water for about an hour and she had finally swum to the deep end of the pool to escape but the men were hot on her heels. She looked around for Maxine but the other woman was lounging on the patio, apparently asleep. 'Don't come any closer,' she said, trying to make her voice sound as threatening as possible.

'Or what?' One of them, she couldn't tell which, made a grab for her ankle.

Tara kicked out. 'I'm warning you,' she called, laughter undermining her serious tone, 'these legs are lethal weapons.' She found herself being backed against the edge of the pool and put out her hand for support.

The two men looked at each other. Like sharks they glided towards her through the water.

'I mean it. Stop you two.' She kicked out again, realising a fraction too late that her action was a mistake.

Immediately Xavier and Guy caught her ankles and held them. Their hands moved up her legs as they came closer, one man moving to either side of her. Tara squirmed but they held her fast, their free hands sliding up her inner thighs, eventually connecting.

'What have we here?' The one whom she believed to be Guy slipped his fingers inside her.

'Ooh!' She cried out and arched her back with surprise and pleasure as the insolent gesture incited a powerful heat in her womb.

Without giving her a moment to recover, the other man slipped his fingers inside her too.

'My brother and I are very close, Tara,' he breathed in her ear, sending ripples of nervous excitement coursing through her whole body.

'You can't do this to me.' Her voice broke as a gigantic wave of pleasure swept over her, almost rendering her senseless.

'And who is going to stop us?' Guy, if it was indeed Guy, looked around. Apart from the sleeping form of Maxine, the place was completely deserted. He released his other hand from her leg, using the pressure in his own thigh to hold her and began to caress her breast. His brother mirrored his actions and spoke to her in the same low tone.

'Do you want us to stop, Tara?'

Slowly, she shook her head. If it meant the world would come to an end right at that very moment she would not want them to stop, the devilish eroticism of having both men inside her at once was too delicious. She let her head drop back and a long sigh of release issued from her lips as they moved against her and within her. Their actions seemed precisely coordinated – choreographed to fill her body with a continuous, rhythmic flow of euphoria. And the effect was sheer bliss.

'Tara, *ma chérie*, you are a lucky bitch.' Maxine's words broke through the thin veil of consciousness that enveloped her.

The other woman slipped into the water beside the three of them, her nipples instantly reacting to the sudden shock of the chill water after the relentless heat of the sun.

Tara smiled lazily, her eyes taking in the questioning expressions of the two men. Still high from the effects of her orgasm, she waved a hand in an expansive gesture.

'Please. Feel free.'

Far from feeling envious, she watched with pleasure as Xavier and Guy treated Maxine to the same delectable smorgasbord of gratification. Eventually, they all floated together in the water, Maxine and Tara smiling contentedly.

'Would you girls like to go out tonight?' one of the men suggested. 'We could show you some of the local night life.'

Tara glanced at Maxine. 'What do you think,' she said, 'should we let them out in public?'

The dark-haired woman nodded and stretched luxuriously. 'Yes but first I must shower.' She swam toward the steps.

'Wait for me, *chérie!*'

Tara glanced across the pool in surprise as one of the brothers swam after Maxine, catching her with easy familiarity around the waist and kissing her deeply. She shook her head, she could have sworn that one was Guy.

Despite her earlier confusion, when they all convened in the large sitting room – fully clothed – she could tell at once which brother was which. She walked straight over to Guy and smiled up at him.

'You look gorgeous,' he murmured as he ran his eyes appreciatively over her body, igniting a familiar warm glow within her.

Tara glanced in the large mirror that hung over the fireplace. She was pleased with her reflection, glad that she had opted to wear yet another new purchase – a simple, fluid sheath dress in cream-coloured satin. Underneath she wore nothing whatsoever. The sound of voices reminded her of Maxine and Xavier and, as they rose to their feet, Tara was struck by their appearance. They made a very attractive couple.

'I love your dress,' Maxine said, kissing Tara on both cheeks as if they had not seen each other in ages.

'Thanks, I was just admiring your blouse,' Tara responded.

The garment of sheer, sapphire blue chiffon worn over a silk camisole of the same shade complimented the French woman's colouring perfectly. Tara took in the whole of Maxine's appearance, including the short black skirt and glossy high-heeled shoes. On many women, she thought, her outfit would make her look exactly what she had been a few years earlier, yet somehow her charisma allowed her to carry if off with a certain dignity. Instead of resembling a call girl she simply looked amazingly chic.

'Are we ready to go?' Xavier looked pointedly at the two women until Tara, realising that she and Maxine were the object of his attention, nodded.

'We're just waiting for you and Guy,' she giggled, knowing her remark would prompt a round of heavy sighs and raised eyebrows.

Guy put his hand around her waist. 'I shall have to spank you for being so impertinent, young lady.' His eyes twinkled with promise and Tara felt her insides melt.

'Perhaps we shouldn't bother to go out at all?' she murmured quietly.

Infuriatingly, Guy simply smiled at her suggestion and looked to his brother. 'Your car or mine?'

Xavier shrugged. 'Yours might be a better choice. I'm afraid I've been having a little steering trouble.' The remark was casually made but Tara noticed how Guy's face suddenly paled. 'God, I'm sorry Guy.' Xavier walked up to his twin and put a hand on his shoulder.

Without needing to be told Tara guessed that a steering problem must have been the reason for the accident that killed his wife. Desperate to change the subject, she complained of feeling faint with hunger.

'Okay, let's go.' Guy put his arm around her again, his renewed smile taking in everyone.

As Guy drove, Tara couldn't help feeling envious of Xavier and Maxine, who kissed and cuddled on the back seat like a pair of sex-starved teenagers and by the time they reached the restaurant she found herself feeling very warm.

They parked in a side street and, while the courting couple went on ahead, Guy and Tara lingered a little. As soon as he had locked the car she put her arms around his neck and kissed him. Hungry with unfulfilled desire, she pressed her body against his.

'I wish you would take me right here, right now,' she murmured, her breath caressing his ear as she slid her hand inside the waistband of his trousers.

For a moment or two he allowed her to caress him, then he took her wrist and withdrew her hand gently but firmly before slipping both his hands under the hem of her dress and cupping her naked buttocks.

'My God, Tara, if things were different you know I would,' his voice was husky as he infuriated her with his reply. Pausing only to slide one hand briefly between her thighs he suddenly became brisk. 'Enough of this. Let's go and eat.'

Quelling an instant retort about him eating her instead, Tara allowed Guy to take her hand and lead her to the restaurant. Xavier and Maxine were already seated and perusing large, complicated-looking menus.

'They serve ten different fish dishes alone,' Maxine remarked as Tara sat down opposite her.

'Oh, good,' Tara mumbled. She was distracted. She felt more sexually aroused and frustrated than she could ever remember and the last thing on her mind was food. Making her choice quickly, she reached for the glass of white wine that sat before her.

Despite her preoccupation, she found herself enjoying the company around her. Xavier proved to be a wicked raconteur of jokes, many of them too

risqué to be told in such public surroundings and
Maxine's stories of her days as a call girl were
equally entertaining. Eventually, Tara found herself relaxing. The good food, the excellent wine
and the general conviviality of the evening all
served to cloak her with the heady glow of
euphoria.

After the meal they walked to a small club where
Tara danced for the first time in years.

'You look as though you're really enjoying yourself,' Guy said. He smiled down at her as they
swayed together on the dance floor, his body pressed
firmly against hers.

'Mm. I am.' Tara nodded dreamily. Although the
manoeuvre hardly seemed possible, she moved her
body even closer to his and rested her cheek on his
shoulder.

'What do you think of Maxine?' Guy asked, stroking her hair and sliding his hand down the length
of her back and across her undulating buttocks in a
single graceful movement.

'She's nice,' Tara said as she looked up at him. 'I
didn't expect to like her at first but I do now.' She
rested her cheek on his shoulder again and replaced
his hand on her bottom. 'Don't stop.'

'Do you find her attractive?' His question surprised her, although it wasn't so much the content
of the question as the way he asked it.

'She's very attractive,' Tara answered, her tone
displaying a note of caution. She wasn't entirely

convinced that Guy wouldn't make a play for the other woman.

'Does she excite you?' His question jolted her from her hazy reverie.

'Me? What do you mean?'

Clasping her shoulders he held her away from him, and stared into her eyes.

'Given the opportunity, would you make love with her?'

'What . . . I mean, pardon..what did you say?' The words fell from Tara's lips in a confused jumble. Detaching herself from his grasp, she strode away from him toward their table. Picking up her glass, she drained it in an instant. Feeling weak all of a sudden she sat down.

Guy sat beside her, his arm encircling her shoulders. 'I think you would derive a lot of enjoyment from an encounter with Maxine,' he said.

She looked at him wide-eyed. She could see from his expression that he was absolutely serious.

'Guy, I have never . . .'

He silenced her by putting a finger to her lips. 'Shh. I thought not,' he said, 'that is why I suggest it.' He glanced to the dance floor where the woman in question and his brother ground their bodies together in perfect harmony. Then he looked back at Tara and dropped his voice. 'Xavier and I have discussed it. We think Maxine would agree and it would certainly be entertaining for us.'

She stared at him in disbelief. 'I see.' She picked

up the nearest glass and gulped it before turning to look straight at him. 'So, not only do you want me to have sex with your brother's girlfriend but you both want to watch us doing it?' She shook her head slowly in disbelief.

Guy smiled lazily. 'But of course. What a waste it would be if we didn't.'

Tara tried to ignore his remark. Despite all her misgivings, his suggestion started to flicker and smoulder like a little flame somewhere deep inside her.

'Okay.'

It was worth it if only to witness the surprise on his face. A long silence passed between them. Eventually Guy found his voice. 'I'll get you another drink.' Picking up her glass he wove his way through the throng of people to the bar.

For a while Tara contented herself by watching the other dancers until she was startled by a strange voice in her ear.

'Would you care to dance with me, young lady?'

She looked up and found herself staring into the deep dark eyes of a young Frenchman.

'*Oui, merci*,' she said. She followed him to the dance floor and, as she slipped into the waiting circle of his arms, she glanced across to the bar. Guy was standing with his back to her talking to the barman. After a swift glance around the crowded room she realised Xavier and Maxine were nowhere to be seen.

Moving to the rhythm of the music, she answered the young man's string of predictable questions, telling him her name, where she lived, and so forth. Politely, but with no real interest, she enquired about him. She discovered his name was Jacques, that he was twenty-six and lived in the next nearest town.

Tara feigned interest, murmuring a response. From over his shoulder she could now see Maxine seated at their table, alone. Moving around a little more she saw Xavier had joined Guy at the bar, they stood close together, their dark heads almost touching as they conversed. Suddenly Guy looked up and saw her dancing with Jacques. He glowered. A small knot of fear and excitement tightened inside her as he strode toward them. When he confronted them, Jacques looked up suddenly, the surprise evident on his face. Tara smiled.

'Do you have a problem, Guy?'

'No. I think it is you who has the problem. Come with me.' He put out his hand but she steadfastly ignored it.

'I'm dancing.'

'Tara!'

On his lips, her name was a warning but still she chose to ignore him. She could feel Jacques' grip around her loosening. The coward was planning to desert her, she thought.

'I shall join you when I'm ready,' she said calmly, her defiant stare holding his eyes, locking into his anger with all the resilience of the immovable object.

He pursed his lips at her reply. 'Very well. But this is not the end of the matter.' Turning abruptly on his heel, Guy strode away.

After a few minutes, Tara thanked her young partner and walked over to join the party, her air deliberately casual as she sat down and picked up her drink.

'*Santé!*' Her smile was a challenge.

'I think it is time we went home, don't you agree, Xavier?' Guy said. He looked at his brother and smiled wickedly, his action causing Tara's stomach to contract. For a moment she had forgotten about their earlier conversation. Damn him, he would certainly make her pay now.

To Tara's consternation, the return journey seemed surprisingly short. Again Maxine and Xavier smooched together on the back seat but she could also hear him whispering to her. The knot in her stomach tightened, obviously Xavier was putting Guy's suggestion to her. Pretending to check her make-up, Tara pulled down the visor and eyed their reflection in the vanity mirror. To her intense disquiet she saw Maxine give a secretive smile and nod her agreement.

Tara swallowed. A lump had suddenly formed in her throat and she couldn't dislodge it. She looked across to Guy's stern profile and placed her hand on his thigh. He did not acknowledge it.

She thought hard about the situation. In a strange

way it reminded her of her dilemma about seducing André. At the end of the day it was up to her if she went through with it or not and she had to admit the outcome of her last challenge had proved to be an extremely pleasant surprise. She felt a sudden rush of moisture at the recollection. All at once she knew, yet again, she would pick up the gauntlet that Guy had thrown down in front of her. There was no way she would give him cause to think he had defeated her.

When they reached the house Tara started to wonder if his suggestion had merely served to tease her. In the large sitting room Xavier and Maxine immediately snuggled up together on the sofa and Guy poured drinks for everyone. To Tara's intense relief, when he had distributed them he sat down beside her and draped his arm around her shoulders. Pulling her to him he kissed her fiercely then pushed her away from him, his fingers gripping her shoulders.

'Don't ever do that again!' he said gruffly.

She considered retaliating but decided against it, she wanted Guy to be her lover not her adversary. Instead she simply smiled and dropped a series of featherlight kisses on his cheek and neck.

In response, he stroked his hand across her breasts, sliding the silky fabric of her dress over her willing body. The gesture automatically aroused her nipples into hard, tight buds and he glanced wickedly at their outline before slipping his hand under the hem of her dress.

She sighed as he caressed the length of her bare thighs and began to probe the hot moist flesh at their apex.

After a long, blissful moment, his eyes slipped away from hers and she followed his glance, noticing how he and Xavier exchanged knowing smiles.

'Come, Tara,' Guy said, his voice soft and meaningful. He withdrew his hand and pulled her to her feet, leading her the dozen or so paces to the sofa.

As she drew nearer so the other man rose, making a place for her beside Maxine. Suddenly she felt her legs turn to water, giving her no option but to sit in the space he had vacated. For a minute or two she sat immobile, her body trembling. She glanced up but the two men were seated some distance away, apparently deep in conversation. Maxine spoke first, her voice barely more than a whisper.

'Don't worry. I'll lead, you follow.' She put out a hand and stroked Tara's hair.

At first Tara flinched at the other woman's touch but almost at once she found herself relaxing under the caress, telling herself it was like visiting the hairdresser. Despite her natural reticence she could feel herself becoming increasingly aware of the proximity of Maxine's body and the heat emanating from it. As the other woman moved she felt herself caught up in a cloud of unfamiliar scent, its musky sweetness enveloping her.

Tara couldn't be sure but it seemed as though it

was she who initiated the first kiss. She who turned her head and smiled with her eyes before covering the other woman's mouth with her own. Certainly it was she who spoke the first soft words of desire.

As though in a dream, their clothes simply melted away and she found herself transported on a journey of exploration into unfamiliar territory. Her fingertips gently tracing the unaccustomed hills and valleys of a body that at once was unusual in that it wasn't male, yet was more familiar to her than any man could possibly be.

Glancing down, she saw Maxine's dark head against her breast, her ruby red lips encircling a nipple, leaving a faint red outline like a blot on a tissue. Arching her back sensuously, she ran her hands over the other woman's shoulders. She played with Maxine's hair, lifting and dropping the unfamiliar weight of her long dark curls repeatedly, enjoying the way the soft tendrils caressed her own body like little fairy breaths, exciting her sensitive flesh into new arousal.

She hadn't yet allowed herself to look at the two men, denying herself the pleasure of their excitement until she felt ready to accept it. Instead she moved her hands lower, tracing the length of Maxine's spine, her fingertips feeling each little knob and ridge of bone. Then she ran her hands up the silky length of her sides, sliding her palms between their bodies to cup the other woman's breasts.

'Ooh!' The exclamation issued simultaneously. Tara's excitement coming from the incomparable pleasure of discovery, to touch a pair of breasts that were not her own. To feel the nipples hardening beneath her fingers yet not experience the effect herself. The pleasure was so acute she felt intoxicated.

Now she allowed her gaze to drift to the other side of the room. The twins sat with rapt expressions, their body language speaking of their desire for the two women who loved before them. Excited anew, she allowed her fingers to drift lower, to open the delicate layers of Maxine's most intimate flesh and search out the swollen bud of her clitoris, her knowing fingertips softly stroking her pliant, perfumed partner to orgasm.

'Oh. Oh, *ma chérie!*' Maxine arched her back and cried out with joy, her response thrilling Tara so much that she felt encouraged to explore further, sinking her fingers into the musky cavern close by. As she delved into the hot wetness she felt the other woman's muscles rippling around her fingers in a second orgasm. The spasming flesh drew her fingers deeper, taking her beyond the limits of her previous voyages of self-discovery.

From across the room came the stereo hiss of sharply expelled breath.

Gradually Maxine's movements abated and she smiled her dreamy thanks at Tara who spread her legs eagerly as the other woman sought to return

235

the gift of pleasure. This time Tara watched the glossy head sink between her thighs, the sight alone arousing her a split second before the light caress of the woman's tongue transported her along a rainbow route of ecstasy.

If she thought she had known pleasure before, then this was surely the pinnacle of all possible delight. There was no way to describe the rapture she felt as the heat within her fanned outward, melting her whole body. The thrill of each soft caress drew a delicate thread of bliss around her – silken skeins of pleasure that gathered in a web of sublime joy as Maxine stroked the tip of her skilful tongue over the sensitive petals of her labia and around and around her throbbing clitoris. Eventually, she screamed out as the heat exploded within her and the pleasure rolled over her in great, pounding waves.

'Mon Dieu, elles sont incroyables.' One of the men spoke but in the ebbing haze of passion Tara did not know who.

She sensed the two brothers moving closer and a moment later masculine arms enfolded her, drawing her almost regretfully away from the warm, soft flesh of her new lover.

'I want to love you tonight, Tara,' Guy whispered the words she had been longing to hear.

'Oh, yes please.' She turned into his arms and kissed him deeply, thrusting her naked breasts against the crisp cotton of his shirt, allowing him to lift her up from the sofa and carry her out of the room and up the stairs. At the door of his bedroom she called a halt for just a second. Although she was convinced that she was with the right brother, the thought that they might have arranged to switch partners arrested her. 'You *are* Guy, aren't you?' she said.

But he was nodding his head and smiling. 'Of course. Remember the café where I first asked you to seduce André? The doctor's examination in my office? Remember the hotel near La Reynard?'

His brief resumé placated her before he overcame her doubts completely by kissing her in a manner that was now so familiar.

'I want you so much, Guy,' she murmured. Even as he lowered her gently to the bed, she could hardly bear to relinquish her grip upon his body. As he locked the door, her eyes travelled over the array of family photographs. Once more she found her attention transfixed by the image of his wife, Marie, whose expression seemed to taunt her. Dead for sixteen years, her presence was overpowering.

Tara saw Guy staring at the photograph too, hardly able to tear his eyes away. When he did she saw the regret and felt it keenly, like a blow to the stomach, before he even moved his mouth to speak.

'I'm sorry, Tara,' he said. At that moment he looked so young, so much like André her heart went out to him.

'It's okay.'

She held out her arms and pulled him to her. For a long time she held him, her body absorbing the violent beat of his heart. How could one woman inspire so deep a love from a man that he was willing to forgo the ultimate pleasure for the rest of his life?

His arms wrapped tightly around her in a gesture of fierce protectiveness.

'I didn't mean to do this to you,' he said at last, his voice full of regret.

'I know,' she murmured. Her words held no accusation as she looked up at him. 'I can't win against her Guy. All the time I thought I was fighting you but it's really her I'm up against, or at least her memory. You must still love her very much.'

'I never loved her. I hated her!'

'Some say love and hate are the same,' she said gently. 'They are both very powerful emotions.'

He shook his head sadly and sighed. 'I know, but I cannot honestly claim to have loved Marie.'

Every fibre in her being urged her to beg him to continue yet something held her back. When the time was right, she thought, he would tell her everything.

That night they did not touch each other intimately but slept in each other's arms. Strangely, as she drifted off to sleep, Tara thought that it was the best night she had ever spent with him.

The following day the atmosphere was once more lighthearted. The four of them swam and sunbathed

– their natural predisposition to teasing and touching each other increased by Tara and Maxine's intimacy.

In the early afternoon, as Maxine held her around the waist and kissed her breasts, Tara watched Guy as he sat reading the newspaper and drinking coffee. Neither of them had mentioned the events of the night before.

'God, I am so sore after last night,' Maxine said, disturbing her thoughts, 'Xavier is such a beast.' She looked up and winked at Tara. 'I take it you had a good night too?'

Tara hesitated but eventually shook her head. She found herself pouring out her heart to Maxine, who pulled her to the most shallow part of the pool and held her close, stroking her hair.

'I just don't know what to do about him, Maxine,' Tara wailed. She was almost in tears as she spoke, such was her frustration.

'I wish I could help you, *ma chérie*, but this dilemma has me stumped.' The French woman smiled apologetically.

They still spoke in French for Maxine's benefit and Tara found herself struggling for a moment with the unfamiliar phrase.

'The trouble is,' Tara said. 'I really enjoy having a man inside me and with André away I'm beginning to miss it a lot!'

'André?' Maxine enquired.

Tara bit her lip. Damn! She hadn't meant to be so

indiscreet. Deciding it would do her good to unbur-
den herself she told the other woman the whole
story.

'So you see what an awkward position I am in,'
she concluded, heaving herself from the water to sit
on the side of the pool.

During the course of her career, Maxine thought
she had seen and heard it all but this was a revelation to her. She said as much to Tara who laughed,
despite her mood.

After a long, boozy lunch Maxine and Xavier went
upstairs for a nap and Tara followed Guy into the
games room.

'Do you play backgammon?' he asked.

'Strip backgammon?' she said, raising an eyebrow.

'No, you little hussy. Just ordinary backgammon.'
She was relieved to see Guy smile again.

'Oh, very well. If that is all you have to suggest,'
she said.

She sat down opposite him and promptly beat him
by five games to three.

'It's a shame our wager the other night wasn't
based on this game,' she joked, remembering how
he had called her bluff with his snooker cue.

He reclined in his chair and eyed her thoughtfully.
'We can made a wager on this game if you wish,' he
said. There was a cunning note to his tone which,
unfortunately, Tara missed completely.

'Okay. What do you suggest?'

She started to set out the pieces once again,

confident that this time she had every chance of beating him hands down.

He pretended to think for a moment, twisting the stem of his wine glass around and around in his fingers. Then he spoke slowly and clearly.

'We will play a total of thirteen games . . . unlucky for some . . .' he said.

'And the prize?' she asked.

'Winner takes all.'

She looked at him for a long moment. 'What does that mean exactly?'

He shrugged. 'Just as it sounds,' he said casually. 'Whoever wins can demand anything of the other person, anything at all. And the loser is honour-bound to comply.'

As he spoke Tara's heart started to beat faster. For some inexplicable reason she was finding it hard to breathe. It was certainly a prize worth winning, for both sides. Deep down she knew that if she won he would keep to his side of the bargain come what may and she didn't doubt that he knew what her demand would be. What worried her was . . . what if she lost? Of all the things he had already asked her to do, what could he possibly ask of her that was even more daunting?

Her lips released the fatal word. 'Okay.'

Guy nodded sagely. 'Good, I knew you would not resist the challenge. When would you like this contest to start?'

With a knot in her stomach she answered him,

her mouth so dry she could hardly speak.

'As the saying goes,' she said, 'there is no time like the present.'

His expression was deadly serious as he nodded. 'Very well.'

They each threw an opening die. Tara smiled triumphantly, six-one in her favour, it was a good start.

Guy threw a three and a one and flashed her a knowing smile that did not quite reach his eyes.

She swallowed. As she suspected, he was not going to make things easy for her by any means.

And so the games went on. Every so often one of them gained a little over the other but there was nothing really in it. By the time Xavier and Maxine put in an appearance they were both level on four games each and had just agreed to take a well-deserved break.

'What's going on here? It looks like serious stuff.' Xavier said, picking up the doubling cube and rolling it casually.

Guy explained briefly.

'My God!' Maxine said exhaling sharply. 'Do you know what you're doing?' She pulled Tara to one side at the earliest opportunity and voiced her concern.

Tara shrugged. 'It's my own fault,' she said, 'I simply can't resist a challenge, especially when it comes from him.' She glanced at Guy who stood by the snooker table laughing with his brother. She added in a more subdued tone, 'I dread to think what he has in store for me if I lose.'

Maxine shook her dark curls. 'Then you had better make sure you win, *chérie*.'

Before supper they played another three games with Tara winning two of them. She smiled broadly. To succeed, Guy would have to win each of the last two games. The scent of victory was so close she could almost bottle it.

As they walked into the dining room, Xavier caught up with her. 'I don't envy you, Tara,' he said in a low voice.

'Why?' She glanced at him in surprise. 'If this is a ploy by your brother to unnerve me, you can forget it. I don't intend to lose.'

Xavier shrugged. 'I know Guy,' he said, 'he's just toying with you.'

'Oh really!' Tara almost exploded with indignation. 'I'm winning, for God's sake, Xavier. Or hadn't you noticed? I do know how to play the game you know.'

'Okay.' He put up his hand in self-defence. 'Just don't say I didn't warn you.' Subdued by the apparently genuine concern he showed her, Tara watched Xavier take his seat next to Maxine and help himself to a piece of bread. The two of them spoke in low voices and she saw the other woman cast a pitying look in her direction. Damn them, Tara thought angrily, now they were all trying to get to her. Throughout the meal she felt every inch the condemned man, or rather the condemned woman. Consequently, her appetite was far from hearty.

243

'More wine, Tara?' Guy asked. He held the bottle over her glass.

'No, thank you,' she said, 'if you think you can beat me by getting me drunk, forget it.'

Guy shook his head in obvious amazement. 'I never intended any such thing,' he said.

By the time they had finished eating, Tara's stomach had contracted so tightly she thought she would burst. With an air of casual indifference Guy stretched and then suggested they conclude their match.

'Unless you simply wish to concede now?' he offered. He smiled arrogantly, knowing that his suggestion would infuriate her.

'I shall not even bother to dignify that remark with a reply,' Tara said. She pushed her chair back.

'Do you mind if we watch you play, or will our presence distract you?' Maxine asked, hovering by the doorway to the games room.

Tara glanced at Guy who pursed his lips and shrugged a typically Gallic gesture of indifference. In reality she felt a little less comfortable with an audience but despite her misgivings she invited Maxine and Xavier to join them. As she took her seat she stared at the board. Two games were all that stood between herself and victory. Or . . .? She gave herself a mental slap, there was no point in succumbing to negative thoughts.

They each picked up a die and threw. Tara breathed a sigh of relief three-one to her – an excellent opener. Guy did not fare quite so well. Six-two was all that he could muster, the throw forcing him to leave an open blot for her to pounce upon. Aha, she thought, as she threw a six-one, the throw was good but it put her in a quandary – either she could be aggressive and take his piece but also leave one of her men defenceless, or she could play the more sensible safety move. Unfortunately, Tara was naturally aggressive.

Returning to the board immediately on his next throw, Guy landed on her open piece and went on to win the entire game.

Tara swallowed hard. She couldn't believe that they were down to a single deciding game. It would have been all the same if they had played just once in the first place. This time when Guy offered her a glass of cognac she accepted. To hell with it! Whatever happened now she would need a drink.

'Are you alright, Tara?' Maxine asked as she placed a perfectly manicured hand on her arm.

For a second Tara simply stared wordlessly at the long, red fingernails, then she looked into the other woman's eyes and gave an imperceptible shake of her head. Aloud she said, 'Of course.'

They rolled the opening dice for the last time and Guy won the throw. Tara could feel her spirits slump but forced herself to be optimistic. It was still anybody's game. For the next few throws it seemed to be just that – there was really nothing to choose between them as they quickly moved their playing pieces into their respective 'homes'. Then Guy began to consistently roll doubles. It was as though he was playing with another set of dice, a loaded set, except Tara knew full well that he wasn't.

Slowly she watched him win, taking away piece after piece while she fretted and fumed as she began to trail behind. Nevertheless, she fought to keep up and eventually found they each had four pieces remaining, hers on the five and six spots and his lower down, two on the one spot and two on the three. If she threw a double six now she would win. With her heart beating faster than ever before she threw – two-one, the worst of all possible throws she could have made! Silently she moved the pieces down the board, then waited and watched for him to take his throw. Double three, it was unbelievable!

'I don't believe you just did that, Guy,' she said, her voice and indeed her whole body shaking.

'Tara, my angel, don't get so emotional,' he replied, 'it's only a game after all.' His tone was so condescending that she wanted to hit him.

She stared at him, anger and fear fighting for supremacy within her, the battle showing in her eyes.

'Well, what is my forfeit to be?' she said. She pushed back her chair and stood, hands on hips, her shoulders squared in defiance.

'Ah, well now . . .' he murmured. Apparently pondering her question, he walked around the table and stroked his hand lightly over her quivering body.

'That is something I shall have to consider very carefully. Very carefully indeed.' Squatting down beside her chair, he looked into her eyes and smiled wickedly. 'Have no fear, *ma chérie*. I shall let you know as soon as I have decided.'

She cursed the fact that they had not put a time limit on the forfeit. If she had won they would be upstairs in his bedroom right at that moment with her claiming her prize. As it was, she would have to bide her time.

Maxine threw her a pitying look, then poured her a fresh glass of cognac. 'I don't envy you, Tara,' she murmured conspiratorially, 'if Guy is at all like Xavier, he will make the most of this opportunity.'

'*I* don't envy me,' Tara admitted, although she kept her voice low so that the men would not overhear.

For the rest of the evening she steadfastly ignored Guy, talking instead with Maxine or watching television. And, when Maxine and Xavier announced that they were going to bed, Tara stood up, intending to go straight to her own room, alone.

Guy, however, had other ideas. He stopped her in the doorway, his body blocking her path.

'Where are you going?'

'To bed of course.' She fought to keep her voice under control.

'I wish you wouldn't behave like such a spoilt child, Tara.'

He sighed in exasperation, knowing his words

only served to anger her more.

'Me childish?' she said as she looked up and stared angrily at him. 'You're the one who likes to play games, Guy, or have you conveniently forgotten that?'

He stepped aside to let her pass.

'Go to bed, Tara. I am not in the mood for another argument with you. If you cannot deal with losing, that is your problem.'

'No.' She knew she sounded like a petulant, argumentative child, just as he had described, but she couldn't bear to let the matter drop and simply walk away.

'Very well,' he said.

He walked down the passageway and entered another room. For several minutes Tara remained immobile, wondering where he had gone and what he was doing. He returned bearing a slip of paper.

He held it out to her. 'Here you are. Now our contract is terminated. You are free to leave if you wish.'

She looked down at his offering. It was a cheque of course, for the balance of their arrangement – another fifty thousand pounds. The words and figures swam in front of her eyes as they blurred with tears. Taking the cheque, she folded it carefully in half.

'Our contract was for the duration of the month,' she said. 'I have barely been here a week.' She fought to keep her voice under control and her gaze steady.

He sighed. 'I told you, you are released from your contract.' His eyes held hers, the deep blue irises glittering more brightly than they had ever done before. 'If you wish to continue you must stop trying to fight me all the time.'

She held his words in her head for a moment before stepping forward. 'Okay,' she said softly, 'I'll try.'

'Then you damned well try hard!' He spoke sharply to her but his lips and eyes smiled as he added, 'Come to bed, Tara.'

She took his hand and climbed the stairs with him. This pattern seemed to be becoming a ritual with them – a blazing row then kissing and making up. The trouble was, none of it seemed to be getting her anywhere. Suddenly, she realised André would be returning the next day. In some ways she was looking forward to seeing him and being with him again, yet she dreaded the added complication of his presence.

Guy must have been thinking much the same thing as he voiced thoughts that were almost identical to hers.

'I won't sleep with him again if you don't want me to,' she offered.

He pondered her words for a moment. 'You must,' he said, 'it would seem very odd if you suddenly withdrew your affection and besides he doesn't deserve such treatment.'

'I know, it's just that . . .' Tara broke off and stared

out of the bedroom window into the blackness of the night. Somewhere outside a owl hooted – probably calling its mate, she thought glumly.

'Don't start romanticising our involvement, Tara.' His voice held a warning. 'We have an arrangement, that is all.'

'Is it?' she said. She turned to look at him, ready for another battle but instead she sighed. 'Look, Guy. I know better than to try and take things any further between us but I cannot simply turn my feelings on and off like water from a tap.'

'But you must,' he said, 'that is our arrangement.' Despite his uncompromising words, he stepped toward her and ran his hands over her breasts. Immediately, they strained to escape the meagre confines of her cotton shirt.

'Guy.' As his name issued from her lips it was nothing more than an exhalation of breath.

'*Tais-toi*, Tara,' he said, starting to undo each tiny button, his hands and eyes fixed on the object of his task, '*tais-toi*.'

Chapter Twelve

Tara was still in her bedroom the following morning when the Citröen arrived, bringing André home. At the time, she had just taken a shower and was pondering what to wear. As she heard his voice greeting Lisette her stomach tightened and the pace of her heart quickened. He had only been away for a couple of days but she had already forgotten exactly how he looked and what he was like.

'*Salut*, Tara!'

She hadn't heard his footsteps on the stairs, or in the passage and he surprised her by suddenly appearing in the doorway. Feeling slightly apprehensive, she tightened the belt on her robe and turned around to face him.

'André, did you have a good time?' she said. She smiled when she saw him, her eyes skimming over him approvingly. He looked even better than she remembered, certainly more self-assured. 'What happened to you this weekend? You look different.'

André shrugged. 'I'll tell you later. Come here.'

251

He kicked the door shut with his heel and held out his arms.

She hesitated for a moment before moving toward him slowly, her heart beating even faster than before.

'I was just about to get dressed. I thought about going into town . . .' she said, her words fading into insignificance. She knew just by the look on his face she wouldn't be going anywhere that morning.

'I've missed you, Tara,' he said, his voice sounding deep and masculine.

'Have you?'

She stepped forward another few paces, reached up and cupped his face in her hands. She stared into his eyes as he gave a silent nod.

Slowly, his hands began to stroke her, smoothing the silken fabric of her robe over her curves.

'You know I want to rip this off you and fuck you like crazy don't you?' he said gruffly.

His words excited her, the force of his passion for her inducing a strong tingling sensation between her legs.

'Your English has improved tremendously,' she joked. There was laughter in her voice until, in a sudden swift movement, he pulled the neckline of her robe apart, forced it over her shoulders and down her arms. The robe pinned them to her sides and forced her shoulders back, thrusting her naked breasts forward to greet his hungry eyes.

'*Mon Dieu!*' he cried.

He sank to his knees in front of her and ran the soft pink tip of his tongue down the valley between her breasts and around each quivering globe. At the same time he pushed his hands up inside the back of her robe and caught her buttocks, pulling her body even closer to his.

Surprise mingled with desire. Feverish with lust, she moved her hands to stroke his shoulders, her fingertips massaging the hard muscle that lay beneath the soft cotton of his plain white T-shirt.

He parted her robe, his eyes seeking out the silky triangle at the apex of her thighs. As he stroked his fingertips lightly over her belly she found herself moaning softly, opening her legs and urging his head closer to her by the gentle pressure of her hands.

She could feel the soft weight of his hair between her fingers and the warm caress of his breath as it whispered across her throbbing sex. Suddenly she felt so hot, so hungry for him. It was as though she had never had a man before, as though she had not been pleasured for hours by his father the previous night.

Always eager to oblige her, he spread open the soft flesh of her outer labia and trailed his tongue over her clitoris. Using the tip of his tongue, he flicked it lightly until she cried out with pleasure. Then he looked up at her face and smiled at the dreamy rapture he saw in her eyes.

'I can't wait. Are you ready for me?' he said.

Her eyes followed his fingers as he unbuttoned

the black denim jeans he wore and pulled his T-shirt over his head. In the next instant he gripped her waist and pulled her down until she squatted in front of him, her knees wide apart showing just how ready she was.

In one swift movement he pushed her backwards and lunged inside her, making her gasp with surprise and pleasure. Joyfully, she thrust her pelvis up to meet his, revelling in the sensation of her body being filled by him. She hadn't realised just how much she had missed it – missed him.

'God, Tara, I've been wanting you so badly,' he gasped as he thrust into her with the tireless vigour of youth, holding back his own burst of pleasure until he was sure she was satisfied . . . for the time being at any rate.

He lay inside her afterwards, his hand idly stroking her breasts. His other hand supported his head as he stared down at her with an expression of gratitude and amazement.

'Was the weekend very tiresome, André?' she said at long last. She stretched languorously beneath him, her smile displaying her state of happy contentment.

'No, not exactly,' he said and shook his head.

She thought he sounded evasive.

'Well, what did you do?' she persisted. 'Did you go out anywhere?'

She had obviously hit the nail on the head because he looked away suddenly and nodded, unable to meet her eyes.

'I met some old friends. We went to a club one night and I ... I ...'

'Go on.'

He looked her in the eye. 'I met a girl. Well, a woman really. She's twenty-two.'

For some strange reason, Tara felt a little sad.

'Did you?'

She couldn't bring herself to say any more than that and a large part of her was totally amazed at her own reaction to the news.

'Yes. She ... we ...'

He broke off but Tara already understood.

She reached up and caressed his face, tracing her fingertips around his hairline and along the length of his jaw, her thumb stroking the fullness of his bottom lip.

'I'm glad André, really,' she murmured. And, with almost ferocious tenderness, she pulled him down to her and kissed him, hard.

With a sigh of regret he withdrew from her. 'I shouldn't have come back and treated you like this,' he said. 'It wasn't fair.'

'Don't be silly,' she chided him softly as she allowed him to pull her to her feet. Walking over to the bed, she lay down and watched him as he stared out of the window at the gardens below. He stood dejectedly, shoulders sagging, and started to speak in a soft, sad voice.

'When I met Angelique I felt as though I was being unfaithful to you. Now I feel as though I have just been unfaithful to her.'

'Stop that. You're being too hard on yourself, André,' Tara said and held out her arms to him as he turned around to face her. 'Sex is supposed to be enjoyable, you know. Don't spoil it for yourself by getting too intense and feeling guilty about it all.'

In that brief moment, as she spoke the words of wisdom, she realised she had been in danger of allowing exactly the same thing to happen between herself and Guy.

'Don't you mind at all about Angelique?' he said.

He walked back to her and lay down on the bed beside her. Opening her robe completely, he allowed his eyes to drift over the entire length of her naked body.

'A little,' she admitted, 'but I am not exactly a one-man woman.'

She didn't bother to elaborate and thankfully André didn't push her. During the past couple of days she hadn't even been a *one-man-at-a-time* woman – although, she had managed to keep it in the family. The thought made her laugh and suddenly the tension between herself and André was broken. She reached down until her fingers closed around the hard familiarity of his erected penis before sliding down the bed so that she could enfold him with her lips as well. In minutes she had brought him almost to the point of release.

'I still think you are the most amazing woman I have ever met,' André said breathlessly, his eyelids heavy with desire.

She smiled at his words and the way he looked and eased herself on top of him. She stretched out full length along his body, loving the sensation of his hard musculature beneath her. Her soft kisses soon became more intimate and she brought her legs up so that she could slip him inside her without breaking the flow of their caresses.

Using slow, purposeful movements, she rocked her hips back and forth. Grinding her pelvis against his, she felt André's hands slide down the length of her back and grip her waist.

With a sudden burst of energy she sat up and arched her back, allowing him to assist her as she raised and lowered her hips in perfect rhythm. She gripped him with her knees and rode him vigorously, suddenly desperate to unleash all the frustrated energy that had built up inside her.

'Oh, yes, André. Harder, harder!'

She couldn't get enough of him, couldn't find the release she needed. Frantically she sought out her own private pleasure zone, her fingers tormenting the hard, swollen bud of her clitoris. In minutes, her self-pleasure became the catalyst for an orgasm of such intensity that she screamed aloud, the sound echoing around the walls of the old house like the wail of a banshee.

'Oh, hell, Tara!'

André was close behind her, his exclamation of pleasure so forceful it almost matched hers.

'It wasn't like this with Angelique,' he murmured

finally as they lay together, spent but happy.

'Of course not,' Tara said, 'you hardly know each other.' She stroked her palm across his chest. 'Give it time. Work at it.'

'Work at it!' André exclaimed. 'You make it sound like learning English. Once a teacher, always a teacher, I suppose.' His laughter was infectious.

'Ah, but haven't I taught you well, André?' she said.

She giggled and he caught her breasts as they trembled.

'You have taught me extremely well,' he replied, his voice thickening suddenly. Covering a nipple with his mouth, he slowly rolled his body on top of hers and entered her for the third time that morning.

Eventually, their bodies gave way to the sort of hunger that could only be satisfied by one of Lisette's excellent lunches.

'I'm sorry I stopped you going into town,' André said as he grinned at her over a plate of cold chicken.

Tara hid a knowing smile behind the forbidding bulk of Lisette's back. 'I'm not.'

Trying hard to ignore the salacious glint in her eyes and the cheeky curve to her mouth, André leaned forward across the table.

'To be honest, I wouldn't mind going into town with you this afternoon.'

'Okay,' she said and put down her knife and fork. 'I'll go and get changed.'

Fifteen minutes later they were pulling out of the garage in the green Mercedes.

Having only been into the local town once before – the day she met Guy in the bar – she hadn't realised that it boasted some excellent boutiques. Now, with her bank balance buoyed by the money Guy had paid her, she had no difficulty making a few purchases.

'Oh, look, André. How gorgeous,' she said, staring with blatant longing at an array of expensive lingerie in a shop window. Each of the garments displayed was beautifully cut and finished. The silk, satin and lace were obviously of the finest quality. 'I must go in,' she added. Her eyes were glazed, as though she were in a trance, as she pushed open the door. Naturally, she expected someone as young as André to be too embarrassed to follow her but he surprised her.

'This would look good on you,' he said. Ignoring the amused stares of the shop's other customers, he held up a black satin corset – boned and laced. It looked old-fashioned yet extremely sensual.

One man accompanying a women who also looked much older than him, probably in her sixties, looked up as André spoke and then swept his eyes appreciatively over Tara before nodding his agreement.

She blushed, reading the message in the man's eyes.

'Mm, perhaps,' she murmured. She took the garment from him and also picked up a contrasting set of bra and knickers in virginal white lace before adding, 'I think I'll try all these.'

The sales assistant directed her toward the back of the shop where a narrow flight of stairs led down to a couple of changing cubicles. As she began to walk down the stairs André caught up with her.

'I can't wait to see what you look like wearing them,' he whispered darkly in her ear, surprising her.

She turned her head quickly, her expression aghast. 'You can't come into the changing room with me!' she said. She hissed the words through gritted teeth, her eyes flashing nervously around. No one was paying them any attention now.

'Can't I?'

He continued to follow her. And, when they reached the bottom of the staircase, he dragged her into a cubicle and pulled the curtain closed.

Stifling a giggle, Tara began to disrobe and was thankful for his help when her zipper caught a thread and became stuck. As she undressed, she gazed at their reflections in the mirror. André sat on a chair behind her, his arms folded, his expression one of casual interest. Suddenly she felt overcome by the eroticism of their situation.

Her heartbeat began to pick up pace as she tried on the black corset.

'What do you think?' she asked, turning this way and that.

'It's fantastic,' he said, 'I thought it would be. Now try the other set, the virgin's clothes.' André smiled wickedly as he handed her the hanger from which the innocent-looking white lace set was suspended.

Quickly she slipped on the knickers and fastened the bra. With a tightening in her stomach, she eyed her reflection in the mirror. It was love at first sight when she saw the way the underwired cups pushed her breasts up and together, giving her a cleavage to die for.

Behind her, André leaned forward and stared at her reflection, his eyes fixed greedily on her breasts. Then he caught her gaze.

'What?' She started to speak but he interrupted her.

'Take them off,' he said glancing at the lacy knickers that barely concealed anything at all. 'Now, come here.'

His tone commanded her and she obeyed, her whole body trembling with excitement as she sat astride him. His hands immediately enfolded the enticing fullness of her breasts as they strained to escape the fragile lace. With trembling fingers she unzipped his jeans and caressed him briefly before slipping the rock-hard length of his cock inside her.

The sight of him watching their reflection in the mirror aroused her and she turned her head to see what he could see. The breath caught in her throat. The sight was so erotic and their situation so dangerous that she could barely contain herself.

'Tara!' he cried out as he thrust inside her violently, groaned and became still.

Thinking that was the end of their diverting little interlude, she waited a moment before rising from his lap. But as soon as she turned around he pulled her back down on to him. This time she was staring right at their reflection. She could see his hands as they eased her thighs wide apart and slipped between her legs. Through heavy-lidded eyes she watched as he spread open her swollen labia to expose her shamefully aroused clitoris. And, with a kind of dreadful fascination, she witnessed the many ways he probed and stroked her tormented flesh until his caresses brought her to a shuddering release.

Eventually, on legs weak with fatigue, she climbed the staircase again.

'I'll take them all,' she said, fighting to find her normal speaking voice as she handed the garments to the salesgirl and extracted a wad of francs from her purse.

From the corner of her eye she could see André surreptitiously emerge from the stairwell and leave the shop. She caught up with him on the pavement outside.

'I can't believe we just got away with that,' she said, 'the shop was absolutely packed!'

Leaning against him weakly, she giggled.

'I know,' he said with a satisfied smile. He put his arm around her waist and led her to a table outside a nearby cafe.

She sat down gratefully and, when the waitress arrived, ordered a glass of mineral water. Then, as an afterthought, she requested a pistachio ice-cream cone as well. André ordered orange juice. As she reclined in her chair and licked her ice cream thoughtfully, she realised André seemed very quiet all of a sudden and wondered what was on his mind.

'What's the matter?' she asked.

'I forgot to mention, Lisette told me my father's brother spent the weekend at the house.'

Tara shrugged. 'Xavier?' she said. 'Yes he did, as a matter of fact. So what?' She swirled her tongue around the ice cream and smirked suggestively at André. 'Guess what I'm thinking?'

He allowed a smile to flicker briefly across his face before becoming serious again.

'I bet he tried to get you into bed.'

'Who?'

'Xavier.'

'Yes, he did. But . . .' Tara allowed the answer to die on her lips, realising just in time that she couldn't very well say, 'Yes, but it was okay, I thought he was your father.'

'But what?' He persisted, leaning forward.

'But . . . But his girlfriend Maxine was there so . . .' She allowed her words to trail off and shrugged, hoping he would assume it meant that Xavier's activities were curtailed.

Thankfully he did. 'Good,' he said, 'I wouldn't like to think of you with my uncle. He's got no scruples whatsoever.'

'Really?' Tara stifled a smile and finished her ice cream. 'Shall we go,' she suggested brightly, 'I feel like a nap before supper.' She took his hand as they stood up and, with a foxy smile added, 'I simply can't understand why I feel so exhausted today.'

When they arrived back at the house Guy had already returned and was sitting outside by the pool. André rushed to see him but Tara hovered, not wishing to intrude. She found it extremely difficult to be in the company of both André and Guy at the same time.

Nevertheless, to her discomfort he called for her to join them. He eyed the carrier bags, obviously recognising the distinctive logo of the lingerie shop.

'I see you have been treating yourself,' he said. 'What have you bought?'

His friendly tone didn't fool her for a minute and she was hesitant about showing him her purchases – lingering over some of the less interesting items, before finally opening the last bag and withdrawing the underwear she had bought.

'Mm,' he murmured softly. He fingered the delicate white lace garments for a moment before picking up the corset. 'Now, this I like very much.'

His tormenting gaze flickered to her face and despite André's presence, or perhaps because of it, she blushed deeply.

Thankfully, Lisette arrived at that moment bearing a tray. She set it down on the table in front of them and cast a disapproving eye over Tara's purchases as they lay in Guy's lap. In very formal French she asked if she should take Madame's shopping up to her boudoir. Stifling a smile, Tara nodded her gratitude.

As soon as she was well and truly out of earshot, the three of them burst out laughing.

'*Seigneur!*' Guy exclaimed. 'Anyone would think you had been sitting there wearing the wretched things, Tara.'

Suddenly he and André stopped laughing simultaneously and stared at her.

She had no difficulty reading their thoughts, except that André no doubt preferred to remember her wearing the white bra-and-pantie set, whilst Guy would be imagining her laced into the black corset. She felt weak, the interest of either man was equally tantalising.

After a moment or two André spoke. 'I am feeling a little tired, papa. I think I shall have a nap before supper.'

He glanced casually at Tara who feigned innocence.

'Actually,' Guy said, pushing back his chair, 'I have a little business I need to discuss with Madame Cochrane.' He turned to look directly at her, his face impassive as he added, 'Perhaps you would be so kind as to accompany me to my study?'

Although she could sense André's anxious eyes upon her and could almost feel his desperation, she found herself trapped in his father's unwavering gaze.

'Of course. I shall come straight away,' she said.

'No doubt you will,' Guy muttered under his breath, his lips curving into a devilish smile.

With an air of regret, André parted company with his father and Tara at the foot of the stairs. Now he had spoken, he had no option but to go to his room. Meanwhile, Guy led Tara down the passageway to the door of his study. Once they were both inside he locked the door.

She glanced around, having never been in this room before. It was only a small room, simply furnished with a wooden desk and a couple of leather chairs. To her surprise he sat down in one of them and motioned with his hand for her to take the other. Crossing her legs carefully, she waited for him to say something.

'I have reached my decision about your forfeit,' he said, coming straight to the point.

He reclined in the chair, one leg crossed casually over the other.

'Yes?'

She looked at him expectantly, her stomach clenching with anxiety. André's return had distracted her from thinking about their wager.

'You will accompany me to a dinner party tomorrow night at the house of a friend.'

'Is that it?' she blurted out.

In all honesty, she was stunned. Knowing Guy, she had expected him to come up with something terrible.

266

'Not exactly,' he said, eyeing her thoughtfully, the wicked smile touching his lips once more. 'All I will say at this stage is that I would like you to wear that corset you have just purchased. Oh, and some stockings. Black of course. Do you think you could manage that?'

Tara swallowed deeply, there was something about his request that really unnerved her and she wished desperately that he would say more about what her actual forfeit would entail. Keeping all this to herself, she nodded.

'*Bon,*' he said. He smiled lazily and moved his chair so that he was seated directly in front of her, then he pushed her skirt up her bare thighs.

Her heart thumping with excitement, Tara simply allowed him to remove her knickers and pull her forward to the edge of the seat. She breathed in sharply as he probed her with his fingers, his other hand busy unfastening the buttons on her blouse.

'What will the rest of the forfeit involve?' she asked hoarsely.

'I don't think you want to know that,' he murmured, unclipping the front fastening of her bra. 'This is a very sensible garment. It makes you so . . . accessible.'

He gave a sigh of satisfaction as he uncovered her breasts, his fingers teasing her nipples until the torment became almost unbearable.

'I do need to know, Guy,' she persisted, her breath coming in short gasps.

As he sank to his knees between her outstretched thighs he silenced her. 'I did not say you don't *need* to know,' he said darkly, 'I said you wouldn't *want* to know.'

Her heart missed a beat at his words but his mouth upon her throbbing flesh erased her fears — for the moment.

At supper that night Guy informed André that his grandparents wanted to take him to Le Touquet for a couple of days. Predictably, André groaned.

'Oh, no, papa. I would rather stay at home.'

Tara concentrated on her meal. She suspected that Guy wanted him out of the way the following night and the reason why he should go to such lengths worried the hell out of her.

Despite André's protests, Guy was adamant.

Later that evening, as they sat together watching television, André whispered to her that he needed to be with her that night. For a moment Tara wavered, all in all it had been a very physical day for her and she almost preferred the prospect of a night alone . . . almost.

'*D'accord*,' she said with a brief nod. 'When you go up to bed, go to my room instead and wait for me.'

At the sound of their low voices, Guy turned around. 'Would either of you care for a drink?' he asked.

Tara nodded. 'Cognac, please.' She stretched unselfconsciously, easing the tiredness from her shoulders and André immediately began to massage her, his fingers expertly loosening the tightly knotted muscles. 'Oh, that's bliss,' she groaned, 'you have such magic in your fingers, André.' She smiled contentedly, almost forgetting that Guy was present.

He turned and for a few moments simply watched silently as his son moved his hands over Tara's shoulders. Then he stepped forward and handed her a heavy cut-crystal glass. The amber liquid sparkled innocently, reflecting the flickering light from the open fire.

Tara breathed deeply, aware of the barely restrained tension that seemed to hang between the three of them.

'I shall arrange for a professional masseuse to come here tomorrow, Tara,' he said. 'You deserve a treat.'

He smiled genially but she still suspected that everything he did or said masked an ulterior motive.

'There's really no need,' she started to say but he interrupted her.

'I think, in reflection, you will be grateful. It is particularly beneficial for your muscles to be completely relaxed.'

She gazed up at him in mute astonishment, her whole body alert to his hidden agenda. Eventually she forced herself to speak.

'Well, in that case, thank you very much.' With a deliberately casual air, she turned her attention back to the film being screened on the television.

For the next hour it took all her willpower to concentrate on the flickering images in front of her and, when André finally yawned and announced that he was going to bed, it was with a feeling of immense relief on her part. In another ten minutes or so she would join him.

As soon as she was certain André was out of earshot she turned to Guy. 'Are you going to tell me what I have to do tomorrow or not?' she said.

His arrogant smile infuriated her as much as his response. 'Not.'

She found her cool exterior crumbling. 'Guy. I'm warning you. If . . .'

Sitting forward suddenly, he interrupted her. 'Do not presume to warn me of anything, Tara,' he said, 'we have a deal. You must simply comply.'

She could see he was intractable on this issue. 'Very well,' she snapped, 'is there anything else I should do – before tomorrow night I mean?'

His reply shook her. 'Get plenty of rest and . . . er . . .' he skimmed her body with an insolent gaze '. . . try to forget the old Tara completely. After tomorrow night I doubt if you will ever be the same again.'

Somehow, she found the strength to get up from the sofa, walk out of the room and climb the stairs. Safe inside the sanctuary of her room, she locked the door and leaned against it. She closed her eyes for a minute, desperate to quell the strong sensation of panic that threatened to overtake her.

'Is everything okay, Tara?'

Her eyes flew open. Through the gloom she could see André lying in her bed, covered only by the sheet. In her anxiety she had forgotten about him.

'Oh, er . . . yes,' she said. She walked over to the bed and began to undress, then she slipped under the sheet beside him. 'I just felt a little dizzy for a moment that's all. I think you have worn me out today.'

She smiled and snuggled up against him, resting her head on his chest.

'We don't have to . . . you know . . . if you don't want to,' he offered. He stroked her hair and for a moment she wished she could simply close her eyes and float away, leaving André and his father, the house in France, everything, far, far behind her.

'Thank you. You are a very thoughtful . . .' she started to speak but hesitated, she'd been about to use the word 'boy' but somehow it didn't seem a very appropriate description of the young man in whose arms she lay, '. . . you're a very thoughtful person, André.' She slipped her hand under the sheet and sought his reassuring firmness. 'Of course I want to.'

Turning around to face him she continued to caress him, her other hand sliding over the familiar terrain of his buttocks, her fingers massaging the taut gluteus muscles. Raising her leg over his hip she eased him inside her and rocked her pelvis very gently until she felt the grip of passion upon them both.

Afterwards, with the exhaustion she felt, she was

certain that sleep would come easily to her but she was wrong. Eventually, realising that the prospect of her forfeit was weighing heavily on her mind, she gave up all attempt to will herself into unconsciousness. Instead she left André sleeping and made her way through the silence of the house to the kitchen where she brewed a pot of coffee.

As she sat at the table, cradling a steaming cup thoughtfully in her hands, she was unaware of Guy's presence in the doorway until he coughed gently.

'You startled me,' she gasped, turning her head.

'If you want to be left alone I'll go.'

'It's okay,' she looked up at his face as he sat down beside her. 'Would you like some coffee?'

'No, thank you,' he said. He covered her hand with his. 'I think I know what this is about. I don't want you to worry about tomorrow night. If you'd rather . . .?'

'No,' she interrupted him vehemently, 'a deal's a deal.'

'I think your bravado is a little misplaced and also a little false,' he said, watching her carefully. 'I keep forgetting how relatively unsophisticated you are.'

'I can take care of myself,' she muttered angrily, pulling her hand away from his grasp and picking up her cup. The liquid was still too hot to drink.

'I didn't mean to imply you cannot,' he said.

Despite her obvious reticence he took her hand again and held it tightly, his fingers clenching and unclenching around her own.

'Is André very disappointed about going to Le Touquet?' he asked, changing the subject completely.

'Yes, a bit,' she said and looked him squarely in the eye as she added, 'Is his trip just a fortunate coincidence or what?'

'Yes, it is a coincidence,' he repeated, 'I'm not that devious.'

'Aren't you?'

By now her coffee was drinkable and she sipped it, wondering if he would say anything in response.

'Le Touquet is a nice place,' he added conversationally. 'It's one of those resorts that suits both the very young and the very old.'

He straightened her fingers between his own and began to stroke them with his free hand.

Tara gazed at their entwined digits. 'I know. I went there once. I thought it was a bit like Brighton.'

His laughter sounded strangely loud in the stillness of the night. 'Oh, *mon Dieu*. Yes. Brighton. You are right.' He glanced sideways at her, his expression becoming serious all of a sudden. 'You are a very enigmatic woman, Tara Cochrane,' he said.

'Am I?'

His words amazed her. She always thought of herself as being very direct, the epitome of the proverbial open book. She said as much to him but he shook his head.

'No, you're not. You harbour a great deal of mystery inside that delectable frame,' he said. His eyes travelled over her body for a second or two, warming her instantly. 'I don't think I could ever tire of trying to discover your secrets.'

She didn't know how to respond, his words had affected her deeply and at that moment she felt as though she wanted him so badly she would do anything, anything at all.

'Will tomorrow night unravel a secret or two for you?' she asked. She moved a little closer to him, suddenly wanting the warmth of his body to penetrate her.

He was thoughtful for a moment, then he nodded. 'Not just for me but for you also,' he said. 'Tomorrow night I think you may discover just how far the limits of your sexuality extend.'

'Really?'

She was desperate to know more but his expression told her that she would get no further information. Impulsively, she strained toward him and surprised him with a deeply passionate kiss.

'You won't get around me like that,' he said, laughing, although she could sense he had been moved by her gesture. He released her hand abruptly. 'André?' he exclaimed in hushed tones.

'André is asleep,' she whispered.

Her lips curved into a smile and she slipped from the chair. Sinking to her knees in front of him, she unzipped his trousers and took him in her mouth.

'This is dangerous, Tara!' he said urgently.

She ignored his protest, noticing how shallow his breathing had become and how his hands gripped her hair with fingers that betrayed his growing desire. Her eyes and the constant rhythm of her mouth and hands told him she was not about to succumb to the threat of discovery. And, as his body yielded to her caresses, she felt an overwhelming glow of satisfaction.

Chapter Thirteen

'Where were you?' André was awake when she returned to her bedroom.

'The kitchen,' she replied honestly, 'I couldn't sleep so I made myself a hot drink.'

She dropped her robe on to a chair and slid her naked body under the sheet beside him once again.

'You should have woken me,' he said softly, as he stroked a gentle hand across her breasts.

She writhed sensuously under his caress. Despite the number of times she and André had already made love that day, her encounter with Guy had left her feeling distinctly frustrated.

'I thought you deserved some rest,' she said.

A wicked smile touched her lips as she parted her legs eagerly for his exploring hands. She didn't trust herself to think about the sort of person she had become. A woman who could move easily from one man to another. Or even to another woman. For a moment her mind dwelt on Maxine.

'What are you thinking about?' André asked

suddenly, interrupting her train of thought.

She glanced at him. 'Nothing important. Maxine, as a matter of a fact.'

'Who? Xavier's girlfriend?'

'Mm,' she murmured, 'don't stop, I was enjoying that.' She pressed his fingers firmly inside her again and ground herself against him.

'Did you get on well together then?' His tone of voice indicated some astonishment at the idea.

'You seem shocked,' she said, 'actually, she and I became very close.' She couldn't help smiling inwardly at the recollection.

Pulling her on top of him, André slid himself easily into the moist velvet of her vagina.

'I wouldn't have thought you two had that much in common,' he muttered.

Her breath caught as he began to thrust inside her forcefully. 'Oh, you'd be surprised, André,' she said, hiding a wicked smile, 'very surprised.'

Eventually, thanks in no small way to André's tirelessness, her body gave in to the need for sleep and it was almost midday by the time she awoke. Seconds after she opened her eyes he appeared in the doorway, fully dressed.

'Oh,' she murmured sleepily before foolishly glancing to the empty place beside her where the sheet was still warm and rumpled from his body. 'What time is it, for goodness sake?' She squinted at the clock and groaned.

André stepped into the room and closed the door. 'My grandparents are already here,' he said, 'they are talking to papa downstairs.' He sat beside her on the bed, his expression regretful. 'I shall have to go in a minute.'

His reminder about Le Touquet served also to remind her of the ordeal that lay ahead of her. Immediately she was assailed by a feeling of panic.

'I wish you didn't have to go,' she said. She spoke desperately, clutching at his arm and meaning every word.

'I know, Tara. But it's only for a couple of days.'

He tried to look optimistic but failed miserably. Reluctantly, he stood up and stooped to kiss her, his breath sweet and minty against the dryness of her lips.

'Bye, André,' she murmured softly, 'take care.'

She lay in the bed for a long time, listening to the strange mixture of voices drifting up the stairs, hearing the front door open, the sound of a car starting and pulling away, the decisive thud as the front door shut firmly once more. A few seconds later and she heard Guy's footsteps on the staircase, then outside her door.

'Are you planning to get up today?'

It seemed strange to see him standing there in her room, almost as though he had taken his son's place.

'Perhaps,' she said airily. Noticing how he still hovered near the doorway, she stretched slowly and luxuriously, the sheet sliding down her naked body as she moved beneath it.

'I will admit, I did say you would need to conserve

your strength,' he murmured, making no attempt to move closer to the bed, nor even to shut the door completely.

Her stomach clenched. She didn't need him to remind her of the coming evening so she decided to taunt him a little, just to even the score.

'Don't blame me,' she said lightly, 'blame your son. Ah, the enthusiasm of the young. He just goes on fucking for hours and hours.' She slid her hand between her legs and smiled sweetly at him. 'Ouch!'

'Do you seriously think you can anger me, Tara?' he said.

His lips formed an arrogant smile but she suspected, from the uncertain undertone in his voice, that she had hit a nerve.

'Anger you, Guy?'

She kicked off the sheet and spread her legs further apart. Her fingers stroked gently, tentatively, as if the delicate flesh really was very sore.

He glanced at her with all the contempt he could muster. 'Get dressed, Tara. Lunch is almost ready and your masseuse will be arriving at two.'

With that he turned on his heel and left.

The masseuse turned out to be rather a butch-looking German woman who, far from relaxing Tara, actually made her feel extremely edgy. All the time the woman's fingers worked her flesh she felt as though she was being assaulted. Halfway through the massage Guy appeared. For a while he watched in silence then he spoke.

'She's not quite as gentle as Maxine, is she?'

He picked up a chair and positioned it near the head of the portable massage table where Tara lay.

Tara cast a warning glance between Guy and the masseuse but he laughed. 'Don't worry about her, she doesn't speak a word of either French or English.'

'Did you want something specific, Guy?' she said, feeling exasperated. 'Or did you just come in here to add insult to injury?'

As if to underline her pun she winced as the woman's fingers nearly dislocated her shoulder.

To her annoyance he gave an amused smile. 'I actually came to tell you to be ready by seven-thirty tonight. My friend's house is about a forty-minute drive from here.'

'Fine.'

At the masseuse's indication she turned over onto her back, biting her lip as she felt a stream of cold oil run down her stomach and over her breasts.

'I almost wish I had become a masseur,' Guy murmured wistfully as his eyes followed the German woman's hands which confidently slicked a layer of oil over Tara's naked body and began to rhythmically knead the pliant flesh of her upper thighs.

At that point she almost asked him to leave but, on quick reflection, decided that his infuriating remarks were preferable to the prospect of being left alone with Atilla the Hun.

'I thought I'd wear the same black dress I wore on Friday evening when Xavier was here,' she mused, her mind suddenly flickering over the memory of their game of snooker. Just the thought incited a tingle between her legs.

'*Bon*,' he agreed, 'but do not forget the corset and stockings. They are very important.'

'Will I be expected to take my dress off then?' she asked casually, thinking perhaps she could trick him into giving her some more information.

'Oh yes,' he said, his laugh disturbing her as much as his words, 'you can count on it.'

To Guy's apparent amusement she took a large glass of wine with her to her bedroom that evening to help calm her nerves while she dressed. As she fastened the corset she eyed her reflection in the mirror. There was no doubt it really enhanced her figure. The boning was artfully contrived to mould her body in all the right places, pushing up her breasts and pulling in her waist to emphasise the generous curve of her hips. With the addition of black stockings and a black lace g-string she looked incredible, even to her own eyes.

She zipped herself carefully into her dress and slipped her feet into a pair of high-heeled black leather shoes. Glancing at her watch she noticed it was already seven twenty-two. Somehow she had managed to remain reasonably calm but now her heart began to flutter. Conscious that she only had a handful of minutes left to herself she quickly checked her make-up and ran a brush through her hair one last time. That was it, she was as ready as she would ever be.

Guy met her at the bottom of the stairs. He nodded approvingly and slipped his arm around her waist.

'You look fantastic,' he murmured, kissing her hair and inhaling her perfume, 'and you smell delicious.'

Despite her nervousness she felt herself succumbing to his praise. As they left the house she thought if anyone was to see them together they would think that she and Guy were simply another pair of lovers about to spend a pleasant evening together. She expected the drive to his friend's house to seem interminable but in fact it passed very quickly. She wasn't sure which was worse.

The house that loomed into view at the top of a long driveway was very similar to Guy's, although perhaps a little larger. As they got out of the car the front door opened and Guy turned to her.

'This is your last chance to back down,' he offered.

She stared at the open door and turned her eyes to his. Her stomach was knotted so tightly, her heart beating so fast, she thought she might collapse right there in the driveway.

'Never,' she said.

Her back straight, her eyes fixed firmly to the

front, she walked across the flagstones and into the house.

Michel Le Broyard turned out to be a very charming man in his mid-forties. He was tall and well dressed and his hair, slightly greying at the temples, made him look very distinguished. After they had been introduced to him, he asked Guy if Tara spoke any French because his English was so appalling.

'*Oui, je parle Français,*' she offered with a tremulous smile.

'Good,' he said with a pleasant smile, 'please come this way.'

He led them into a richly appointed sitting-room, much larger than the main one at Guy's home and completely furnished and garnished with antiques.

'Oh, what a lovely room,' she breathed, forgetting for a moment to be nervous.

Then she looked around properly and noticed the four other men.

Identically dressed in immaculately tailored dark suits, they were younger than Michel – in their mid- to late-thirties, she guessed.

Michel waved his hand casually around the room. 'Etienne, Marc, Jean-Pierre, François,' he said.

Each man nodded in turn as their host pronounced his name and Guy smiled back.

Tara stared mutely at them. She felt an overwhelming sense of disquiet at their presence, particularly as she seemed to be the only woman at the gathering.

'Where are their wives?' she whispered to Guy, as Michel left them alone for a second to fix them a drink.

He shrugged. 'At home I should think. Where else?' He smiled as Michel appeared with a glass of whisky for each of them.

'I don't . . .' Tara started to say, then decided that one alcoholic drink was as good as another under the circumstances.

'Come and sit here with us, Tara.'

The one called Jean-Pierre patted the space on the sofa between himself and the one called François.

'Go on,' Guy murmured in her ear as she hesitated.

Trembling, she crossed the room and sat between the two men, her legs crossed primly together at the ankles. She hadn't known what to expect but if she thought the men were going to pounce upon her as soon as she sat down she was pleasantly surprised.

For a few minutes they talked across her and to the others, discussing the details of a company take-over bid. As they talked it gave her the opportunity to appraise each one. The untamed-looking François, she decided, was the youngest, although Jean-Pierre was definitely the most handsome with short, black, wavy hair and two glimmering dark pools for eyes. Etienne was fair in colouring, looking almost Nordic rather than French. And Marc was similar in appearance to François but with longer, curlier hair and a more developed sense of style.

285

All in all they were an attractive group and, if circumstances had been a little different, she might have enjoyed flirting with one or two of them. As it was, the prospect of her unknown forfeit occupied her thoughts.

She couldn't help wondering how much they knew about her. Had Guy told them of the reason for her holiday? Did they assume she was his girlfriend – or a whore? She suddenly felt desperate to ask the man who had brought her there but he was talking to Michel and apparently uninterested in her activities.

'Guy certainly knows where to find the most beautiful women,' Etienne said.

As he spoke he leaned forward, his eyes blatantly covering her body. His remark only served to add weight to her earlier thoughts.

'Have you know Guy long?' she responded. If she wanted to know more she would have to find out from them, she decided.

'Of all of us I think Jean-Pierre has known him the longest,' François said, 'I believe you went to university together didn't you, JP?' He smiled across her at his companion.

The handsome man grinned broadly. 'Yes, it was a very educational time for us all round.' He laughed, displaying perfectly even, white teeth.

Tara decided then and there if her forfeit turned out to be that she was expected to go with one of them then she would prefer it to be him. Unintentionally, she found herself leaning slightly more toward him, crossing her legs in his favour. He appeared far from perturbed by her subtle overture.

'And how long have you known Guy?' he asked, his eyes dropping to her cleavage before returning to her face.

So, they didn't know about her arrangement with their friend.

'Just a few weeks,' she murmured, growing warm under his unrelenting gaze.

'Monsieur Ricard is a fast worker.'

François gave a dirty laugh that immediately made her want to retaliate.

At the sound of his name and the sudden loud burst of laughter, Guy looked up.

'Is someone taking my name in vain?' he asked.

Etienne winked at him and glanced at Tara. 'François was just saying that you are a fast worker,' he said.

Only a glimmer of a smile touched Guy's lips but he nodded his assent, adding, 'Of course, it depends on the woman.'

Tara wasn't sure how to interpret his remark. A movement glimpsed from the corner of her eye caused her to look up suddenly. The man called Marc had shifted in his seat crossing one leg casually over the other. He had been so silent she had forgotten he was there but now he fixed her with a piercing stare.

'Do you know why you are here?'

His question was shocking, like a slap across the face and she didn't know how to answer him.

'For dinner?' she said. She raised her eyes to meet his, feeling instantly that he was laughing at her.

He inhaled deeply and simply stared. To either side of her she felt the two men stiffen, as though they were predators suddenly sensing their prey. At that moment all she wanted to do was leap up from her seat and run away. Only stubborn pride and determination kept her there.

From somewhere outside the room a gong sounded, summoning them all to the dining room. As she expected, it was as well appointed as the rest of the house, although the table at which they sat was small and round.

To her dismay, Guy did not sit next to her. It was some consolation that one of her neighbours was Jean-Pierre, whilst to the other side of her sat the disturbing figure of Marc. Despite her pronounced state of anxiety she found she had an appetite of sorts and the food was so delicious she could almost pretend to herself that her only reason for being there was to enjoy an excellent meal.

Nevertheless, she took the precaution of anaesthetising herself with plenty of wine. And, as the meal progressed, she found herself loosening up a little, the alcohol giving her the courage to participate in the small talk that circulated the table.

'Your French is excellent, Tara.' Jean-Pierre said, leaning close to her and whispering in her ear, his breath inciting a tingle of anticipation deep within her.

'Thank you,' she responded quietly. She treated him to a brilliant smile that didn't go unrewarded. Under the cover of the table top he placed his hand firmly on her thigh.

'It looks as though Jean-Pierre is eager to finish his meal and get straight on with dessert,' Marc observed, his tone slightly mocking.

Naïvely, Tara interrupted. 'Why, what is for dessert?'

All eyes turned to her but Marc took obvious delight in uttering the fateful words.

'You, Tara, you are our dessert.'

The five dark-suited men suddenly took on the appearance of ravens. Gathered expectantly around her they waited to dine on her flesh.

'Oh no!'

Shaking her head slowly from side to side she pushed her feet against the carpeted floor, trying to distance herself from the table, from them.

Suddenly events began to move at a lightning pace. From nowhere a veritable army of servants appeared and began to clear the table with indecent haste. Rooted to the spot, Tara stared at the activity. But Guy was at her side in a flash.

'You don't have to go through with this,' he said.

She looked at him gratefully, ready to ask him to take her home. Then she realised he expected her to concede defeat. She shook her head once more, partly in disbelief at the turn of events, partly in denial of his request.

'Give up, Tara,' his voice urged her.

'No,' she said, shaking her head more decisively, 'I can't. I won't.'

She stared wide eyed at the men gathered there. She watched as Marc and Michel moved to the table and began to fiddle with a mechanism on its pedestal. They slowly revolved the round polished wood top to reveal an altogether different underside. Covered completely in red velvet the new table top was also equipped with four strategically placed black leather restraints.

'Oh, my . . .' she began, her words expelled slowly in one long gasp of fear.

She stared at the fate that awaited her. Her stomach churned. Her legs trembled violently. And her heart was beating faster than she had ever known it to before. Yet also, from somewhere deep inside, she felt the undeniable flicker of excitement – a flicker that began to grow and spread as she felt their hands upon her, removing her dress, carrying her to the table, strapping her wrists.

She could see Guy standing apart from them, watching mutely as his friends disrobed her. They pulled down her g-string so that all she wore was the corset and stockings, then pushed her legs apart and strapped her ankles. Unable to bear his expression of disbelief she looked up, noticing that François stood over her, his hand poised to touch her breast.

'Do it, François, touch me,' she ordered.

She shuddered in disbelief at the sound of her own voice but the young man needed no further encouragement. He stroked the smooth mounds of her breasts eagerly as they swelled generously over the black satin cups. A moment later, she felt other fingers between her legs and she saw that it was Jean-Pierre. Good, she thought, I'd like him to be the first.

For a while all the men, except for Guy, watched as she was stroked and fondled by Jean-Pierre and François, then Michel's voice cut through their low murmurs of appreciation.

'Would anyone like a glass of cognac?' he said. 'We do, after all, have the entire night at our disposal.'

Despite her growing arousal Tara quaked at his words. Their attentions were bearable at the moment but she didn't know if she would be able to withstand them for too long. Etienne nodded, as did Guy, and the two men walked over to the open drinks cabinet that stood against the far wall. Marc remained, impassively watching Tara as she writhed under the hands of the other two men. Without taking his eyes off her he spoke.

'Please be so kind as to bring me a glass, someone. I want to stay here and watch Jean-Pierre fuck her.'

As if his words were a command, she saw Jean-Pierre climb onto the table between her legs and unzip his trousers. Her mind whirled, she felt appalled by what was happening to her and yet so excited that her whole body throbbed and burned with latent passion. Even Marc had excited her by his presence and the insolence of his remark. She decided she was looking forward to welcoming him inside her, she couldn't wait to see his arrogant expression crumble as he came.

In the long slow minutes before the first man penetrated her she felt almost overwhelmed by the agonising throbbing of her sex. The fact that she could hardly move her body at all only served to heighten her excitement.

She heard Guy utter her name but she blocked her ears to the sound. Instead she concentrated her gaze on the hovering figure of Jean-Pierre who, just for a moment, suddenly seemed a little uncertain, as if he thought he might have made a mistake. She narrowed her eyes and captured him in an unwavering stare.

'What are you waiting for, Jean-Pierre?' she whispered harshly. 'Why don't you just do it? Why don't you just fuck . . .?'

His sudden movement took her breath away. She saw the men converge upon her as they watched their friend take her, or she him. Playing to her audience she bucked her hips as far as the restraints around her ankles would allow, urging him deeper and deeper inside her.

It was over in seconds, her strong muscles expertly milking him as she came.

Guy stood over her as his friend withdrew. 'Okay, Tara,' he said firmly, 'you have proved yourself. Your forfeit is over. Now let us go home.'

'No, Guy!' she cried. Her eyes glittered with the excitement of danger, the adrenaline now coursing through her body at the speed of light.

'Leave her alone, Guy. She's enjoying it and so are we.' Etienne moved to the foot of the table and started to unzip his trousers. 'I must say you have really chosen well with this one,' he added. 'She must wear you out.'

Tara caught Guy's eye but her expression did not betray him. With a shrug he moved away from the table, leaving Etienne free to pursue his own aim. Again she gasped as she felt the sudden intrusion of his hardness inside her.

'Don't expect me to come as quickly as Jean-Pierre,' he warned.

'Mm. If you say so,' she said and smiled like a cat.

François, who had left her alone for a few minutes, returned to stand by her head. He stroked himself absently as he watched Etienne thrust inside her. Tara slid her gaze upward to meet his face.

'Would you like to be next?' she offered.

Wordlessly, he nodded and she opened her mouth to take his erection while his friend thrust inside her. After a few minutes she gripped Etienne's cock so forcefully inside her that he came at once.

She sensed it would be different with François and she was right. Not content with thrusting mindlessly inside her, he freed her breasts from the meagre confines of the black satin and licked them hungrily. At the same time, one hand delved between her legs, seeking out her clitoris. The throbbing bud was so hot and swollen that she groaned with unrestrained lust.

Wave after wave of pleasure overtook her as he caressed her and thrust inside her. Now the evening was really becoming enjoyable. Arching her back she urged her body closer to his, wanting him to know how much she appreciated his attention to detail. As his unceasing caresses took her beyond the point of reason the nectar flowed from her and she writhed desperately, wishing she could be free of the restraints so that she could move against him properly.

As if he sensed the reason for her frustration, Marc stepped forward. 'I think it's time we dispensed with these don't you?' he said, laughing wickedly as he added, 'I don't think Tara is planning to run off anywhere.'

'No. Oh, thank you,' she gasped, immediately clasping François' buttocks in her hands as soon as her wrists were free and wrapping her legs around him the moment her ankles were similarly liberated.

'Oh, *mon Dieu*. You are *fantastique!*' François groaned and buried his head in her hair as he gave in to his own desire.

After the young man had withdrawn from her and as no others attempted to approach her, Tara climbed gracefully from the table. She stretched slightly, trying to ease the tightness in her muscles

– it hadn't been the most comfortable of situations. She stood for a moment, hands on hips, her smile encompassing all the men present.

'Would somebody mind pouring me a drink?' she said pertly. 'All this fucking has made me thirsty.'

A soft murmur of laughter rippled around the room. Being the perfect host, Michel brought her a glass of cognac, his hand straying briefly between her legs as he handed her the glass.

'Mm,' she murmured, closing her eyes and allowing herself to drift on the wave of pleasure that his caress induced. 'Where would you like me, Michel?'

She opened her eyes suddenly and looked straight at him.

Without saying a word, he took her glass, passed it to Etienne, then turned her around. With the flat of his palm between her shoulder blades he pushed her forward over the table with a force that surprised her.

'Open your legs,' he commanded.

She didn't hesitate and her heart began to pound anew as his fingers slid into her, making her ready. With a warm rush of elation, she felt him spread her open and lunge into her, his hands gripping her waist as he thrust deeply. Unfazed by his ardour, Tara arched her back, amazed at her own capacity for gratification. Her body felt so hot and desperately insatiable. And she moaned loudly, as though the noisy exhalation of breath could somehow dissipate her surging passion.

She glanced briefly over her shoulder to where Guy sat.

Apparently unconcerned by her behaviour, he sipped his drink, occasionally exchanging a few words with Jean-Pierre.

His casual air no longer fooled her. She knew beyond a shadow of a doubt that he had expected her to take up his challenge and then back down. He certainly wouldn't have expected her to enjoy her forfeit. Thinking about Guy made her come and, within seconds, she felt Michel's body tense as he too climaxed.

Four down, one to go, she thought to herself as she retrieved her drink and sank down into the blissful comfort of a soft leather chair. She sprawled carelessly and took a grateful sip of the smooth, fiery liquid. All evening she had been aware of Marc's eyes upon her but now she felt his gaze more keenly than ever before, particularly as he was the only one who had not yet taken her.

At that moment he moved in his chair and the pace of her heart quickened. She watched him guardedly as he stood up and walked towards her. As he bent over her she expected him to tell her that he was ready for her but to her surprise he did not speak but simply placed his hands on her thighs and spread them apart. Then he walked back to his chair and sat down again.

Tara struggled to control the fierce trembling that seemed determined to overtake her and the tears of humiliation that sprang to her eyes. She didn't like what he had done. And, although it seemed incredible, she felt more violated by that simple act than by anything else that had happened to her so far that evening. All the other activities she'd enjoyed but being put on display like this unnerved her. She was aware of him staring at her and steeled herself to meet his gaze. The moment their eyes met, he put out his hand.

'Come,' he said. As she stood up obediently, a hush fell over the room. Guy moved forward in his seat but Marc shook his head. 'Leave her, Guy. She is a woman who knows what she wants.'

'Yes. But . . .' Guy began, his voice faltering.

Tara was amazed at his response. She wasn't used to seeing Guy back down in the face of anyone or anything.

'She won't forget this in a hurry.'

She heard François' words but didn't hear the reply.

Naturally, she expected their coupling to take place in the same room, in full view of the others, so she was surprised when he led her to the door.

'Where are we going?' she said, trying but failing to keep her voice steady.

'Be quiet. Only speak when you are spoken to!'

He tightened his fingers around hers until she winced.

'That's enough, Marc!' Guy cried. He was on his feet now but the other man ignored him.

Tara looked back as he guided her forcefully from the room, her eyes locking for the merest fraction of a second with those of Guy before having to relinquish them completely. As they approached the imposing staircase she looked back again. In all honesty, she had expected at least one of them to have come after Marc by now. It was obvious that his actions concerned them but still no one tried to stop him.

He led the way up the staircase and along a passageway to a luxurious sitting room.

'Is this Michel's room?' she said. She glanced around at the gleaming antiques, the ornate furniture, the heavy brocade curtains.

To her annoyance he ignored her question and silently led her through another doorway to a room which was dominated by a huge four-poster bed.

'I said, is this Michel's room?' she repeated, the annoyance she felt at being ignored showing in the tone of her voice.

Suddenly, he turned around and glared at her. 'Don't raise your voice to me,' he said.

His eyes were ice cold as he raked them contemptuously over her and she shivered, more conscious than ever of her state of undress.

'I'm cold,' she complained instead, realising that the room held none of the natural warmth of the bedrooms in Guy's house.

'I'll warm you in a minute,' he promised, a wicked smile touching his lips, 'wait there.' He disappeared into the sitting room and locked the door. Tara followed him, not trusting him for a second. When he saw her behind him he strode toward her and grasped her around the top of her arm. 'Don't you ever do as you are told?'

Despite her fear, his words and the way he spoke infuriated her.

'How dare you?' she said, her voice low. Using all her strength, she tried to wrench her arm from his grasp. 'Let me go. I want to go back downstairs.'

To her surprise he released her arm.

'Get on the bed.' Excitement glittered in his eyes but his voice was still perfectly controlled.

'No. I won't.' She shook her head and started to stride purposefully toward the door. 'I told you. I want to go now.'

'And I told you to get on the bed!'

Before she could argue a second time he picked her up and literally threw her on to the dark brocade coverlet of the high bed.

She started to scramble to the edge of the bed but he moved swiftly, pinning her down with his body as he tied her wrists to the solid oak bedpost behind her head. For a brief instant his action reminded her of the time Guy had tied her wrists and despite her trepidation she felt a small tremor of something that definitely wasn't fear.

'Untie me, you bastard!' she shouted, kicking out at him as she had at Guy. But instead of holding her legs until she conceded as Guy had done, he simply turned her over as if she were a rag doll and bound her ankles as well.

'You are just making things worse for yourself,' he warned.

'Worse?' she almost laughed. 'Why don't you just screw me and get it over with?'

'All in good time,' he said. His tone infuriated her even more than his actions, so much so that she decided to retaliate properly.

'What's the matter, Marc?' she taunted. 'Don't tell me you can't do it. Don't tell me you can't get it up!'

Despite her bravado, she cowered as he threw her a look of pure fury.

'You bitch,' he said, his voice low and menacing, 'now I will have to make sure you pay for that remark.'

To her surprise he turned on his heel and strode from the room.

Chapter Fourteen

In the few brief moments that Marc was out of the room, Tara tried desperately to free herself from the cords tied around her wrists. He had left plenty of slack in them, giving her some freedom of movement but she still could not escape. Her heart beat a rapid tune against her ribs, partly from exertion and partly from the feeling of panic that threatened to overwhelm her. Almost sobbing with anger and frustration, she buried her face in the unyielding richness of the coverlet.

'I don't know why you are trying to get away. You know as well as I do that deep down you're enjoying this.'

His voice surprised her but she didn't look up. She couldn't bear to see his arrogant expression and didn't want him to guess her feelings. Almost against her will, she let her mind dwell on his words. Was she enjoying it? Did she actually like being his captive?

'You're wrong,' she said, 'let me go!'

She started to wriggle again, even though she knew her efforts were useless. Without looking up she could sense him moving toward her and smell the scent of him in the air around the bed. Her stomach contracted tightly with a mixture of fear and anticipation.

'I am never wrong. Especially where women are concerned.'

His voice was dark and suggestive as he trailed a finger slowly down her spine and allowed it to rest at the sensitive little place at the very top of her buttocks. She felt his tongue touch her there, his breath warm against her shivering flesh. He continued to speak in the same low, hypnotic tone, almost lulling her into a trance.

'I have seen the excitement in your eyes, Tara. When you were strapped to the table. When each of the others took you. That sort of excitement cannot be faked and should never, ever be denied.'

She shook her head. 'I was just doing it to get back at Guy. I never intended to enjoy it.'

'Ah but you did enjoy it. Didn't you, Tara?'

'Yes.'

Her voice was small in reply. If he had ripped the corset from her body then and there she couldn't have felt nearly as naked as she did right at that moment, or as vulnerable to him. It was as though he had stripped away her skin and flesh and could see right inside her soul.

'You are a wicked girl, Tara,' he murmured in a

voice as dark and sinful as treacle.

She sensed him moving around the bed again but she still didn't trust herself to look at him. Surely at any minute he would unzip his trousers and thrust himself inside her and then it would all be over.

'Tell me you're a wicked girl, Tara. Speak!'

For a long time she wavered. It wasn't in her nature simply to obey but his tone thrilled her.

'I'm a wicked girl.'

He nodded, a smile of satisfaction spreading across his face, although she couldn't see it.

'Yes, you are,' he said, 'and what happens to wicked girls, Tara?'

He stroked his hand across her naked buttocks and slid it between her legs.

'I don't know,' she mumbled into the coverlet. As she shook her head her blonde curls danced playfully.

'You do know, Tara. Think. What happens to wicked girls?'

'A punishment of some kind?'

She suddenly realised where their conversation was leading. Or rather, she allowed her conscious self to acknowledge it. Deep down she had known all along.

'Yes, they are punished. Men like me have to punish wicked girls like you.'

Before he had even finished speaking she felt the first lash sting her buttocks.

'Ouch . . . you . . . bastard!'

She turned her head to glare at him. In his hands he held a black leather belt.

He brought the belt down again.

'Don't you dare speak to me like that. You must show respect.'

'Ha!' Tara exclaimed, she wasn't in the habit of showing respect, 'you must be joking. You must . . . ouch . . . ooh . . .'

The belt struck her twice in quick succession and she felt a sudden rush of moisture between her legs.

'Oh God!' She groaned loudly as the belt stung her buttocks a fourth time, inciting a fresh burst of moisture and a heat that spread throughout her body like wildfire. Feeling hopelessly depraved, she thrust her bottom into the air and begged him to do it again.

'Good, Tara. Good.'

Marc leaned over her, dropped a couple of feather-light kisses on her glowing buttocks and began to anoint her with a little cold cream, his skilful hands massaging it soothingly into her grateful flesh.

A long sigh of pleasure issued from her parted lips as she writhed under his hands, wishing he would touch her more intimately.

'I want you, Marc,' she whispered hoarsely.

'I know,' he said, 'all in good time.' He continued to massage her buttocks until he was satisfied that the job was done. Then he unfastened the corset and turned her around so that she lay on her back, vulnerable to his insolent gaze. 'You are certainly a prize worth winning,' he mused thoughtfully.

'You . . . you know about the wager between myself and Guy?' she said, amazed.

He nodded and stroked a lazy hand across her breasts.

'Of course, Guy has to confide in someone. I am his closest friend after all.'

'But I thought Michel . . . or Jean-Pierre?'

'They are good friends and, as you know, Jean-Pierre has known Guy for a greater length of time than any of us but he and I have a certain . . . shall we say . . . rapport.'

'Have you been lovers? Are you gay?'

She thought it unlikely but then again perhaps it would explain a few things.

'Hardly,' he said, laughing genuinely for the first time, 'but we share the same tastes in a lot of things. Particularly women.'

As he spoke he lay down beside her and began to stroke his hand between her legs. His fingers delved into the tightly closed pouch of her sex, opening it up a little and tormenting the sensitive flesh within.

She moaned softly, writhing under the unexpected artistry of his touch.

'Promise you will not try to kick me if I untie your ankles?' he said.

Tara smiled tremulously, hopeful of what would happen next. 'I promise.'

Swiftly, he unfastened the cord and spread her thighs wide apart. In an instant his fingers were inside her. Two fingers scissoring open then twisting and turning, stimulating the sensitive walls of her vagina. Without disturbing his manipulations of her lower body, he moved alongside her again, seeking her breasts with his free hand and pinching each nipple hard.

'Ohh . . . yes . . .' She ground her pelvis against his hand in ecstasy.

'I think madame likes a little pain,' he said, smiled wickedly and pinched them again but just a little harder. 'Am I right?'

'Yes. Oh, yes. I love it when you do that.'

She felt so hot, so excited that she thought she would explode.

'You wish Guy would fuck you don't you?' he said, his question taking her totally by surprise.

'You know?'

He bent his head and gently bit her nipple. 'I told you. Guy and I have no secrets. I know everything.'

The amount of inflection he put into the last word made her temporarily forget her rising desire.

'Do you know the real reason for my visit to Guy's house?'

'Of course. André is a very lucky boy.' He bit her other nipple.

'Oh!' She didn't know if it was his action, or the breadth of his knowledge that surprised her.

'In case you are wondering, I also know about you and Maxine. Even you and Xavier. You have been a busy girl, haven't you?'

Before she had the opportunity even to absorb his

words, let alone answer, he unzipped his trousers and thrust inside her.

She couldn't help noticing straight away how large he felt inside her, how he filled her almost to capacity.

'Is it my imagination or are you particularly well endowed?' she said, trying to peer between their bodies to the place where they were joined.

'So I've been told,' he replied.

To her immediate disappointment he withdrew from her. But then he moved his pelvis level with her shoulder and held himself to her face for her inspection. She stared at his extraordinary penis in obvious fascination. Although it was of average length, it was very, very thick. With all the succulent promise of a salami.

'Can you release my hands? I want to touch it,' she said. She looked up at his face, realising that she had nothing really to fear from him.

She could hardly wait for him to untie her so that she could wrap her fingers around the stem. Flicking out her tongue impulsively, she licked the smooth glans, its taut flesh glistening tantalisingly under the sheen of her own juices. She began to feast upon him greedily but with delicate precision, taking care to savour each pearl-like droplet that appeared from the tiny opening at the very tip.

'You didn't go to all this trouble for the others,' he groaned, his hands enfolding hers as they enfolded him.

'They didn't deserve it the way you do,' she said.

She smiled sweetly and covered him with her lips.
Cradling the weight of his testicles in her hands she
licked and sucked him as though he was the most
delicious prize on earth.

'Ooh, Tara. You're such a naughty girl!' He gripped
her hair as he exploded in her mouth and afterwards
looked down at her and his diminishing erection
with obvious dismay. 'You appear to have deprived
yourself, young lady.'

'I should hope I am more depraved than deprived,'
she retorted lightly as she slipped her chilled body
under the coverlet. 'I know, why don't you tell me a
little about Guy while you recoup your strength?'

'What do you want to know?'

Pulling the cover over both of them he slipped his
hand between her legs again, picking up from where
he left off.

'I want to know why he won't, or can't, make love
to me.'

'Because of Marie. I thought you knew that!'

Tara sighed, partly from pleasure and partly from
frustration at the mention of Guy's wife.

'I still don't understand why someone who has
been dead for sixteen years and who claims he never
loved her in the first place, should have such a hold
over him and over his sexuality.'

'Marie was a bitch. She stole his masculinity and
wrecked the marriages of a few others.'

'Really, so how do I get through to him?'

Infuriatingly, Marc shrugged. 'I think the only

way is to break through his own personal pain barrier but don't ask me how.'

Tara fell silent for a little while. She felt for his cock and smiled. Good, he was growing a little harder. Then she looked at him slyly from under her lashes.

'I think I might have been a naughty girl again, Marc,' she said.

'Really – how?'

She felt him stiffen in her hand.

'Oh, I'm sure you'll think of something.'

With a peal of laughter, she rolled on to her stomach and wiggled her bottom in the air.

On the fifth lash of his belt they were disturbed by the sound of agitated rapping on the outer door. Marc glanced at his watch.

'I thought this might happen,' he said, 'they've sent a search party to rescue you.'

Tara glanced at him over her shoulder, her smile wicked. 'Send them away. I don't want to be rescued. I'm enjoying myself.'

He glared at her with mock ferocity. 'How many times do I have to tell you. Don't give me orders.' He brought the belt down again but there was laughter in his voice.

She wriggled delightedly. 'I'm serious, Marc,' she said, 'I don't want to join the others again, yet. And besides...' she raised her eyebrows and pouted slightly '...you haven't fucked me yet.'

'Okay. Wait here,' he ordered. Pausing only to pull on his trousers, he left the room and she heard muffled voices. 'They wanted to know if you were still in one piece,' he confided as he walked back into the room and unzipped his trousers again.

'What did you tell them?'

He treated her to a lascivious smile. 'I said you were begging for mercy but that I hadn't finished with you yet.'

'Oh, God,' she said with a nervous giggle. 'Guy is going to kill me when he finds out the truth.'

'Then don't tell him,' he said, 'I certainly won't.' Reaching down, he picked up the belt again. 'Now, where were we?'

Eventually she asked him to take her, admitting that she couldn't wait any longer.

'I'm so hot for you, Marc,' she gasped, writhing under him as his massive bulk filled her to capacity once again.

'I know,' he said, without a trace of arrogance. He reached down and spread her legs wider, his fingertips skimming her throbbing clitoris.

With an overwhelming surge of passion she thrust her pelvis against him, bringing her knees back to her chest to give his impressive dimensions ample room for manoeuvre.

With a groan of determination he thrust deeper into her, the movement tugging at the delicate flesh around her clitoris, making her come in a surge of heat and dark, animal lust. It was with some reluctance that she finally allowed him to set her free.

Five shocked faces turned to greet them as they returned to the sitting room. Tara entered slightly ahead of Marc, her body clad once again in the corset. No one spoke but as she turned to accept a second glass of cognac from Michel, she heard a simultaneous sharp intake of breath. She glanced over her shoulder automatically to see what had caused the response and was surprised for a moment to see them staring at her buttocks. Then she realised what had prompted their reaction. She couldn't see the red stripes across her flesh but she was certain that was the reason for their gasps.

Although she hardly felt more than a slight sting whilst standing up, as soon as she sat down she immediately winced as her delicate flesh came into contact with the cold leather.

'Tara, are you alright?'

Guy was by her side in an instant, his expression one of anger and concern.

For a split second she glanced at Marc who shrugged in a non-committal manner.

'I don't really know,' she murmured softly, thinking it was the safest answer she could give under the circumstances. Unable to meet Guy's stare, she took a large sip of her drink.

Guy glanced at his friend, his eyes glittering with barely concealed outrage. 'I think you and I shall have some business to discuss tomorrow,' he said.

To give Marc his due, he played his part well.

'She deserved everything she got,' he asserted and cast a withering glance at Tara who fought desperately against the urge to smile back at him.

Michel walked over to them carrying Tara's dress and g-string and, with a look of sympathy, he handed them to her.

'Get dressed, Tara,' Guy said, 'I'm taking you home.' He spoke softly but decisively and instinct told her it wasn't a time of dissent.

Draining her glass, she stood up and slipped on the g-string. An act that elicited a round of murmurs as she bent over to step into it. Finally she pulled up her dress and zipped it.

'My shoes?'

She glanced around and noticed them laying under the table. In a flash, Guy retrieved them for her and slipped them on her feet. Like Prince Charming, she thought absently to herself.

Minutes later they were outside in the driveway. As they reached the car he opened the passenger door for her. Feeling a little guilty, she watched as he winced in sympathy when she slid her bottom across the seat. With bated breath she allowed her eyes to follow him as he walked round the car. His expression was stern as he slid into the driver's seat next to her. He pulled the car door firmly shut and suddenly they were all alone.

If she expected him to say something to her

straight away she was disappointed. Instead he started the engine, slammed the car into gear and turned it round in a cloud of dust. In no time they were out on the open road. She turned her face to look at him but he stared straight ahead and didn't even glance up to the rear-view mirror. The roads were narrow and dark and from a long distance away she could hear the faint rumble of thunder.

'It looks as though we're in for a storm,' she murmured quietly.

He didn't speak a word until they arrived back at the house. Once inside, he took her into the kitchen and filled the kettle with water.

'What are you doing?' she asked.

'I'm making some tea,' he said calmly. 'Would you like some?'

'You're making tea?'

She almost laughed aloud. His action was about as far removed from her expectations as it could get. Yet, on reflection, she realised that one of the main things that attracted her to this man was his ability to surprise her.

'Take your clothes off, Tara,' he said, his voice low.

'I beg your . . .' she began, surprised yet again by his sudden volte face and unsure if she had heard correctly because he still had his back to her.

'I said take off your clothes.' Suddenly he let out a long sigh. 'It's nothing sexual, I just want to see what that bastard did to you.'

'Oh,' she said, feeling slightly idiotic.

Slowly, she started to disrobe, feeling almost as embarrassed and exposed as she had that day in his office. When she had removed everything he held out his hands.

'Come here.'

'He only hit me on the bottom, nowhere else.'

She didn't know what her motives were – whether she wanted to reassure him, or save Marc from his friend's wrath. When she stood before him, naked and trembling, he turned her around, stroking his fingertips lightly across the tracks in her flesh.

'Couldn't you get away?' he said, 'I know how you like to put up a fight.' Despite his concern he allowed a glimmer of a smile to touch his lips and eyes.

Tara shook her head, the ends of her hair stroking her bare shoulders.

'No. He tied me to the bed. I couldn't do anything except . . . except . . . take my punishment.'

She stared straight at him, wondering what was going through his mind at that precise moment.

'I see.'

He left her standing there while he walked to the kettle and placed a tea bag in each cup before pouring boiling water over them.

'If you don't mind, I'll just go and put on my robe while the tea is brewing,' she said.

She didn't wait for his assent but gathered up her discarded clothes and almost ran from the kitchen. About ten minutes later she returned, the comforting warmth of her robe and the cup of tea that he placed in front of her both doing their part to ease her tension and fatigue. Impulsively, she told him that she had asked Marc about Marie.

'Did you?' he said. He had been staring thoughtfully into the depths of his cup but at her admission he looked up surprised. 'I didn't realise that while you were being whipped and abused you also found time for a cosy chat.'

For a moment she wondered if he had seen through her deception but he made no further comment.

'He said Marie was responsible for wrecking a number of marriages,' she continued. 'Is that true?'

She sipped her tea feeling thankful for its warmth. Outside she could hear the first soft patter of raindrops as they hit the flagstones.

Guy was silent for a moment, considering her question. 'Yes, it is true,' he replied at long last, 'she became an almost fatal attraction for many men.' He noticed her enquiring look and continued. 'One or two of her lovers' wives threatened to kill their husbands for their infidelity with her. A couple of the other men she became involved with tried to commit suicide.'

'My God, she must have been one hell of a good lay!' Tara exclaimed without thinking.

Far from being shocked, Guy gave a small laugh. 'According to her lovers she was. Some of them even thought her epitaph should have included the words, *"elle baise bien"*.' He looked at her, his expression suddenly sombre again. 'I only have their word for it of course. I never found her to be a good fuck at all.'

Tara stretched out her hand to him. 'I am,' she said softly.

He opened his mouth, about to ask her what she meant before he realised and slowly shook his head.

'I don't know how many times I have to reject you, Tara, before you accept it once and for all.'

The finality in his speech and the idiocy of his attitude struck her to the core. In a fit of rage she pushed back her chair and stood up abruptly.

'Are you going to bed?' He sipped his tea and gazed up at her, his expression inscrutable.

Shaking with anger she glared at him across the table. 'No, I am not going to bed. In fact I don't intend to spend another minute in this house.'

She marched to the kitchen door and wrenched it open, the sudden blast of rain-soaked air causing her to waver just for a split second.

'Tara, don't be so stupid.'

Oh, the bastard, how dare he call *her* stupid! The unfairness of his words drove her out of the house and across the gardens. And her anger and frustration gave her the impetus to keep going, despite the fresh gathering of dark rain clouds in the purple sky and the ominous rumble of thunder coming ever closer.

She didn't know where she was going. She just knew she wanted to get away. A brief glimpse over her shoulder showed that Guy was not following her and for a moment she didn't know whether she was relieved or disappointed. She should never have gone there to his house, never accepted his offer, or his challenge. All along she had known it was sheer madness.

Her legs took her over a low wooden fence and into the woods. If she remembered correctly, the main road was somewhere to the east of the trees. She started to veer in that direction, squinting up at the sky as large persistent drops of rain began to fall. Damn, now she would get wet into the bargain.

With a typically dramatic turn of thought, she imagined herself getting pneumonia and expiring pathetically at Guy's feet. Huh! Then he would have two dead women on his conscience. She laughed aloud at the force of her imagination until, overhead, a fork of lightning illuminated everything in a fleeting burst of eerie light and stopped her in her tracks. She heard the crack it made and then another crack but this time like the sound of a twig. Suddenly it occurred to her that there was someone else in the wood.

Desperately, she urged her legs to move faster. The hem of her robe became wet and heavy as it dragged through the sodden grass. She tried to gather the material in her hands and keep the hem raised but it seemed elusive somehow, as though her fingers had lost the power to grip anything. Despite feeling weighed down, she ran on through the trees and out into a clearing. In the gloomy distance she could make out some large shadows and concrete structures. Oh, hell, she was completely lost.

'Tara!'

She heard Guy's voice in the distance but she kept on pushing forward frantically – thinking that at least if she made it to one of those strange shapes it would shield her from his view.

He was coming closer, she could sense his presence, almost hear his breathing, yet she still couldn't see him anywhere. Suddenly another fork of lightning lit up the sky, its illuminating force suspended in the firmament just long enough for her to see the tall figure of her pursuer just a hundred yards or so behind her. As she turned around quickly her breath caught, without realising it she had stumbled into the middle of a graveyard and the concrete structures she had been so desperate to reach were tombs.

With her heat thumping wildly in her chest she made her way forward hesitantly. Brought up on a diet of black-and-white horror films her worst nightmare had always been to find herself in a graveyard at night. No. Correction. Add thunder and lightening and the fact that she was being chased to the scenario. That was her worst nightmare.

'Go away, Guy!' she called out with false bravado, a sudden roll of thunder almost drowning her voice.

'No. I've come to take you back to the house.'

She heard him but she could no longer see him.

With her heart in her mouth, she took a couple of tentative paces backward. Reaching behind her, the fingers of her left hand came into contact with the smooth marble of a tombstone. She hardly dared to look around, instead she called out to him again.

'I'm not coming back. Leave me alone.'

'Tara. I am serious. Stop being so stupid.'

His voice sounded so close, as though he were almost on top of her. But she was so angered by his words that she screamed until she thought her lungs would burst.

'Stop it! Stop calling me stupid!'

Suddenly she felt fingers close around her arm and she screamed again.

'Tara!'

She felt his palm connect with her cheek and a fierce sting spread outward, bringing tears to her eyes.

'You bastard!' She turned on him and began to lash out. 'How dare you hit me! You arrogant, supercilious, French pig!' She almost spat the final insult at him.

'Have you finished?' His voice was calm and, to her annoyance, she could hear the undertone of amusement in it.

'I've finished with you,' she said.

It had stopped raining now and the sky had started to clear, making him visible to her all of a sudden. She began to walk away from him, then something made her turn around. The marble headstone beside her, or rather the name on it, caught her eye. Marie Ricard.

He followed her gaze. 'She didn't deserve to be interred with the rest of the family,' he said flatly. His glance took her eyes to the large stone vault that bore the Ricard name.

'So, this is your family home?' Just for a moment she forgot her anger.

Guy nodded. 'Yes, it is. But I still had to buy it. I didn't inherit it. My parents disowned me when I married Marie.'

'If your parents are dead then André's grandparents must be Marie's mother and . . .?' she said, her voice trailing off as she marvelled at the sort of man who could maintain a good relationship with the parents of someone he had detested just so that his son would not be deprived of the relationship. 'That's pretty amazing, Guy,' she said softly.

Typically, he shrugged.

For a moment or two they simply stared at each other in silence. A thought began to formulate in her mind which was so dreadful and shocking she knew she couldn't ignore it.

Keeping her eyes locked with his, she untied the belt on her robe and allowed the sodden garment to drop to the floor. His steady gaze didn't waver and she marvelled at his self-control. She bent her knees and began to lower her body slowly and deliberately until she was lying flat on the smooth slab of granite that covered Marie's grave.

'What in God's name?' Guy took a step forward, his expression a mixture of shock and horror. Yet, she thought – she hoped – she could detect something else there too.

Slowly, she began to caress her own breasts. She moulded them in her hands, her fingers teasing the nipples until they were fully erect. As she felt her arousal growing she started to writhe sensuously, her flesh recoiling at the sensation of the cold, clammy stone beneath her. He stared at her in mute astonishment but she deliberately ignored him, concentrating instead on her own pleasure. She slid her hands down the length of her undulating torso, her legs opening wider to greet her questing fingers. As the cool night air caressed her swollen outer lips, she slipped three fingers into the hot canyon of her sex.

The pleasure was immediate and she cried aloud. With delicate fingers she spread her labia apart and began to stroke herself, teasing her clitoris until it throbbed remorselessly. Little whimpers broke from her parted lips as she circled the shameless nub of flesh, wetting it with a slick coating of her own juices.

Through heavy-lidded eyes, she saw Guy's fingers working his belt free. A further tremor of excitement ran through her at the sight of the strip of leather and a moment later he unzipped his trousers and knelt between her open thighs. Wordlessly, he stared at the glistening opening of her vagina. He saw how enticingly it beckoned to him, how her whole body craved him.

She could sense his inner turmoil and didn't want to hurry him. Hardly daring even to breathe she continued to stroke herself, letting him know that she was preparing herself for him. Eventually, she felt his hands upon her and she almost came from that single action alone. It was a struggle but she held herself back, waiting to see if this time he would do more than simply touch her.

With only a fraction more hesitation he positioned himself over her and thrust himself inside her and up to the hilt.

'Oh ... my ... God ...!'

A raging inferno swept through her and exploded in her pelvis. He was inside her, actually inside her and it felt so wonderful and so right.

'Tara.' This time he spoke her name with passion, not anger.

She put her hand up to his lips. 'Don't speak, Guy,' she said softly, 'just make love to me.'

Bringing her legs up she gripped his hips with her knees, urging him deeper and deeper inside her. She wanted to feel all of him. To take every last little bit and eat him up. Desperately, she clutched his shoulders and rocked against him, straining her body up to meet. his. She envied the way that he could enter her body when she wished she could press herself inside him too.

For a man who had held out for sixteen years

she thought he showed remarkable staying power, thrusting deeply and rhythmically inside her until he was certain that she could come no more before allowing his own orgasm to burst forth.

For a while they lay together, his body on top of hers and inside her, their breathing and their hearts taking forever to slow down to a normal pace. Eventually, though, she began to shiver.

He propped himself up on his hands and looked down at her. 'Oh, *mon Dieu*. I am so thoughtless.' Immediately, he withdrew from her and stood up. For a second he stared down at her flushed and trembling body, then he relented. 'Here, put this on.' He slipped off his jacket and held it out to her.

'Thank you,' she murmured, for once feeling almost shy in his presence.

Although it barely covered her, she was grateful for its warmth. Bending down she picked up her sodden robe and rolled it into a ball, then she looked up at him, wondering what would happen next.

He put out his hand. 'Let's go home,' he said.

Chapter Fifteen

Heedless of the wet grass and earth beneath her bare feet, Tara walked back to the house with Guy, her hand locked tightly in his. Once inside he stared at her for a few minutes but this time she was unable to interpret his expression.

'I will make you some more tea but first of all I am going to run you a hot bath,' he said.

Instead of going straight to her room he led her to his own. Walking purposefully into his bathroom, he strode to the large white porcelain tub and turned on the taps.

'You'll find soaps and shampoo in there.' He nodded toward a wooden cabinet on the wall.

After he had left the room she sat down on the edge of the bath, her mind whirling with countless thoughts. Her biggest question was still, what next? She didn't want him to think that she expected him to be beholden to her in some way, just because she had succeeded where others had failed. On the other hand, she had worked damned hard to get to that point and a single night of passion simply would not suffice.

Her body aching with cold and fatigue, she climbed in the tub and relaxed her chilled body in the blissful warmth of the water. She had just finished washing her hair when he returned bearing two mugs of tea.

'I didn't think a cup would be enough,' he said with a smile, as he set the mugs down on the top of a wooden cabinet.

Tara looked up at him as he stood over her, staring at her body through the clear, steamy water.

'There's plenty of room for two, you know.' Her voice was soft and inviting.

Quickly, he stripped off his clothes and as Tara obligingly moved forward he sank into the water behind her. Putting his hands around her breasts, he pulled her back against him and picked up the bar of soap.

Her breasts grew slippery and warm as he began to lather them thoroughly.

Tara sighed softly. She felt as though she could die quite happily from the effects of so much pleasure.

'Are you feeling a little better now?'

His hands slid rhythmically over the slippery surface of her breasts as he spoke into her ear in a low hypnotic tone.

'Oh, yes,' she breathed and turned her face to look at him. At that moment, she found herself wishing they could stay like that forever. Their naked bodies immersed in a warm cocoon. His hands upon her. His blue eyes crinkling at the corners with easy humour.

Smiling gently at her response, he slid his hands lower to lather her stomach. Tiredness seeped through him and tugged at his eyelids as he watched the soap bubbles lift almost instantly from her skin and float to the surface of the water.

'You surprised me tonight Tara,' he said.

She knew she must have done more than surprise him. She had even succeeded in shocking herself by some of her actions and reactions to the unusual situations she had faced.

'Really?' She squirmed under his touch as he allowed his fingers to delve into the secret cleft between her legs.

'Yes, you know you did. Particularly when you went with Marc.' He laughed suddenly, the sound incongruous to the subject matter and his previous reaction to that particular situation. 'Do you want to hear something amusing?'

She nodded silently and he continued.

'I half expected you to tell me that you had enjoyed being whipped,' he said. All at once his caress became a little more deliberate. His hands spread her thighs as far as the confines of the tub would allow and his fingers similarly spread open her labia. Satisfied that she was properly exposed, he began to stroke the sensitive flesh that he uncovered, his fingertips circling the very edge of her vagina with maddening precision.

Her heart started to beat a little faster but she said nothing, waiting to hear what else he had to say on the subject.

'Yes. I know it sounds incredible,' he added, 'but after the way you reacted when the others strapped you to that table top and then ... well, I wouldn't have expected you to be fazed by a little domination.' His fingers sought her clitoris and began to work their magic there. 'Do you know how I felt as I watched you being fucked by all those men, Tara?'

She shook her head. Her mind was only half on his words as she felt the rapid build up of warmth in her sex and the way her clitoris swelled and throbbed under the skilful caress of his fingertips.

'Which one did you enjoy the most?' he persisted. 'Jean-Pierre, François, or what about Michel? Let's face it, he wasn't very subtle was he, Tara? He took you like an express train.'

Remembering the way Michel had slammed into her from behind made her come instantly, yet still Guy's fingers kept up their relentless stimulation of her delicate flesh.

'That's enough, Guy,' she gasped, grasping his wrist but he pulled her hand away.

Without releasing her arm he stood up suddenly, dragging her out of the water. Only pausing to wrap her in a large towel, he carried her into the bedroom where he deposited her on the bed like a damp bundle of rags. With a sense of déjà vu she felt him bind her wrists. Although yet again, excitement overtook her feelings of panic.

'What are you doing?' she asked. She wriggled uselessly. She already knew it was pointless to struggle, nevertheless it was a reflex action.

He knelt over her. 'You were lucky they didn't all want to put their cocks in your *derrière* as well,' he said teasingly.

He moved a little closer and she glanced up at the length of hard muscle just inches from her face.

She felt a little tingle, wondering briefly why the men hadn't sought to do that. Feeling almost transfixed by the sight of Guy's erection swaying from side to side in front of her, a picture of herself sucking Marc's cock suddenly flashed into her mind and she gasped.

'What is it? What are you thinking?'

She jumped guiltily as he spoke, wondering whether she should tell him.

'Nothing, really.'

To her surprise he didn't press her and instead moved down her body again, still straddling it, until he was hovering over her stomach – his testicles just brushing her skin.

'Marc told me once that one of his favourite tricks is to really squeeze the nipples, or even bite them,' he said lightly. 'Did he do that to you?'

She hesitated for a moment, wondering if he was really ready to hear the truth about her experience at the hands of his friend.

'Yes. Yes, he did.'

'Was it painful?' His fingers crept over her breasts, lingering at the very tips.

'Of course.' She held her breath, knowing exactly what he intended to do next.

'And did you enjoy the pain?'

He took the tight red buds of her nipples and pinched them harder and harder until she closed her eyes against the piquant agony, her sex burning with renewed arousal.

'Yes,' she said, her voice the merest whisper.

Satisfied with her response he let her go and moved to the side of her, turning her body over so that she lay on her stomach. With gentle fingers he traced the swell of her buttocks, the evidence of her *ordeal* now hardly visible.

'You enjoyed being whipped as well didn't you?' he said.

She couldn't decide from his tone whether he would be angry if she told him the truth or not, so she remained quiet.

'I asked you a question, Tara.'

He raised his voice a little but still she didn't answer. In any event speech would have been difficult, by now her heart was beating so fast that she could hardly breathe.

'Answer me, damn you!' he thundered. 'You enjoyed it, didn't you?'

She glared angrily over her shoulder.

'Yes, I did enjoy it. It was tremendous. Wonderful.

The most exciting experience of my life. Now are you satisfied?'

She could have ripped her tongue out.

'No, Tara. I am not.'

The quietly controlled response took her by surprise. Once again he turned her over so that she lay on her back. She suddenly felt tired of fighting him and simply allowed him to work her body. With an air of quiet determination he untied her wrists once more.

'Do you want me to go?' she said. She held her breath, but he didn't answer her.

Instead he prised her legs apart and pushed against her shins until her knees were fully bent, the red swollen flesh of her vulva totally exposed to him. With a jolt of surprise and pleasure, Tara felt him lunge into her for a second time that night, his rock-hard cock filling her completely, as though her body was its rightful place.

'I want you to come, not go,' he said, his tone fierce with concentration, 'I want you to enjoy it as much with me as you did with Marc and the others. And André. And Xavier.'

He continued to pound remorselessly inside her.

'Okay. Okay. I get the message,' she gasped breathlessly. Suddenly, her glimmer of a smile was wiped out by the force of passion and she cried out, 'Oh, Guy. Oh, yes. All I ever wanted was this.'

She felt the waves of pleasure build and build, her mind focused on the rhythmic thrusting of his cock inside her. The way it felt. So strong and hard. She opened her eyes briefly and looked up at his handsome face hovering over her. She felt transfixed, his eyes such a deep blue, like the Mediterranean.

I'm drowning, she thought and the pleasure-heat exploded.

With a dispassionate expression on his face, he watched her come. And without withdrawing from her he pulled her to him and slid his legs under her, covering her breasts with his hands as she sat astride him.

'You are an amazing woman, Tara Cochrane,' he said, 'I knew it would be fun getting to know you.'

Releasing her breasts he pulled her to him, his mouth seeking hers.

Concerned that she might have caught a chill, Guy insisted that she stay in bed for a couple of days and gallantly volunteered to keep her company. His only reasons for leaving her were calls of nature and occasional visits to the kitchen to collect a tray that Lisette had prepared for them, or another bottle of champagne. Eventually, however, they were both forced to acknowledge that André was due home and so reluctantly returned to a more public existence.

They sat in respectable conviviality by the pool sharing a pot of coffee. Tara wore only her brief white bikini bottoms and a matching diaphanous chiffon blouse to protect her modesty and her shoulders from the harsh rays of the sun. Cradling her coffee cup thoughtfully between her hands, she asked Guy what they were going to say to his son when he returned.

Guy gave his customary response. He shrugged.

'Shrugging isn't a satisfactory answer, Guy,' she said, sipping her coffee and pretending to glare at him. 'Imagine if I just went through life shrugging every time a difficult situation cropped up.' She aped his action and then burst out laughing. 'Stop looking at my breasts!'

'How can I when you shrug so beautifully,' he said as he leaned forward and cupped his chin in his hands. 'Do it again.'

Giggling, she complied with his request, glancing down as her chest heaved and wobbled.

'*Merde*, that is a wonderful sight!' he exclaimed. He reclined in his chair looking totally relaxed. 'In answer to your question, I think we must play the situation by ear, as it were. Wait for the right opportunity to say something.'

'And what if he comes back here all youthful vigour and raging testosterone, expecting to fuck my brains out?'

'How could I blame him?'

His response was typically flippant, although she could see he was disconcerted by the possibility. Or rather, the probability of her prediction.

'I suppose we'll just have to cross that bridge when we come to it,' she said, moving to one of the thickly

333

padded sun-loungers that edged the pool. With a sigh she lay down and closed her eyes, suddenly feeling very drowsy. 'Wake me up when he returns.'

To the surprise of both of them, André didn't return alone. At the familiar sight of the Citröen, Tara craned her neck and was intrigued to see that beside him sat a young dark-haired girl. She emerged from the car like a colt, all long brown legs and silky hair. And that was when Guy noticed her. His greeting was an irresistibly seductive smile but to his frustration André stepped between them.

'Papa. Tara. I would like you to meet Angelique,' he said.

The young man was beaming from ear to ear and Tara guessed that his trip to Le Touquet had not been as arduous, or as boring as he had feared.

Of course, Guy knew nothing about the young girl's existence in his son's life but Tara stood up and held out her hand. With a deep-seated sense of personal interest in André's welfare, her eyes quickly appraised the girl's pretty, pouty face before skimming over her neat figure which was clad in impossibly small cut-off denim shorts and a skimpy white T-shirt that left nothing to the imagination.

'Hello, Angelique,' she said in her friendliest voice. She smiled broadly before throwing a glance in André's direction and raising an eyebrow. With an even broader smile, she noticed he had the grace to blush.

They all sat down at the table and, after half an

hour or so of polite conversation, Angelique excused herself and went inside the house to use the bathroom. As Guy had already disappeared to take a telephone call, Tara was able to seize the opportunity to talk to André alone.

'I take it you had a good time in Le Touquet after all?' she said.

Her voice was soft and gentle as her smile. She didn't really expect a reply and reclined easily in her chair, hardly aware that his eyes kept straying to her breasts – the full tanned globes clearly visible through the transparent material of her blouse.

'Mmm,' he murmured, nodding absently. A wicked glint flickered in his eye as he added, 'I forgot what wonderful breasts you have. Angelique's are so small. In fact, her whole body is very undeveloped in comparison to yours.' His voice was filled with an admiration and undisguised longing.

Tara forced a laugh, desperately trying to ignore the frisson of excitement that his presence caused. Despite all that she and his father had been through, she was surprised to find how much André's presence affected her physically as well as emotionally.

'Size is not really an issue, for either men or women.'

'I know but I just realised how much I had missed them. I have already forgotten exactly how they feel.'

He leaned forward, obviously about to touch her

but at that moment Guy appeared.

Just for an instant, his eyes narrowed slightly as he looked from his son to Tara.

'Where has your girlfriend disappeared to, André?' he asked.

He sat down again and, confident that his movements were adequately concealed by the table top, began to stroke his bare foot purposefully along Tara's thigh.

'Call of nature, papa.' The young man blushed and sat back in his seat, his eyes straying to the house, obviously anxious for Angelique to reappear.

'Have you asked her to stay?' Guy enquired, his impassive expression successfully hiding the fact that all his efforts were concentrated on tormenting Tara.

'Sort of,' André said, 'but I wanted to see what you had to say about it first.'

Tara noticed that he looked anxious again and for a moment she forgot her rising excitement as her heart went out to him.

'I don't mind.' Guy insinuated his foot between Tara's thighs as he spoke, his toes wriggling provocatively against the soft mound of her sex. 'Do you want her to share your room, or shall I ask Lisette to prepare one of the guest rooms?'

Poor André, Tara thought, trying not to look at his face as he blushed even harder than before. Little did he realise that his father would be relieved if he said he wanted to sleep with his girlfriend.

Then Tara would not be put in the difficult position of having to refuse him.

'Er, my room. If . . . if you really have no objections, Papa?' André said.

His father smiled. 'No. Far from it. You may go and fuck her now if you wish.'

'Guy!' Tara exclaimed, she couldn't let him get away with that remark.

Predictably, he shrugged.

A few minutes later Angelique reappeared and André leaped from his seat. 'I'll just help her with her bag and things,' he said, his voice trailing off in embarrassment.

As soon as they were alone Tara looked at Guy and pursed her lips reprovingly.

'You were not very subtle, Guy. The poor boy is as embarrassed as hell.'

'Give him an hour or two with that little peach and I think he will get over it.' He smiled lasciviously, then he turned to her. 'Have you had enough of the sun by any chance?'

Despite her disapproval, Tara smiled back. 'No. But I think you have.'

As they lay together in Guy's bed, temporarily sated by yet another frantic bout of lovemaking, Tara looked at him, realising that she had to get some answers from him.

'Guy?'

'Uh huh.'

He turned on his side and gazed down at her face, his fingers marking out a lazy path that meandered lightly across the twin peaks of her breasts.

'I think perhaps I should go home.' There followed a minute or two of silence and eventually, when he showed no indication that he intended to reply, she strove to fill the gap. 'I've enjoyed being with you very much but . . .'

'But what, Tara?' he interrupted suddenly. 'Surely you are not tired of me already – am I not enough of a man for you?'

Far from being calm, he suddenly seemed extremely agitated.

'Don't be silly,' she said, 'that's not it at all.' Desperate to placate him she put her hand up to his face, her fingertips scraping over the sand-paper texture of his jaw. 'I just don't think that either of us is cut out for commitment.'

'Probably not,' he agreed, 'but why should you have to go home?'

His easy acceptance of their unsuitability for a permanent relationship rocked her. Although she would never acknowledge it, she realised that in her subconscious she had probably been harbouring the old romantic notion about their eventual union.

'I just thought it would be easier on all of us,' she said, 'that way there's no need to explain anything to André. No pressure on you to keep sleeping with me . . .'

Swiftly, he interrupted her. 'Are you joking, woman, do you think I find it a trial having to satisfy your gorgeous body for hours on end?' His eyes swept her nakedness. 'Do you think I dislike having your mouth around my cock, or your legs around my neck? *Mon Dieu!*'

'I didn't quite mean it like that,' she giggled, feeling inordinately pleased by his response and not a little aroused by his reaction and the way he continued to look at her.

Noticing the subtle change in her expression, the way her eyes had suddenly become dreamy with lust, Guy allowed his fingers to skim down the length of her torso, their journey ending at her silky mound. Automatically, she parted her legs for him.

'I don't want you to cut this holiday short just to spare André's feelings,' he murmured, 'but on the other hand, if you are just trying to be polite because you don't really want to spend the next couple of weeks with me . . .'

'Oh, no.' Shocked by his words she rolled her body over, pushing him onto his back and sitting astride him. 'I can't get enough of you, Guy. Surely you must realise that by now?'

'I hoped but . . .' He shrugged yet again and treated her to a winning smile.

To silence him, Tara reached down behind her, grasped his cock firmly around the base and slipped it inside her. With fierce determination she began to grind her hips.

Despite the fact that Tara and Guy had managed to resolve their own personal dilemmas, supper that evening was a strained affair. To André's annoyance and Tara's own disquiet, the young Angelique made it obvious that she found Guy attractive. As they adjourned to the games room, Tara took Guy aside.

'That girl is upsetting André,' she whispered, her naturally protective urges coming to the fore.

'Oh, I don't know,' he said, 'I think she is actually rather lovely.'

He smiled wickedly and deliberately glanced at the butterfly tattoo on Angelique's lower buttock as she leaned across the snooker table.

Deep down Tara hoped he was only teasing, yet she couldn't help feeling a frisson of disquiet at the way he responded to the young girl. And it was obvious that he enjoyed her attempts at flirtation. Consequently, it took the entire force of her will-power not to act like a jealous lover. At least she could masquerade her feelings behind a noble profession of outrage on André's behalf.

'Guy, you wouldn't, would you?' She couldn't seem to release the knot in her stomach.

To her annoyance he shrugged. 'Perhaps, perhaps not.'

Composing his features into a deliberately casual expression, he strolled across the room to stand behind Angelique. And he threw Tara a devilish smile as he put his arms around the young girl to assist her with her next shot.

Pretending not to notice, Tara drank a whole glass of cognac in a single swallow.

'You and my father are lovers aren't you?'

Tara started with surprise at André's voice in her ear. Her first reaction, of course, was to deny the accusation. Yet something in his tone told her it was not an accusation at all, simply a statement of fact.

'Yes,' she said.

She couldn't bring herself to look at him, even if she could bear to take her eyes off Guy for a second as he laughed and treated the unsuspecting Angelique to the irresistible force of his most seductive technique.

'When?'

Now she looked up at him, confusion written all over her face. 'When what?'

'When did you become lovers?' André asked, eying her intently. 'Was it while I was away in Le Touquet – or perhaps before then, while we were still in England?'

Under the odd circumstances of her relationship with Guy she wasn't entirely sure how to answer him. Eventually, she admitted to him that she had started sleeping with his father when he went to Le Touquet, which in a way was the truth.

'You can't have missed me a whole lot then?' he said, just for a moment displaying all the unjustified petulance of a child.

Realising that she was treading on precarious ground, she chose her words carefully.

'I told you right at the start of our . . . er . . . affair,

341

that we are both free agents. And that we should always endeavour to live for the moment.' She didn't bother to draw his attention to the fact that he had also been seeing Angelique at the time. Gently, she placed a hand on his arm and added, 'Why don't you take Angelique up to bed and leave your father to me?' At that moment she realised she felt more like his mother.

With a grateful nod he walked over to the side of the snooker table where, by this time, the young girl had almost wrapped herself around Guy. He spoke a few words to her and Tara watched the exchange, noticing how the girl seemed angry for a moment before conceding and taking André's hand.

After they had left Guy remained where he stood, staring blankly at the half finished game on the green baize.

'I'll play you Guy,' Tara said softly.

He turned to look at her. 'Is this just a friendly match? After all, we have nothing left to use as a wager.'

'Yes, we do.' Tara began to place the coloured balls on their correct spots.

'I don't . . .' he began in confusion but she silenced him.

'Angelique,' she said, her reply barely a whisper, 'if you win, you get carte blanche from me to pursue Angelique. If I win, you must promise to leave her alone, to give André a proper chance with her.'

Guy let his breath out slowly. 'That's some bet,'

he said, 'particularly as you know I am the better player.'

Tara nodded. 'That may be but the stakes were never as high before. This time it is André's happiness that is at stake. It is in all our interests that I win this time.' Purposefully, she gathered all the red balls together in the triangle and positioned them on the table. 'You break.'

By the time she got to take her first shot Guy was already leading by eighteen points. Desperately, she fought to keep up with him, the adrenaline coursing around her body as she sank several reds and blacks in quick succession on her third go.

'You don't intend to give up easily, do you?' Guy said.

He smiled as he took aim for the last red ball on the table. He missed and the smile died.

Hardly daring to allow herself to breathe let alone get excited, Tara took up her cue and sank the ball into the centre pocket. The white ball came right back to her and hovered conveniently close to the black. Seven more points. With her heart beating faster and faster with every subsequent shot Tara cleared the table completely.

'Well done, *ma chérie*,' he said quietly.

She knew Guy had not expected to lose and one quick glance at his face told her he was far from pleased by the result.

'I had no option,' she replied firmly, 'I had to win.' She hung up her cue on the rack on the wall and stood at the opposite end of the table, simply staring at him. Something about his demeanour told her that they had reached a watershed. She turned away.

'Where are you going?' He started to walk around the table, his fingertips trailing along the green baize cushion.

She turned back and looked him straight in the eye. 'I'm going to bed and then tomorrow I shall leave.'

For several moments they simply stared at each other.

'Get on the table,' he commanded softly.

She felt her stomach clench. 'What? I . . .'

Guy shook his head impatiently. '*Au nom de Dieu, Tara, tais-toi!*'

In an instant, he rounded the corner of the table, gripped her arms and lifted her on to the table top as if she weighed no more than a feather.

With rapidly mounting excitement she allowed him to rip the clothes from her body and move her limbs until she lay naked and spread-eagled in front of him. Then, through heavy-lidded eyes, she watched as he removed his own clothes and covered her with the smooth hardness of his torso. There was no finesse in his actions, yet she felt her passion soar as he plunged into her, driving her crazy with the power of his thrusts.

'I owe you this one, Tara, don't you remember?' he muttered darkly.

344

Lifting her hips to meet him, he took her over the brink of ecstasy.

Lost in the rapture of the moment, she moaned and writhed uncontrollably, her body only becoming still and silent when she had conceded all her passion to him.

Looking up at his face, her senses drowning in the deep blue eyes and her body melting under the heat of his special smile, she finally allowed herself to simply enjoy the moment for what it was — a very special, very private lesson in pleasure.

Adult Fiction for Lovers from Headline LIAISON

PLEASE TEASE ME	Rebecca Ambrose	£5.99
A PRIVATE EDUCATION	Carol Anderson	£5.99
IMPULSE	Kay Cavendish	£5.99
TRUE COLOURS	Lucinda Chester	£5.99
CHANGE PARTNERS	Cathryn Cooper	£5.99
SEDUCTION	Cathryn Cooper	£5.99
THE WAYS OF A WOMAN	J J Duke	£5.99
FORTUNE'S TIDE	Cheryl Mildenhall	£5.99
INTIMATE DISCLOSURES	Cheryl Mildenhall	£5.99
ISLAND IN THE SUN	Susan Sebastian	£5.99

All Headline Liaison books are available at your local bookshop or newsagent, or can be ordered direct from the publisher. Just tick the titles you want and fill in the form below. Prices and availability subject to change without notice.

Headline Book Publishing, Cash Sales Department, Bookpoint, 39 Milton Park, Abingdon, OXON, OX14 4TD, UK. If you have a credit card you may order by telephone – 01235 400400.

Please enclose a cheque or postal order made payable to Bookpoint Ltd to the value of the cover price and allow the following for postage and packing: UK & BFPO: £1.00 for the first book, 50p for the second book and 30p for each additional book ordered up to a maximum charge of £3.00.
OVERSEAS & EIRE: £2.00 for the first book, £1.00 for the second book and 50p for each additional book.

Name ....

Address ....

....

....

If you would prefer to pay by credit card, please complete:
Please debit my Visa/Access/Diner's Card/American Express
(Delete as applicable) card no:

Signature .... Expiry Date ....